The Nature
of Small Birds

Books by Susie Finkbeiner

All Manner of Things
Stories That Bind Us
The Nature of Small Birds

The Nature of Small Birds

A Novel

Susie Finkbeiner

Revell
a division of Baker Publishing Group
Grand Rapids, Michigan

© 2021 by Susie Finkbeiner

Published by Revell
a division of Baker Publishing Group
PO Box 6287, Grand Rapids, MI 49516-6287
www.revellbooks.com

Printed in the United States of America

Library of Congress Cataloging-in-Publication Data
Names: Finkbeiner, Susie, author.
Title: The nature of small birds : a novel / Susie Finkbeiner.
Description: Grand Rapids, Michigan : Revell, 2021.
Identifiers: LCCN 2020058630 | ISBN 9780800739355 (paperback) | ISBN 9780800740061 (casebound)
Subjects: LCSH: Adoption—Fiction. | Vietnamese Americans—Fiction. | Vietnam War, 1961–1975—Psychological aspects—Fiction. | Racially mixed families—Fiction. | GSAFD: Christian fiction.
Classification: LCC PS3606.I552 N38 2021 | DDC 813/.6—dc23
LC record available at https://lccn.loc.gov/2020058630

"The Language of the Birds" by Amy Nemecek was first published in *The Windhover* 25.1 (February 2021) and is used by permission of the poet.

This book is a work of fiction. Names, characters, places, and incidents are the product of the author's imagination or are used fictitiously. Any resemblance to actual events, locales, or persons, living or dead, is coincidental.

21 22 23 24 25 26 27   7 6 5 4 3 2 1

For

Elise Marie,
Austin Thomas,
and Tim Spence.

My three small birds.

The Language of the Birds

On the fifth day, your calloused fingers
stretched out and plucked a single reed
from the river that flowed out of Eden,
trimmed its hollow shaft to length and
whittled one end to a precise vee
that you dipped in the inkwell of ocean.
Touching pulpy nib to papyrus sky,
you brushed a single hieroglyph—
feathered the vertical downstroke
flourished with serif of pinions,
a perpendicular crossbar lifting
weightless bones from left to right.
Tucking the stylus behind your ear,
you blew across the wet silhouette,
dried a raven's wings against the static,
and spoke aloud the symbol's sounds:
"Fly!"

AMY NEMECEK

CHAPTER One

Bruce, 2013

No matter how the world has changed over the course of my life, somehow crayons still smell the way they did when I was a kid. A fresh pack of Crayolas sits open on the kitchen table, and I roll the one called "Macaroni and Cheese" between thumb and finger.

My youngest granddaughter sits next to me, coloring heart shapes and smiley faces all over her piece of printer paper. We're busy making cards for her great-grammy—my mother—whose birthday is over the weekend. So far Evie's got more wax on the page than I do.

"How old is Great-Grammy gonna be?" Evie asks, switching to a light shade of brown.

"Eighty-five," I say.

She looks up from her coloring to give me a drop-jawed look. "That's really old."

"Well, let's not say that to her, all right?" I give her a wink.

Evie gives me a thumbs-up before going back to her work.

Boy, do I love spending time with this girl.

"You're doing a good job," I say, tilting my head to look at her picture.

"Thanks," she says. "Do you think Great-Grammy will like it?"

"Of course she will."

A gust comes in through the open window, making the corner of Evie's paper flicker just a little bit. Outside, the tops of the trees sway and the leaves that have already fallen to the ground ride the wind across the yard.

Man, do I love fall in Michigan.

I fit my crayon back in its place between the deep orange and goldenrod yellow. "You know what. I'm getting thirsty."

"Me too," she says, letting her shoulders slump as if she's been laboring over that card all day.

"How about I make us some hot cocoa?" I narrow my eyes at her. "Would that be all right with you?"

That gets her to perk up right away, and she tells me, "Yes, please."

As soon as the weather drops below sixty degrees, Linda makes sure we're well stocked with the fixings for hot cocoa. The mix, marshmallows, the works. Our oldest, Sonny, likes to point out that it wasn't this way when she was a little girl. I like to remind her that we weren't grandparents then.

I hardly get the cupboard open to pick two mugs before I hear a thunk on the window. A quick look and I see a little sparrow, unmoving, on the grass, wings splayed on either side. Its head is turned at a funny angle.

"What was that?" Evie asks, eyebrows scrunched together.

"You stay right there," I say by way of answering. "I'll go check it out."

I rush to the family room and push open the sliding door, stepping out onto the patio.

The late morning has a hint of chill to it as if to remind me that winter isn't as far away as I might like to think. I wish I'd slipped on a pair of shoes. Socked feet aren't always the surest, especially on leaf-covered grass. Last thing I need is to fall, especially while I'm supposed to be taking care of Evie. At my age—sixty-ahem years old—it's not so easy to recover from a tumble.

Trying my best not to startle the bird—a house sparrow—I lower myself, pressing one knee into the ground, hoping to see a sign of life.

"Grandpa?" Evie's on the other side of the window, fingers curled and pressed against her cheeks. "Is it dead?"

"I don't think so, honey," I say, smiling at her. "How about you see if Grandma has a dry washcloth in the drawer. All right?"

She nods, but the look in her eyes says she's feeling more than a little bit worried. I'm more than a little relieved when I notice the slight rise and fall of the sparrow's chest. She's breathing. That's something at least. By the time Evie comes out, cloth in hand, the sparrow's managed to get herself sitting up.

"She'll be fine in a few minutes," I say, as calm and gentle as I can so as not to startle the bird.

I use the washcloth to pick up the sparrow. She rests in my cupped hands, and I resist the temptation to run the tip of a finger over her feathers. They look like they'd be soft to the touch.

But birds like this one are wild, not meant for the affections of humans. Instead, I just watch her, hoping she recovers from the shock she's had this morning.

"'There is a special providence in the fall of a sparrow,'" I whisper after a minute.

"What's that mean?" Evie asks.

"Well, it's from a play called *Hamlet*," I say, noticing how the sparrow blinks at the sound of my voice. "It just means that God sees everything and cares, even if it's just a little critter smacking into a window."

Evie doesn't take her eyes off the bird and doesn't give me any indication that she understands. That's all right. Sometimes I have a tough time comprehending it too.

The sparrow gives a little tremble, and I make a shushing sound like the one I always made when comforting one of my girls when they fell off their bikes or stubbed a toe.

"That's it," I say when she tries her wings, stretching them with a little twitch. Keeping them spread, she gives a tiny, tentative hop.

Then a second hop with a bit more certainty.

"Can we keep her?" Evie asks, putting a hand on my shoulder.

"I'm afraid not, honey." I shake my head. "She wouldn't like being a pet, I don't think. She needs to be free."

I flatten my hands, hoping to give the sparrow a better surface to take off from. She's hardly an ounce; I barely notice the weight of her at all. But when she pushes off to fly, saying goodbye with a little trill, I miss how she felt in my hands.

We watch her go, Evie and me, until we lose her in the branches of the ancient sycamore at the far end of the yard.

My sweet girl lowers her head to my shoulder, and her sniffles let me know that she's crying. Well, I feel like crying too, just for a different reason.

"I wanted to keep her," she says.

"I kind of did too," I say. "But it wouldn't have been good for her."

"Will we ever see her again?"

"I bet we will, sweetheart." I put my arm around her and kiss the top of her head.

I look back toward the spot where I last saw that bird, not saying that house sparrows are a dime a dozen, if that.

Still, it's something to see them fly.

Linda's car is in the garage when I get home from dropping off Evie and running a few errands. When I come inside the house, I hear her singing along to the radio in the kitchen. Her voice is a deep, satiny ribbon of alto that I could listen to all day long. It's an old Carpenters tune, and her tone is every bit as smooth as Karen's was.

She perks up, ending her song, when she sees me. I wish she'd just keep on singing, but it would only embarrass her if I said so.

Years ago, before she met me, she'd had dreams of playing alongside the likes of Dusty Springfield and Janis Joplin. It isn't lost on me that she chose to settle down and start a family with yours truly instead of heading out for the San Francisco music scene.

I admit that I'm biased as the day is long, but she could have made it out there.

"Hey there," she says, rolling a ball of ground beef between the palms of her hands. "Did you have a nice day with Ev?"

"I did," I answer. "We rescued a stunned bird."

"How about that?" She drops the meatball into the pan. "Did she want to keep it?"

"Yup. But she understood when I said we couldn't."

"She's a sweet girl," she says. "You don't mind meatballs for supper, do you?"

"Nope," I say.

"Good. I wouldn't want you going hungry." She winks at me before pinching another hunk of ground beef and rolling it.

"Mindy eating with us?"

"As far as I know."

Our middle daughter's been back home for a couple of weeks—temporarily, of course—and we're still figuring it all out. We're doing our best to have an abundance of grace for her right now. It's got to be tough to be forty-two and starting all over again.

As far as grace goes, I'm happy to extend it to Mindy. That husband—soon to be ex—of hers, however, is a different matter altogether.

I clear my throat, trying to convince myself to forgive anyway. Man alive, it's hard.

Harder still for Mindy, I have to imagine.

I'm the father of three. All daughters. So far all the grandkids I have are girls. I have become a man well acquainted with all things pink and frilly and sweet. More than once I've woken from a nap on the couch to find my toenails painted red. Over the years I've grown accustomed to posters of teenaged heart-throbs plastered on bedroom walls and the way girls have of showing their emotions. I've learned to appreciate a good rom-com and that it's all right to cry at the end when the pair lives happily ever after.

Every once in a while somebody asks if I'm disappointed that I never had a boy. Nah, I tell them. I'm pretty content. I like my life as is. I'm used to it.

What I'm not used to, though, is the blazing anger I feel when somebody hurts one of them.

And I'm especially protective of Mindy.

She's come so far from the tiny girl we met thirty-eight years ago. She'd shaken so hard when they'd put her in my arms. Mindy had felt so light. Lighter than any four-year-old I'd ever known.

But as tiny as she was then, the burden she bore was heavier than any I've ever lifted.

It doesn't seem right that she's got to go through this too.

Had I known it would end up like this, I might have tried to stop her from marrying Eric. I might have done a better job of protecting her.

Mindy didn't make it home to eat with us, but at least she sent a text message to let us know as much. Work is keeping her busy these days, which I guess is a good thing. She just got promoted to senior editor over at the local paper—the *Bear Run Herald*—and our high school football team is having a winning season for the first time since the late 1980s. She's got plenty to keep her distracted.

Neither Linda nor I hear her Prius roll into the driveway around nine o'clock—those cars are spookily quiet, if you ask me—so when she comes into the family room, she gives me a start.

I may or may not have been halfway into a nice little snooze in my La-Z-Boy.

"I'm sorry," she says, laughing. "I guess I snuck up on you."

"It's all right," I say.

"Hi, honey," Linda says. "You want me to warm up some supper for you?"

"Oh, I already ate," Mindy says. "Thanks, though."

She drops into the couch cushions, her satchel still strapped across her shoulder. I hit mute to quiet the program Linda and I were watching.

"Everything all right?" Linda asks.

"Yeah." Mindy nods. "Crazy, but all right."

She nudges up her glasses with her finger.

"You're doing a real good job at the paper," I say. "We're proud of you."

"Thanks, Dad." She pulls her legs up under her.

We three sit and watch the movement on the silent TV for a couple of minutes, and I think about turning the volume on again. But right when I'm about to hit the button, Mindy clears her throat.

"So, I read an interesting article today," she says.

"One for the *Herald*?" Linda asks.

"No. Just one I found online," Mindy answers. "I was doing a Google search and came across it. It's about this guy who was adopted from Vietnam from the Babylift. Um, like I was."

"Oh," Linda says.

"I guess he found this website for people like us who were looking for their family over there." She licks her lips. Then she cringes. "Not that I'm looking for anybody in Vietnam or anything. You know."

"Uh-huh." Linda pulls the lapels of her robe closed around her neck.

"Anyway, somehow he—the guy in the article—got connected with his birth mother and he went to Ho Chi Minh City to meet her." Mindy lifts her shoulders and smiles. "Isn't that wild?"

"Yeah," I say. "After all these years."

"I know." Mindy reaches up and scratches the top of her head. "I wouldn't have thought something like that was possible. But, um, I found that website. It was linked at the bottom of the article. You know how they do that?"

I push the footrest down and lean forward in my seat.

"Did you find anything?" Linda asks.

"Oh no. Not really." Mindy clears her throat again. "I wasn't really looking. Just poking around. I . . . I . . ."

"It's all right if you are looking," Linda says. "We'll understand."

"That's right," I add.

"I know." Mindy bites her bottom lip. "It's scary to even think about, though."

From where I'm sitting, I can reach her hand. So I take it in mine, her fingers cold against my warm skin.

"What's scary about it?" I ask. "Are you afraid you won't find anything out?"

"No." She smiles the way she does when she's holding back emotion. "I'm afraid I will find something or someone. It's dumb."

"No it isn't."

"I was just curious. That's all." She squints her eyes. "I don't want you to think that you aren't enough for me."

Linda leaves her chair so she can sit beside Mindy, putting her arm around her. "We would never think that."

"You know we'll support you in whatever you do," I say. "If you want to look, I say go for it."

"There's just so much going on already with work and Eric . . ."

Her hand trembles in mine, and I tell her that everything's going to be all right. Good even. Maybe not right away, but eventually.

"I probably wouldn't find out anything anyway," she whispers.

"But what if you did?" Linda asks.

"I don't know." Mindy turns toward Linda. "I guess I'd have to think about taking a trip there. Maybe."

"By yourself?" I ask.

She's an adult. I know this in my head. She's an adult who needs to be free to make her own choices and to take a risk now and then. It's silly. I know it. Still, worry burrows deep in a man's heart when he becomes a father, and it's not so easily coaxed out.

"No. Of course not." She shakes her head and wrinkles her nose. "Do you think Sonny would let me go without her?"

She's got a point. She really does.

Then she pulls her hand out from mine and pushes up her glasses again.

"Tomorrow's going to be another late night," she says. "There's a home game against Fort Colson I'm supposed to cover."

"Busy, busy," Linda says, getting up from the couch. "I think I might have some popcorn. Anybody else like some?"

She goes to the kitchen, and within a minute I hear the microwave going.

"Dad," Mindy says.

"Yeah?"

"Maybe just don't say anything to Grammy about the Babylift stuff. Okay?" She shrugs. "She wouldn't understand."

"No, she would not," I say with a bit of a chuckle.

There are many words one might use to describe my mother. *Understanding* certainly isn't one of them.

CHAPTER TWO

Linda, 1975

If only it had been warmer, I would have rolled my window down and let the sun-kissed breeze whip around me as I sped down the highway. But, as was often the case in Northern Michigan, early April was still on the chilly side—hardly above freezing!—and I wasn't completely out of my mind.

So, to make up for the lack of rushing air, I turned up the radio and sang along with B-b-b-Bennie and the Jetsssss, tapping my fingers on the steering wheel along with each bum-bum-ba-da-bum of the piano.

My cherry-red Dodge Dart may have been fifteen years old and showing its age in rust spots, but it still had pretty good get-up-and-go. Had I been alone, I would have blown the stink off, taking her all the way up to fifty-five on the highway. But since Sonny was in the passenger seat, I decided to keep it down to the speed limit.

Having a kid in the car was a good reminder to drive safely. Especially when that kid was five going on thirty-five and had absolutely no qualms about tattling on her mommy. And who did this particular five-year-old most like tattling to? None other than my no-nonsense, take-no-prisoners mother-in-law, Hilda.

The glare of that woman could wither me faster than anything else in the world.

By the time I pulled onto my in-laws' street, my hands felt buzzy from the shake-rattle-and-roll of the steering wheel. I turned the radio down and eased off the gas pedal so the muffler might not grumble quite as much.

The last thing I needed was to add even more to Hilda's running list of my offenses against her. The first was my stealing of her son from her—he, in fact, married me quite willingly—closely followed by my choice to occasionally wear slacks to church. Other transgressions included not peeling the potatoes before mashing them and serving them with less than silky-smooth gravy.

Oops-a-daisy.

My one shining moment, though, was in giving her a grandchild.

Every moment following Sonny's squalling entrance into the world, however, was fair game to be added to the list, including my inability to quickly produce a second baby for Hilda to grandparent.

Not that it was for lack of trying.

It was a wonder there hadn't been a full investigation into my single-handed crimes against humanity.

I parked next to Hilda's Ford Fairlane wagon—it was, of course, a sensible shade of eggshell and without a speck of dirt or a splatter of bird poop—and put the engine into park.

Hilda and Ivan's house looked like it belonged in *Better Homes and Gardens*. Not because it was anything spectacularly fancy, but because of how well taken care of it was. The hedges were always trimmed just right, the yard tidy, the garage kept cleaner than my kitchen. Everything had a place and was only out of that place if in use.

There was nary a hint of clutter in Hilda Matthews's house.

Bruce claimed it had always been that way, even when he and his brother and sister were growing up.

It was intimidating considering how cluttered our place tended to get. It seemed we were constantly crowded by a stack of books on the coffee table or a pile of shoes by the door, not to mention Sonny's Barbie dolls.

Then again, our house was so small it looked a mess even if merely two things were out of place. It was six hundred square feet filled with a thousand square feet worth of stuff, but it was ours. I had to remind myself often that we wouldn't live there forever.

For the meantime, I just had to make the most of it and try to hide the clutter whenever I saw that eggshell-colored Ford pulling into my driveway.

The moment I cut the engine, Sonny burst out the passenger-side door and bolted for the house, letting herself in without so much as a single knock or ring of the doorbell.

"Sonny," I called after her, an act of futility to be sure.

She was five and cute, but that didn't mean she would get away with breaking and entering.

I rapped my knuckles on the door that Sonny hadn't bothered to close behind her, proving that she was, indeed, born in a barn.

"Hello?" I called, stepping inside and feeling a sinking sensation of dread.

"In the kitchen," Hilda answered. "Make sure you shut the door behind you, for Pete's sake."

If I could have been sure she wouldn't see it, I might have rolled my eyes. But I could have no such certainty. Unreasonable as it may have seemed, I was convinced that nothing—but nothing—escaped the notice of my mother-in-law.

Instead, I shut the door and hung my purse on the coat-tree in the entryway before heading to the kitchen.

Hilda stood at the stove, moving her wooden spoon through something thick and bubbling in her blue enamel pot, and I chased away the images of every witch from the Grimm Brothers' tales.

"Did Sonny come through here?" I asked.

She shook her head. "She must have found Father in the living room."

I knew she meant my father-in-law, Ivan, her husband of just over thirty years. It gave me the heebie-jeebies when she called him that.

"What's for supper?" I asked. "It smells great."

"Sonny's favorite," Hilda said. "*My* spaghetti."

I tried not to let her emphasis on "my" sting me. We both knew that my daughter wouldn't touch any spaghetti I made with a ten-foot pole. I thought of the last time I'd tried feeding it to her. The evening ended in tears and tantrums, not all of them on Sonny's part. She'd gone to bed that night without taking a solitary bite.

When Hilda had heard about it, she told me that I must never, ever allow my child to rule the roost like that. She'd said that was a lesson learned better sooner than later.

I hadn't learned that lesson at all.

Instead, I'd learned to never tell her things like that again.

Hilda held out her wooden spoon with a dab of red sauce on it, holding her hand under to catch any drips. "Would you taste this and let me know if it's missing anything?"

"Sure."

It was perfect. Of course. That show-off.

The first Friday of every month was family dinner night at Bruce's folks' house. They'd put the leaf in the dining room table and grab the spare chairs from other rooms so the seven of us could all have a seat.

Before long we'd have to find a high chair for my sister-in-law's soon-to-arrive little bundle.

Never in my life had I seen a pregnant woman quite as adorable as Dana. Never had I known an expecting father as smitten and nervous as her husband, Chris.

Under the table I pressed a hand against my stomach, wishing I could have just one more, thinking of how many times I'd begged God to give Sonny a brother or sister, just to be disappointed whenever my time of the month came along.

"How much longer do you have?" Bruce asked his sister from across the table. "You look like you're ready to pop."

"Bruce," I scolded, drizzling sauce on top of my pasta.

"It's all right," Dana said, rubbing her hands on the dome of her tummy. "I am very ready to have this kid. But I've got a week left yet."

"I smoked four cigarettes a day when I was expecting each of you," Hilda said, handing the basket of dinner rolls to Chris. "I never got *that* big."

She pointed with her eyes at Dana.

"Well, I think she's the most beautiful girl in the world," Chris said, plopping two rolls onto Dana's plate. "More beautiful now than ever."

Dana leaned toward him, planting a kiss on his cheek that

earned an eye roll from her mother. Hilda wasn't one for displays of affection.

Out of the corner of my eye I spied Sonny on the other side of the table, sneaking her grandpa the entirety of her green beans. The little stinker. And he put them all—every last one of them—directly into his mouth to conceal their little exchange. The big stinker.

Sonny put a hand over her mouth, watching Ivan—or Grumpy, the name she'd called him since she started to talk—chew his way through the waxy veggies. I decided that I would need to have a conversation with her later about pawning her beans off on a man who she knew could never refuse her a single thing.

"Anybody read the paper today?" Bruce asked, twisting his fork in his pile of spaghetti.

I shot him a pleading look. Nothing good could come of a conversation that started like that. In fact, such topics as politics, Vietnam, and religion had been banned from Hilda's table since the year before when Nixon resigned the presidency. About such things there were as many opinions as there were behinds in the chairs.

But, of course, he took no notice of my silent begging. Either that or he ignored it and relished the idea of stirring the pot.

"A plane leaving Vietnam crashed just a minute or two after takeoff," he said, shaking his head.

"Bruce . . ." Hilda said, her tone one of warning that made my skin raise in goose pimples.

"It was full of kids they were bringing to the States to be adopted," he went on. Then he sighed and rested the fork against the rim of his plate. "Imagine that. Putting a kid on a plane to fly, what is it, five thousand miles over the Pacific . . ."

"Seven thousand," Chris corrected.

"All right then. Seven . . ."

"I don't know why you're talking about this at my dinner table," Hilda said before taking a bite of her roll.

"Because it matters, Mom," he said. "Why were they even bringing them here in the first place? Because they think we can raise them better than the people in their own country? Or are we just trying to make ourselves feel better for what we've done to them?"

"Hey, I'm sure there's a good reason," Chris said, putting his hands up as if surrendering. "If you'd seen all the kids there, lots of them living in the streets on their own, you'd understand."

Chris never said much about his thirteen months in Vietnam, and I guessed it was hard for him to think about, let alone articulate. Dana had confided in me that he often jumped at loud noises—a car backfiring or a popped balloon—and that he had trouble sleeping most nights.

She'd made me promise not to tell Bruce about it, though. Chris was so embarrassed and would have been mortified if everyone knew. But I sometimes thought that maybe it would make Bruce go easier on him.

But Bruce was twenty-eight and full of ideals and beliefs. It was just that sometimes they got away from him and he carried on just to win the argument. I tried clearing my throat to get his attention so I could give him my "chill out" face. He didn't hear me.

"How'd they become orphans in the first place?" Bruce leaned forward, arms resting on either side of his plate. "That's on us, isn't it?"

"Well, we aren't fighting a war all by ourselves," Dana added. "There's the North and the Vietcong and . . ."

Ivan leaned toward Sonny, whispering something in her ear. Then he picked up their plates, letting her grab the silverware, and the two of them headed to the kitchen, where they could shut the door and enjoy a bit of lighter and undoubtedly sillier conversation.

"Maybe this whole thing would have blown over long before now if we'd just kept our noses out of it," Bruce said.

"Bruce, honey . . ." I said, trying to get through to him. "Not at the table. All right?"

No one acknowledged me.

"Right. Great idea, Bruce," Chris said, nodding his head. "We should have just let the Communists take over another country on their way to invading us."

"I don't know why you boys insist on going on so at my dinner table," Hilda said, slapping the edge of the table with every syllable like a confused Morse code.

I considered for a full minute taking my plate and retreating to the safety of the kitchen and the blissful ignorance Sonny and Ivan enjoyed. But then I realized that if I left there would be no one to rein it all in if the arguing got out of hand.

Blessed are the peacemakers.

Even if all they want to do is run away.

"You know, Bruce," Chris started, "it's sure easy to sit there and talk about a war you didn't have to fight."

"Well, it's not like I ran off to Canada." Bruce crossed his arms. "All I did was get into college."

"While your brother enlisted."

"If I could have gotten him out of it, I would've."

"He didn't want out of it," Hilda said. "He wanted to serve his country."

"He could have served in other ways."

I lowered my eyes, thinking of the American flag folded into a triangle that Hilda kept in her cedar chest along with Dale's dog tags. Bruce believed his brother's life was wasted over there. I bit the inside of my cheek, praying that he wouldn't say as such out loud.

"So you would have gone in his place?" Chris asked. "I don't think so, buddy."

"Come on," Dana said, putting a hand on her husband's arm. "Let's all settle down a little."

"Bruce, I know you think you served your country by holding up a peace sign in DC." Chris snorted. "But you don't know the first thing about sacrificing for freedom."

"Oh, so riding around on a tank, blowing up villages, is how we promote freedom?"

"Bruce," I said, surprised he would ever say such a thing in front of his mother.

"I will not have this talk at my table!" Hilda yelled.

I froze, not daring to take a breath for fear of her wrath turning in my direction. Bruce, on the other hand, threw his napkin on the table and crossed his arms, and Chris proceeded to tear his dinner roll into tiny pieces.

No one said another word.

If a pin had the nerve to drop, the sound of it would have hit like the clattering of a cymbal.

Hilda sat on her throne at the head of the table, sitting ruler straight, and I imagined she was just waiting for someone to say something else. I prayed that Bruce would keep his yapper shut.

The door to the kitchen opened a crack, and Ivan peeked in. "Who won?" he asked.

"Who do you think?" Hilda asked.

"That's my girl," Ivan said with a crooked grin. Then, when

he closed the door, he declared, "Sonny, I was right. Grammy won. Pay up."

Dana and I met eyes. She rested a hand on her stomach and blew out a stream of air. For half a second I worried that all the fighting had sent her into labor. But then she picked up her fork and spun it in the pile of spaghetti on her plate before shoving a huge mess of it into her mouth.

"Now, are you all finished?" Hilda said, dabbing her napkin at the corners of her lips.

"Sorry, Mom," Bruce said, his voice as sheepish as I'd ever heard it. "I shouldn't have said anything."

"I forgive you," Hilda said. "Now, apologize to Chris."

"I'm sorry." He glanced at Chris out of the corner of his eye.

"Christopher?"

"I'm sorry, Bruce," Chris said.

The only sound in the room was the clinking of silver on Corelle dishes.

It wasn't the first time we'd finished family dinner with a few bruised feelings, and I doubted it would be the last.

I just hoped that Hilda had something good for dessert.

Once we got home and Sonny into bed, Bruce showed me the headline on the very front of the paper about the airplane that crashed in Vietnam. I tried my best to read it but couldn't get past the first paragraph without my eyes becoming too blurred with tears.

"These were kids who already had families here in America ready to adopt them," Bruce said, handing me the hanky from his pocket. "It's clean."

"Thanks," I said, rubbing it under my eye, blackening the

cotton with my running mascara. "Did it get shot down? Does it say?"

"No. They're still trying to figure it out."

"How awful." I sniffled. "Haven't they already been through enough there?"

My eyes cleared up long enough to look at the picture they'd placed above the fold of the paper. In the top righthand corner were two palm trees growing tall on the hillside. I let my eyes focus on them a moment before moving them lower.

Billow of smoke over rage of fire. Shattered pieces of the plane lay strewn among the grass and in the mud. Two Vietnamese men stood, in uniform, looking at the mess of tragedy around them. Only one of them was turned toward the camera, the expression on his face completely helpless.

"They don't know a whole lot yet," Bruce said, quieting his voice. "There may have been a hundred who died. Mostly kids. Some of the orphanage workers. It's horrible."

I left the living room, standing in the hallway until I was able to collect myself. Then I turned the knob on Sonny's door as quietly as I could, sneaking in and hoping not to wake her.

She lay in bed, her sheets a tangle around her legs and arms, half her stuffed animals on the floor. Even in sleep that child was in motion.

Doing my best not to disturb her, I pulled the covers up so they'd keep her warm, at least until she started thrashing again. I found her very favorite rag doll under her bed and looked at it for a moment.

It was the doll Hilda had made for Sonny's first birthday. The brown yarn hair had seen better days and the bangs stood up on end from years of being smooshed and pulled.

The doll had eyes the color of Hilda's, a deep and chocolatey brown instead of a blue-green hazel like Sonny's. All through my pregnancy, Hilda had insisted that the baby was going to have her eyes. It wouldn't have surprised me if she'd prayed for it.

When Sonny's eyes ended up being the same color as Ivan's, Hilda had taken it personally.

Only my mother-in-law could have felt slighted by the color of a child's eyes.

When I moved Sonny's arm to tuck the doll in with her, she stirred, looking at me through half-open lids.

"Hi, Mommy," she said in her dreamy voice.

"Hi, Sonny-One-So-True," I whispered.

"Is it time to wake up?"

"Not yet."

"Okay."

She let her eyelids close and her mouth hang open as she drifted back into whatever dream she'd visit next. I couldn't help but wish I knew what amazing picture shows played in her head every night.

Soft as could be, I pushed a tangle of hair away from her sweaty forehead and kissed her cheek, wishing I could gather her in my arms and hold her while she fell back to sleep.

But she was too big for that anymore.

CHAPTER Three

Sonny, 1988

Mindy stood in the doorway of our bedroom, arms crossed over her stomach and her backpack slung over her right shoulder. She didn't say anything. All she did was watch my reflection in the mirror.

"Don't stare at me," I said.

"Can we be on time today?" She leaned against the door-jamb. "We've been late every day this year."

"Have not." I unscrewed the top off my mascara, moving my face as close to the mirror as I could get. "Stop being such a spaz."

"I'm sick of getting tardies, Sonny."

Moving the mascara wand away from my lashes, I rolled my eyes. As if the secretary would ever think it was Mindy's fault that we were late. As if Mindy could do anything wrong at all. Not sweet, innocent, punctual Mindy Matthews.

I glanced at her reflection in the mirror. She didn't wear

makeup. Not even eyeshadow. And the most she ever did to her hair was pull it back into a scrunchie.

Somehow—maddeningly—the understated look worked for her. If I ever stepped out of the house without foundation and blush and eyeliner and the works, people would have asked me all day if I was sick and/or dying.

It was so not fair.

"Go ask Mom to drive you," I said. "Duh. It's on her way to work anyway."

"She's got an appointment."

"What appointment?"

"With the obstetrician. You know, the baby doctor."

"Um, of course I know that," I said.

What I didn't say was that I only knew that because of *The Cosby Show*, and I was pretty sure that all obstetricians did was stay up late to deliver babies and then come home to solve all their family's problems.

That and wear really, really grody sweaters.

Mom's doctor was a woman, though, so I thought maybe she had a little more fashion sense.

Whatever.

Mindy cleared her throat, and I decided that I wouldn't give her the satisfaction of annoying me. But when she started tapping her fingernail on the face of her watch nonstop, it made my blood boil.

"That's not going to make me get ready any faster!"

I hadn't meant to yell. Not really. But she was making me crazy, and I couldn't seem to hold back.

Mindy glared at me before turning and stomping her way down the stairs.

"Sorry for ruining your life," I called after her.

Like, three seconds later—okay, maybe that was an exaggeration, but still—she blared the car horn from the driveway so I'd know where she'd decided to wait. Then I heard the grumpy, coughing sound of my car starting up.

I dropped the pin I'd been using to separate my lashes as I released a sound of aggravation that came directly from my gut. I had to pay for gas out of my babysitting money and she knew it. The way that hunk of junk El Camino guzzled gas, she was costing me at least a dollar.

Double-checking my hair and giving it another spray or two of Aqua Net, I decided I looked as good as I could and closed my bedroom door behind me.

When I got most of the way down the stairs, I saw Mom hanging half out the door, waving at my sister.

"Mindy," she called, her voice way too sweet. "Can you please come inside? Now."

I swung my backpack up onto my shoulder and took it a little slower down the steps.

My mom was, without a doubt, the cool mom. The nice mom. The keep-the-peace-at-all-costs, former-hippie mom. Well, at least she was when the pregnancy hormones didn't take over, making her a giant mood monster.

I'd learned to give her lots of space when she was mad, and I froze in place, hoping all her wrath would pour out on Mindy instead of me.

"Sonny, I know you're there," she said. "Stop lollygagging and get down here so we can talk this through."

I sighed, cursing whatever parenting book mom had read for teaching her about "talking things through."

"I'm coming, I'm coming," I said, rushing down the last few steps.

Mindy stepped in through the front door, shoulders slumped, school bag dangling from her hand.

"Girls, I'm sick to death of you two fighting every single morning," Mom said, looking between Mindy and me, one hand pressed against her belly. "Knock it off, okay?"

"Well, if she wouldn't nag me—" I started.

"I'm not the one who makes us late every day," Mindy interrupted.

"Yeah? Well, wait a couple of months and I'll be gone at college and you won't ever have to be late again," I shot back. "I'm not going to miss you."

Mindy's mouth dropped open, and she held her stomach like I'd sucker punched her in the gut.

I felt like trash as soon as the words were out of my mouth.

"What an awful thing to say," Mom said. "You don't really mean that."

"Maybe I do." I stuck out my hip and crossed my arms. "And maybe I'd be a lot nicer if I didn't have to share a room with her."

"Sonny . . ."

"She's got to get used to sleeping in a room by herself sometime," I said. "What's she going to do when I'm gone?"

"We'll figure it out when the time comes," Mom said.

"It's just not fair." I wanted to pout but knew I was way too old for that. "She could move into the guest room. We, like, never have guests. It's empty all the time."

"We're turning that into the baby's room."

"How come the baby gets its own room and I don't?" I crossed my arms. "It's not fair."

"Don't talk to me about what's not fair," she said.

"I just want my own space for once in my life."

"You know she has nightmares . . ."

"Don't talk about me like I'm not right here," Mindy said. "I'm not a little girl."

"Then grow up and stop being so afraid of everything," I snapped.

That was enough to start us into a jibber-jabber of bickering, both of us talking over each other. After just a couple minutes of that we both ended up crying, and I was sure I was wrecking my makeup.

"Stop!"

Mindy and I both shut our mouths. Mom never—I mean, like, never—yelled.

She clenched her fists and closed her eyes, her face getting redder by the minute. I half expected steam to shoot out of her ears like Yosemite Sam.

"Mom?" Mindy said. "Are you okay?"

I opened my mouth to snap at my sister. Something to the effect of her trying to make me look bad by acting concerned about Mom.

But then my mother hissed—actually hissed—my name.

"What?" I said.

"This is going nowhere," she said, grabbing her purse. "Give me the car keys."

"What?" I asked again, dabbing under my eyes and glad to find that the waterproof mascara did its job.

"Mindy, give me the keys." Mom put out her hand, palm side up.

Mindy, ever the compliant goody two-shoes, gave them to her.

"I'll see you girls this afternoon." She dropped the keys into her purse. "We can hash this all out later if you both still care about it."

"But how are we supposed to get to school?" I asked, know-ing how whiny my voice sounded.

"Walk."

"You can't be serious. Why are you so horrible?"

"Excuse me?" Mom crossed her arms over the shelf of her stomach. "I wasn't the one screaming and honking horns first thing in the morning."

"Whatever, Mom." I squinted at her. "You're so unfair."

"Really? You think so? Back to the fairness argument?" She shook her head. "Maybe the fair thing would be to ground you for the weekend?"

I rolled my lips between my teeth and bit down so I wouldn't let anything else slip out. That weekend, of all weekends, I couldn't afford to get myself grounded.

My parents sent Mindy and me to a Christian school that, in an effort to be separate from the world, didn't allow homecom-ing dances or prom. But every once in a while, a girl from our school would get asked to go to the prom at the public school by a boy in her youth group or that she met while working at the mall.

Each of the last three springs my friends and I went to Deb to try on every single formal they had, dreaming of being lucky enough to be asked to a dance.

That year, my senior year, I was the luckiest girl. I was going to prom.

And the boy who'd asked me to go? Kevin Woods. *The* Kevin Woods, who wasn't only the most popular guy in Bear Run. He was the most popular guy in the tri-county area.

All right, so he was the one who told me that. It didn't make it any less true even if he was bragging.

Mom and I locked eyes like a standoff in one of the old Westerns Grumpy was always watching. I knew she was waiting for me to crack and say something bogus so she could ground me.

Lucky for me, she wasn't even close to as stubborn as I was. She blinked first and I knew I'd won.

"You girls better start walking," she said before giving us hugs and telling us that she loved us. "Someday you'll realize how lucky you are to have each other."

I really wanted to respond with a sassy "as if." Lucky for me, I stopped myself before I could even open my mouth.

When she shooed us out, my car keys secure in her purse, I realized that I hadn't won. Not really.

I looked back once while Mindy and I walked down the driveway just in time to see the guilty look on Mom's face.

She hadn't won either.

There were certain bummers about going to a Christian school.

First, it cost a lot of money, and unless your parents were rolling in it like Scrooge McDuck, you had to go without certain things like vacations to Florida and designer jeans.

Second, the depressingly small dating pool. Add to that the fact that I'd known most of the guys in my class since we were five and had borne witness to their nose pickings. It was hard to see a guy as having boyfriend potential with that image stuck in your mind.

Third, practically everyone remembered the time I peed my pants in the first grade. I was pretty sure that took me out of the running for coolest girl by a mile.

Fourth—and nowhere near last—was that there wasn't a bus we could ride to and from school. Usually that didn't present a problem. It was just a seven-minute drive if the El Camino was warmed up enough.

That morning, though, it was a major problem and the biggest of all bummers.

"This is going to take forever," I said, shuffling my feet on the sidewalk.

"It's just three miles," Mindy reminded me. "It's not that bad."

"We're never going to make it." My stomach growled and I was suddenly aware of how hungry I was. "I forgot to eat breakfast."

Mindy stopped, swinging the pack off her back and reaching in, pulling out a granola bar.

"Here," she said.

She always did that. Whenever we fought, she had to make it up to me somehow. She'd do all my chores or slip money into my wallet. Something. Anything to make me happy with her again, even if usually I was the reason we were fighting in the first place.

If I hadn't felt guilty for being so mean before, I always did when she did things like that.

"Thanks." I took it from her, and we started walking again. "I'm sorry I was a jerk."

"It's okay. I'm used to it." She kicked a stone with the toe of her white canvas tennies. "I'm not afraid of everything, you know."

"Yeah," I said, tearing off the wrapper and breaking the granola bar in two, handing one half to her. "I know."

Mom and Dad worried about Mindy. A lot.

I mean, I got it. Sort of. She had a ton of nightmares, and when we were little she did some weird things that I didn't think I'd ever really understand. Mom said it was because of what happened to her before we adopted her. But when I asked what happened to her, Mom just said she wasn't sure.

As if that helped me understand anything.

"I can move into the guest room if you want," Mindy said. "I mean, until you leave or the baby comes."

I chewed a mouthful of granola bar before answering, trying to figure out what the right thing to say was.

The sidewalk ended and we moved to the gravel along the edge of the road. We weren't even halfway there.

I was about to tell her that I'd help her move her things. That I'd even drive her to the hardware store as soon as I got my keys back to help her pick out paint to cover up the hideous burnt orange that was currently on the guest room walls.

But then I heard a *meep*, *meep* and turned to see a banana-yellow Gremlin pull up beside us. I had never been so relieved to see that strange little car.

Reinforcements had arrived.

"What in the world are you girls doing?" Amelia asked. "Did the El break down?"

"If only," I said.

"Get in." Amelia reached across the seat to unlock the passenger side door.

"Thanks," Mindy said.

The first time I met Amelia Parlette was on the very first day of kindergarten when the teacher put us at the same table. We'd been best friends ever since. We'd even arranged to be roommates for our first year at college.

How lucky could I be?

"Shotgun," I called when I opened the door.

When Mindy sighed, looking at the cramped back seat, I reminded her that she was smaller than me.

On Fridays the school served hot lunch, and it was always the same. Boiled hot dog on a bun with a handful of chips and some dried-up carrot sticks for one buck. Add a quarter and they handed you a little carton of white milk.

Mom always gave Mindy and me $1.25 on Fridays for lunch, and I found it a better investment to get a candy bar and can of Cherry Coke from the vending machines, saving the quarter in my pocket.

When Mindy rolled her eyes at me for it, I told her that it couldn't be any less healthy than a hot dog, reminding her of what they put into those things. Ew.

Amelia and I always sat at the same lunch table—the third one from the doors—with basically the same group of friends every day.

One of the advantages of going to a small school was that the odds of being near the top of the popularity ladder were pretty good. It wasn't like we were *the* popular kids. The Velthouse sisters were leaps and bounds out of our league. But we weren't the least popular, so that was something.

I was already in my seat when Mike Huisman and his little group of friends sat across from me. They proceeded to dare each other to eat their hot dogs in three bites or less.

"You guys are disgusting," Amelia said, crinkling her nose.

Mike just laughed and said, "Thanks," with his mouth full of bread and meat product.

"Hey, Sonny," one of the Jennies said from the other end of our table. "I heard you're going to prom with Kevin Woods."

I nodded while I took a drink of my pop, doing my best not to have a smug look on my face.

SUSIE FINKBEINER   39

"How do you even know him?" asked a girl named Becky.

"Just around," I answered.

I was not going to admit that my uncle set us up after selling Kevin a used Mustang at his dealership. That was way too embarrassing.

"Do you have a dress?" the other Jenny asked, scooting closer with her plate and carton of milk.

"It's so pretty," I answered. "I'll bring pictures once my mom gets them developed."

"You're so lucky," Becky said.

I looked across the table where Mike sat rolling his eyes and shaking his head.

"Oh my gosh, Sonny," he said with a fake Valley girl voice. "I can't believe you're going to prom with Kevin Woods. He's so cute. I would, like, die if he even looked at me."

"What's wrong with you?" I asked, glaring at him.

"Nothing. What's wrong with you?" He picked up his empty plate and stood from his seat. "By the way, I'll see you there."

"What?" I asked.

"I got a date to the prom too."

"With who?"

"It's actually *whom*," he corrected. "And it's none of your beeswax."

"He's so immature," Amelia said once he'd walked away. "Can you believe you ever went out with him?"

In my defense, it was freshman year. I hadn't known anything back then.

CHAPTER Four

Bruce, 2013

Fiona's Kitchen is the kind of greasy spoon where the menu is written on a chalkboard and hasn't changed in twenty years. The coffee's strong, the bacon crispy, and the hash browns come with cheese on top whether you ask for it or not.

Everybody who comes for breakfast—the only meal she serves—better bring cash. That's the acceptable form of payment. Period.

I must say, though, the cinnamon rolls Fiona makes from scratch every day are more than worth a trip to the ATM.

I park down the street and hoof it a couple of blocks to the restaurant, book under my arm, humming the Rascals' "It's a Beautiful Morning" all the way.

Somebody drives by, giving their horn a friendly beep, and waves at me. I return it even if I don't see who it is.

Fiona's is bustling today. I can tell as much as I round the corner and see the lack of parking spaces out front. When I get closer, though, I see there's a booth clear to the back that's empty. I make a beeline for it as soon as I get through the doors.

"Morning," Fiona calls to me from the pass-thru window

where she's hefting an armload of breakfasts for delivery to one of the tables.

"Hi, Fi," I say back.

"Be right there with your joe."

"No hurry."

In my seat, I put my book in front of me on the table—an ancient collection of Rilke I've had since sometime in the late sixties when I first started reading poetry beyond what my high school teachers had assigned. My dad had handed it to me off his shelf, saying he thought I'd take a shine to it.

He was right.

A crack in the spine makes the book open to page fourteen. I don't read the whole poem at first. Instead, I take in the lines about God cupping his hands around "each fledgling thing."

At some point in my life, I took a yellow highlighter to those words. I guess they meant something to me then. They sure do now.

Fiona comes by with a cup of coffee that leaves no room for cream. Just the way I like it.

"Thanks," I say, looking up from my book.

"Yup," she answers. "You want to put in your order now or wait for your dad?"

"I guess I should wait." I peek at my wristwatch. "Seems he's running a little behind."

It doesn't worry either of us that Dad's late. The past year or so he's started having a hard time getting someplace on time unless Mom's there, giving him what-for and keeping him on track. Every once in a while he even gets lost—no, that's not the right word. He gets turned around.

Nothing to cause anything more than slight concern. Not yet, at least.

"Just let me know when you're ready." Fiona nods at the book. "I'll leave you to it."

She moves on to the next table over, and I go back to my reading.

When, a minute or so later, the phone buzzes in my pocket and I see that the call's from Dad, I get a little flutter of anxiety.

"Dad?" I say once I answer the call. "Everything okay?"

"It's your mother," he answers, voice shaky. "She's taken another fall. Ambulance is on the way."

"All right." I swallow hard. "I'll meet you at the hospital."

"Yup."

He hangs up and I push myself out of the booth. Gathering my things, I reach into my wallet and pull out a five to leave on the table.

"Everything all right?" Fiona asks as I head out.

"I hope so," I say. "Sorry. I left money on the table for the coffee."

"I'm not worried about it." She half smiles. "Take care. Whatever it is."

I leave without telling her thanks.

If I know Fiona, she won't feel the least bit slighted by it.

Making my way back down the street, I wish I'd parked a whole lot closer. But how was I to know?

Dad sits in the recliner next to Mom's bed, holding her hand. He hasn't looked away from her since the nurses let us in here. It's one of a handful of instances in which I've witnessed any measure of physical affection between them. And Mom's sleeping through it,

They've got her on some pretty hefty meds and warned us that she might not wake up for the rest of the day.

It's probably for the best. She would throw an unholy fit if she woke up to find us staring at her. She'd insist on being allowed to go home.

But they aren't going to release her. Not for a couple of days yet. And then only to a long-term rehabilitation center. All signs point to her having had a stroke. Not her first, but her first that led to a broken bone—her ankle.

Dad's jaw tenses and relaxes. Tenses and relaxes. He's got to be thinking what I am. That this very well may be the beginning of Mom's decline.

And I have to think that if she starts to go, he won't be far behind.

Against all reason and despite Mom having grown into a bit of a crab apple, Dad is still as devoted to her as ever. The way he looks at her reminds me who she used to be when I was a kid. Stern, sure, but loving.

I like to imagine that he still sees that younger version of her, the one from before grief took up housekeeping in her heart, turning it hard.

Gosh, I miss how she used to be.

"Dad, are you hungry?" Linda asks, putting her hand on his forearm.

It's the first time in forty-five years of being his daughter-in-law that she's called him that. It comes as a surprise to me. Maybe to Dad too. He seems to snap out of an open-eyed sleep and turns toward her.

"Oh, I don't know," he says.

"I think you should eat," she says. "I'll see what they have in the cafeteria."

"All right." He pats his back pocket. "I'm sorry. I think I left my wallet at home."

"That's okay." She smiles. "I've got plenty of money."

"I'll just take a sandwich, then, I guess."

"Sure thing."

She kisses his temple and he shuts his eyes, pushing his lips together, the corners turned down into a frown.

"Thanks, Linda," he says.

Once Lin is out of the room, Dad leans forward and lets go of Mom's hand. He takes off his glasses and rubs at his eyes with his knuckles. When he drops his hands to his lap, I notice that his eyes are watery. I don't know if that's from all the rubbing or if he's crying.

"You okay?" I ask.

"Sure," he answers after a few seconds. "You called Dana, didn't you?"

"Yup. She and Chris should be here in an hour or so."

"That's fine." He turns his attention back to Mom.

For most of my life I've had a difficult relationship with my mother. It's a hard thing to admit, especially with her looking so helpless in the stark white sheets of a hospital bed. I've never said it out loud, but I sometimes wonder how my dad stuck it out for all those years with her.

He takes her hand again, lifting it to his lips and holding it there for a full minute.

He loves her and it doesn't matter that I fail to understand it.

As hard as she makes it, I love her too.

I'm not ready to let her go.

CHAPTER Five

Linda, 1975

I sat beside Dana on the bed in the hospital room she shared with a handful of other moms and their newborn babies. The whole maternity ward smelled soft and warm like Johnson & Johnson, and I breathed it in. Just the smell of it took me back to right after Sonny was born. I ached in the center of my chest for that time.

Goodness, my little girl was growing too fast.

Baby Teddy's mouth opened wide in a yawn. I met eyes with Dana in wonder. It didn't take much for me to be completely and utterly amazed by a baby.

"He's beautiful," I whispered, rubbing the bottom of the tiny foot that Dana had uncovered for me to see. "Just perfect."

"Do you want to hold him?" Dana asked, not waiting for me to answer before putting him into my arms.

He was absolutely perfect.

"Hi, Teddy," I whispered, running a fingertip over his soft, peach-fuzzy cheek.

"Say hi to your Auntie Lin," Dana whispered to him.

"Oh goodness, I'm an aunt."

"You'll be the very greatest ever."

I hoped so. I loved this little human so much already.

I held him for as long as I could, marveling over his soft skin and impossibly small fingernails, trying to notice every single thing about him. I held him until he started squawking and the nurse hustled in to bustle me out.

On the way to pick up Sonny from Hilda's house, I turned up the radio and sang along to every single word of that corny *Brady Bunch* song they played all the time that spring, feeling the sunshine day deep down in my soul. It didn't matter that I didn't know all the words or that I looked ridiculous bopping along to the bouncy beat.

I couldn't remember the last time I felt so full of complete and unabashed happiness.

Bruce stood at the dresser we shared, emptying his pockets like he did every night. He dumped the handful of coins into the canning jar we used for our rainy-day fund and put his wallet next to my jewelry box. Last of all was his Swiss Army knife.

Ever the Boy Scout.

I lay in bed, propped up on one elbow. When he turned and looked at me, he gave me a puzzled look.

"What?" he asked.

"Huh?"

"What are you smiling so big for?"

"Oh. I don't know," I said. "Am I smiling?"

"Yup." He narrowed his eyes, right hand working at the button on his left sleeve.

"Do you think we should have another baby?" I asked.

"What's that?" he asked, his eyes widening.

"I asked if you think we should have a baby."

Just the idea of it made me feel buzzy all over with excitement. All day long I'd imagined how this conversation would go. So far, though, I was the only one smiling at the prospect. Bruce didn't seem so certain, pulling one side of his mouth down.

It was something Hilda did when she was unsure of something, and it took all the happy, sunshine-day feelings from me.

"Forget it," I said. "I shouldn't have said anything."

"No. It's fine," he said. "I just wonder if it's a good idea. You know, after what the doctor said."

I knew very well what that humbug of a doctor said. That my inability to conceive was an indication that something was wrong. He worried that I'd have a miscarriage if I were to get pregnant again.

"He could be wrong," I said, trying not to sound like I was pouting.

"I guess so."

I sat up, hugging my knees to my chest. Bruce left the room and I heard the water running in the bathroom followed by the sound of him brushing his teeth.

"All right, why do you suddenly want a baby so badly?" he asked, coming back into the room.

A nugget of possibility sparked in my chest and I couldn't help but smile.

"I always want a baby." I sighed. "I miss having a baby. Babies are so dreamy and wonderful."

"And messy and stinky and demanding."

"Well, so are you, but I still like you." I batted my lashes at him. "Just joshing."

"I'm not the messy one." He proved his point with a nod of the head at my side of the dresser, where the jewelry and scarves and makeup were all jumbled together.

"You knew I was like this when you married me," I said. "Anyway, I wish you could have seen Teddy today."

"Oh. So I have him to thank for this." Bruce winked at me.

"Don't you think Sonny's ready to be a big sister?"

"Maybe the real question is if she's ready to stop being the only child," he said. "She's got it pretty good right now."

"I'm serious." I pushed the bangs off my forehead.

Bruce sat on the edge of the bed, hands on his thighs. He didn't say anything and he didn't look at me.

"Having a baby on our own isn't the only option," I said. "We could adopt."

He nodded. "That's true."

"What are you thinking?"

I reached forward, touching his shoulder. He turned and we locked eyes. I regretted saying anything at all.

"It's not a great time to take a leap like this, Linda."

I pulled back the covers and slipped in under them, rolling away from him, not wanting him to see how disappointed I was.

He was right. Obviously he was.

We were making it, but just. Our salaries together made all our payments and bought groceries, but there was hardly anything left over. Thank goodness the school let me teach music twice a week to cover part of Sonny's tuition.

Bruce definitely had a point.

Oh, but it was infuriating that he was always right.

"Eventually things will pick up at work," he said. "I'm next up for a promotion."

"You've said that for three years."

"I know."

"The least they could do is give you a raise," I said. "You've been there plenty long enough for it."

"Well, I don't have much control over that kind of thing."

He didn't say anything all the while he changed out of his clothes, tossing his socks and shirt into the hamper—a child of Hilda Matthews never threw their clothing on the floor. He didn't say anything when he climbed under the covers and arranged his head on the pillow. And he didn't react when I reached over and clicked off the bedside lamp.

"Honey?" I whispered after a few minutes in the dark. "Are you upset with me?"

"Nope."

"I shouldn't have said anything about another baby." I pulled the covers up over my shoulder. "I was just being impulsive."

"Well, my answer isn't no," he said. "It's maybe later."

He tossed and I turned, neither of us able to fall asleep.

"You still awake?" he asked after a little while.

"Yeah," I answered.

"What's on your mind?"

"It's silly. You'll think I'm being ridiculous," I said.

"I promise I won't."

"The possibility . . ."—I paused, taking in a trembling breath—"of never being able to have another baby feels like mourning a death."

I very rarely cried that hard, especially in front of Bruce. Or anyone for that matter. He did his best to calm me down, holding me tight and whispering in my ear. Once all the tears were cried out, he kissed my forehead.

"I promise that we'll have another someday," he said. "I can try and find a second job and we can save up . . ."

"You don't have to do that," I said.

"I want to."

I couldn't see his face for how dark the room was, but his words sounded so sincere that I had to imagine the earnest expression he wore.

"Maybe a little boy?" I whispered.

"Maybe."

He fell asleep but my mind kept spinning, so I went to the kitchen to warm up a glass of milk.

When I put my hand on the fridge, I saw that Sonny had been playing with the alphabet magnets. She'd rearranged a handful of them to spell "SONNY LOVES MAM."

I knew she'd spelled my name that way because she'd already used both of the *O* magnets.

I traced the letters with my fingertip.

If raising this girl was the extent of motherhood for me, then it would be enough. I could be happy and content and fulfilled.

My sweet girl. She was enough.

CHAPTER Six

Sonny, 1988

Mindy zipped me into my prom dress and I smoothed the bodice over my stomach. The metallic blue fabric was smooth and shimmery. The black tulle under the skirt was itchy against my legs, and I hoped it wouldn't bug me all night. Not only that, the shoes we'd had dyed to match my dress pinched my toes and rubbed at the back of my heels.

I looked at my reflection in the full-length mirror, thinking that it was worth any amount of pain and blisters just to be going to prom.

I fanned a hand in front of my face, trying to keep down the flush that was creeping up my neck.

"You look nice," Mindy said, circling around me and fussing with my skirt.

"Thanks," I said, drooping my shoulders.

I wasn't going for "nice."

I was going for something right out of a Molly Ringwald movie. I was going for nothing short of perfect.

Shutting my eyes, I daydreamed about how I wanted everything to go.

Dad would call up the stairs that my date had arrived, and

I'd check everything—hair, makeup, nails, breath—one more time before making my entrance. I'd take my time walking down the steps, fingertips skimming the railing, the skirt of my dress flouncing.

Kevin would look up at me from the landing, and his jaw would drop.

"You look beautiful," he'd say, holding out a wrist corsage that exactly matched the blue of my dress.

Then we'd walk out to his car and . . .

"Sonny," Mindy said, interrupting my daydream.

"Yeah?" I opened my eyes to see her so close to my face it made me jump.

"He's here." Then she clapped and almost skipped to the door. "Come on."

I totally forgot to do my last check. By the time I thought of it, I was already at the top of the stairs.

Feeling a little lightheaded, I held the railing in a death grip and my hand made a skidding sound against it as I slid it down, sounding like what Mom would have called a "rude noise." Mindy giggled behind me and I turned and shot her my look of death.

It didn't work. She kept laughing at me.

"I'm ignoring you," I hiss-whispered at her, then took another step down.

Once I was halfway down the stairs, Mom snapped a picture and I smiled just a second afterward.

"Oh, honey, you look so pretty," she said, replacing the disposable flash cube from the top of the camera before taking another. "All right. Hold on. I want to get one of you standing right there. Don't move."

Snap. Flash.

And again.

The woman was going to blind me before I even stepped out the door.

"Mom," I said in a whiny way that let her know I was mildly annoyed with her.

"Okay, okay." She smiled at me and wiped under her eye.

I wanted to tell her not to cry, but something else caught my attention.

Him. Kevin. Standing at the foot of the stairs and looking like Rob Lowe in *The Outsiders*. Well, except that his hair wasn't greasy and he was wearing a tux instead of a T-shirt with the sleeves torn off. But still.

Oh, Sodapop.

"You look hot," Kevin said.

My dad cleared his throat. Loudly.

"I mean nice," Kevin corrected himself.

Nice.

Great.

The problem with going to prom at another school was that I didn't know anybody. The problem with going to prom with the most popular boy from that school I didn't go to was that he was too cool to dance to any of the fun songs and I had to sit next to him on a metal folding chair, watching everybody else having the time of their lives.

Kevin just sat there, slumping in his chair, every once in a while admiring the cloth-covered buttons of his shirt and the shiny cummerbund around his waist. He didn't even offer to get us little cups of punch. I probably wouldn't have wanted it anyway. I'd learned from watching teen movies that the punch at all public-school proms was spiked. Still, it would have been nice to be asked.

"This is lame," he said while everybody danced to "Walk Like an Egyptian." "I hate this band."

I had to force my mouth to stay closed so it wouldn't hang open. What kind of person didn't like the Bangles?

It wasn't until the DJ started playing "Take My Breath Away" that Kevin showed any interest at all. Something at the middle of the dance floor caught his eye and he sat up straight.

"Come on," he said, grabbing my hand and pulling me toward all the swaying couples.

Not entirely used to wearing heels, I tottered and he caught me just before I tumbled.

"Easy there, sport," he said.

Sport? Had he just called me sport?

I had to, like, make a major effort not to roll my eyes at him.

All my annoyance with him melted away when he put his arms around my waist and I got a case of the swoony butterflies in my stomach. We moved back and forth a little and he whispered in my ear, telling me to link my hands around his neck. Then he pressed me against him.

It was the closest I'd ever been to a boy, and I felt special that this boy—Kevin Woods, for goodness' sake—*wanted* to be that near. To me. It was nearly unbelievable that he thought I was pretty enough, good enough, to be with him. I thought that maybe he'd want to be my boyfriend or something. Part of me had an instant daydream that he was *the one*.

I dared myself to rest my head on his shoulder the way I'd seen girls do in the movies, but I chickened out. I'd save that move for later. From the way he kept pulling me closer and closer, I thought he would want to dance with me all night long.

When the song ended and Kevin let me go, I looked up at his

face and smiled. But he wasn't looking at me. When I turned to see what had his attention, my heart dropped.

She was beautiful. Not in the way that eighteen-year-olds were supposed to be. But more like a movie star. And not like a cute movie star, but a glamorous one like Michelle Pfeiffer or Kim Basinger. When she laughed, her perfect smile showed off perfectly straight teeth, and her red dress fit her exactly like it should have.

"Oh my word," I said under my breath when I saw who she'd been dancing with.

Mike Huisman. He hadn't mentioned at lunch the day before that his date was Miss Universe. He leaned over and whispered something in her ear that made her throw back her head and laugh like she'd just heard the funniest thing in all the world.

I wondered how anyone could look that pretty when they laughed. It was super annoying.

"Who's that girl?" I asked.

"My ex," Kevin answered.

Of course. It figured. Blonde and gorgeous and perfect. She was, like, made for him.

"Oh." I swallowed back a lump of either dread or jealousy. Something like that. "I have to go powder my nose. I'll be right back."

I stood in front of the bathroom mirror, seeing that my hair was too brown and my dress too little-girlish. My makeup was too last year and my face was just too ordinary. Looking at my reflection, I saw a hundred little imperfections and wondered why in the world Kevin would want to be with me after being with *her*. I couldn't even compare.

But he did want to be around me or else he wouldn't have asked me out. Right?

When I left the bathroom, "Raspberry Beret" was playing and Kevin was nowhere in sight. I stood near the chairs where we'd been sitting, trying to find him on the dance floor or by the punch bowl or in the clusters of kids milling around.

But he wasn't there.

For that matter, I couldn't see Miss Beautiful-Ex-Girlfriend-in-the-Red-Dress either.

I crossed the gym to the double doors where we'd come in, hoping maybe he'd gone outside for some fresh air. But when I looked out into the parking lot, I didn't see anybody. And the spot where Kevin had parked his Mustang was empty.

Backing up against the wall, I slid down, sitting cross-legged on the floor and trying to figure out what to do. It took a whole lot of clenching my teeth to keep from crying.

A cluster of girls talked all at once and walked past, pushing through the doors and seeming not to notice me. An adult rushed after them, yelling that they weren't allowed to smoke in the parking lot.

Yup. That was what I had expected of public school.

After just a few minutes, Mike came walking out of the gym, a plastic cup of punch in each hand. He handed one to me before sitting beside me.

"Don't worry," he said. "It's not spiked."

"Thanks," I said, taking a sip. I hated to admit it, but it wasn't all that bad.

"Well, I've got some bad news." He put his cup on the floor. "Kevin and Allie left. Together."

"Who's Allie?"

"She *was* my date." He rolled his eyes. "I should have known better."

Then it hit me. I'd been dumped. Abandoned. At the prom

for a school I didn't go to. And I was stuck sitting in the hallway like a dweeb with a boy whose greatest accomplishment was being able to burp the alphabet.

I could have screamed.

"I can drive you home if you want," Mike said.

"That's all right." I took off one of my toe-pinching shoes and turned it upside down until the dime fell into my hand. "I'll call my dad."

"I'll wait with you until he gets here then." He shrugged.

"If you want to." I got up and grabbed the receiver of the pay phone on the wall.

"Hey, Sonny," Mike said.

"What?"

"You look really pretty." He swallowed. "Like, twenty-two-and-a-half times prettier than Allie."

"Thanks," I said, dropping my dime into the slot. "You look pretty too."

Mike gave me half a smile, watching while I worked my other foot out of my darn shoe.

There really was no reason to give myself a blister.

Dad didn't ask me what had happened when I got into his truck and I was so glad. And he didn't steer us toward home. Instead, he swung around the McDonald's drive-thru, ordering chocolate shakes and French fries.

I held the bag and the drink carrier on my knees until we got to the little park just down the road from our house. It officially closed at dusk, so nobody was there. And nobody would come along and ask the director of the parks department to leave.

It was just Dad and me and a handful of fireflies.

He helped me up onto the tailgate of his truck, and I handed him his shake.

"My date was using me to make his old girlfriend jealous," I said after half my fries were gone. "And then he left with her."

"What a rotten thing to do," Dad said, shaking his head.

I shuddered, the milkshake making me cold.

Dad unbuttoned his flannel and draped it across my shoulders, promising that he wouldn't be too cold in his T-shirt.

"Thanks, Dad," I said.

"No problem." He slurped the last of his shake.

"I should have known better."

"What's that?"

"I mean, why would a guy like Kevin want to be with somebody like me?" I pulled the collar of Dad's shirt tighter around my neck. "I was so dumb to think he might actually like me."

"Sonny . . ."

"No, seriously."

"Any guy who doesn't want to be with you is a fool," Dad said. "And that kid is a darn fool."

I rested my head on his shoulder, kicking my feet back and forth lazily.

When I was younger and something was upsetting me, I'd ride my bike here and swing, pumping my legs as hard as I could until I forgot everything except the way the air felt on my face and how it blew my hair every which way.

It was the closest I'd ever get to flying.

I thought about asking my dad if we could go on the swings, just for a few minutes.

But I wasn't a little girl anymore.

CHAPTER Seven

Bruce, 2013

It's the kind of autumn day that tricks a man into thinking it's far warmer than it really is. Still, it's beautiful outside and the sun is shining, so I take the back way, avoiding the highway that cuts through town. Creedence Clearwater Revival is on the radio, and Linda's on the passenger side. I long for the days when my old Chevy pickup had a bench seat and she could sit right next to me and I could have my arm around her.

We traveled a lot of miles that way, my babe and me.

But, safety measures as they are these days, she's on her side of the truck and I'm on mine, both of us singing about the rising of a bad moon, all manner of cup holders and gearshift and storage compartments between us.

I won't complain about the heated seats in this thing, though. Those are pretty nice in winter.

"How about we drive past the old place? We've got plenty of time," Linda says, grabbing my hand. "I haven't seen it in forever."

"Sure." I take the next right, headed that way.

It's funny how, even though I haven't been within five miles of the old house in years, I don't have to give a thought to which way to steer the truck.

We moved into the house on the highway leading out of town about a year after we got married. It was no bigger than a postage stamp, but the lot was decent sized and there wasn't a neighbor for a mile in each direction. The property was hemmed in by sugar beet fields.

Plus the price was right for our budget. If nothing else, that was the deciding factor.

Linda did her best to make it homey. It was one, maybe two steps up from being a shack, but somehow she made it warm and cozy.

Man, I have such good memories of that place.

As soon as we get within sight of it, I think it may have been a mistake, bringing her out here.

It looks as though nobody's lived here in a long time.

"Pull in," Linda says.

I do as she asks. Disheartened as I am by the appearance of it, I'm curious.

The weeds have overrun the yard, the paint peels from the wooden siding, the windows are fogged up with grime. And as I step out of the truck, I can see that a thick branch from the old maple broke off and crashed into the roof.

"Well, that's a shame," I whisper, although I'm not sure why.

It little matters that an old abandoned house is ruined.

I hesitate. Linda, though, gets out of the truck and makes her way up the graveled driveway. Shoulders slumped, hands in her back pockets, she turns back toward me and crinkles her nose.

"A bit of a bummer, huh?" I ask.

"Yup."

I put my arms around her.

Once I let her go, she takes a deep breath.

"Oh, Bruce, it smells the same as it did then," she says. "Don't you think?"

I sniff the air and catch the earthy aroma of the fields and the crisp and clean air.

"Suppose so."

She touches the crumbling lattice I nailed to the side of the porch when we first moved in.

"Remember the morning glories we used to weave into this?" she asks, hooking her fingers on one of the slats. "They were so pretty."

"Yup," I say, making my way over to stand beside her. "The girls used to sneak out, hoping to catch sight of a hummingbird."

"They pretended the birds were little fairies."

"I'm not altogether convinced that they aren't." I wink at her.

Kicking aside some rotten walnuts and thick fall of leaves, we make our way around the yard, letting ourselves remember. Here, where the girls built their snowmen in the winter and stacked leaves to jump into in the fall. There, the tree that Sonny fell from and broke her arm. And over there where Mindy turned her first cartwheel.

The tire swing I hung from the old weeping willow is long gone, but if I shut my eyes, I can still see it in my memory. The girls on either side of it, their feet dangling in the middle, their hands holding tight to the rope.

"Faster!" they'd yell at me, squealing when I pushed them higher and higher.

If I'm still enough and concentrate hard enough, I can almost hear the echoes of their little-girl voices.

The house was never anything to speak of. It gave me more

grief in fixing rusted-out pipes and drooping floorboards than was ever worth it. Every spring we'd have to put down ant traps in the kitchen, and in the winter we'd set out some for the mice.

Still, there was something special about living at our own little chateau in the middle of nowhere.

"Why did we ever move from here?" I say, more to myself than anything.

"Well," Linda says, taking my hand, "we outgrew it."

"Yeah. I suppose we did."

"It was a good place for us for a time." She leans her head against my shoulder.

We wander around the yard a little more, rub the meat of our hands on the windows to look inside, sigh when we see the damage from the branch that fell into the roof.

"Ready?" Linda asks, taking my hand. "We'll be late."

"Sure," I answer, letting her lead me back to the truck.

It's melancholy making, walking away from our old place. But we can't stay here all day.

We've got a party to go to.

Linda makes much of birthdays. She bakes cakes and hangs streamers and blows up balloons until she's red in the face and seeing stars. She's got a knack for picking out the exact right gift without spending a fortune. It's her mission to make sure the birthday boy or girl feels sufficiently celebrated.

I can't think of a soul who wouldn't know they were loved by the end of one of her parties.

I can, however, think of one who is nothing short of a humbug about her birthday. No surprise, it's my dear mother.

She thought she got out of having a party thrown in her honor just because she's currently in the rehab facility. No such luck. We may be a week late, but we brought the streamers and cake to her.

Linda decided to skip the balloons just this once.

All of us crowded into Mom's room, with barely space to turn around, we watch Dad help her tear open her presents—a blanket for her lap, a pair of mittens, a new heating pad. It's clear that she's complained to everybody about always being cold in this place.

"Thank you," she says after each one. "This will be useful."

That, as a matter of fact, is the highest praise she can bestow on a gift.

Once she's done, Linda asks if she's ready for some cake, sans candles. We didn't want to set off any fire alarms.

"Wait," Mindy says, stepping around her nieces, a beautifully wrapped gift in hand. "Just one more."

She places it on my mother's lap. It's small. About the size of a paperback. I don't guess that it's a book, though. Mom never really had much use for reading when there was so much housework to be done. Mindy knows that as well as I do.

"You need a little help?" Dad asks, reaching over to tear a bit of the wrapping paper.

"I can do it." Mom swats at him with her good hand, the other resting lamely on her leg. "Don't baby me."

Mindy squats beside Mom's wheelchair, hand on the armrest, eyes on her grammy's face. It takes a good amount of time for Mom to get enough of the paper torn to see what's inside. That's all right. Nobody's interested in rushing her. Well, none of the grown-ups, at least.

"What is it?" Evie asks, lifting up to tiptoes to see.

"A picture," Mom says, holding it up to her face and squinting. "Huh."

"It's from Easter," Mindy says. "Remember when I set up my camera? It was on a timer. Remember that?"

Mom shakes her head. Even if she doesn't remember, I do. It took us a good half an hour to corral everybody and get them situated so we would all be in the shot and looking in the same direction. Mindy set the timer and ran to make it in before the camera took the picture.

After about two dozen tries she eventually ended up with one that was good enough.

"I thought you'd like to have a picture of all of us for your room," Mindy says. "You could put it on your bedside table."

"Isn't that nice?" Dad says. "Hilda, isn't that something?"

Mom nods and hands him the picture in its frame. "You can take it home."

"Well, dear, she wanted you to have it here in your room."

"Is there cake?" Mom asks.

"We have to sing first," my granddaughter Faith says.

Mindy takes that as her cue to step to the side. She sings along with the rest of us, but the smile on her face isn't real. I've been her dad long enough to know that much.

Sonny and Linda serve the cake on little red plates, and Holly makes sure everybody gets a scoop of ice cream to go with it.

While Mom's busy trying to get a forkful of frosting into her mouth, I grab that picture and set it up next to her clock on the table next to her bed.

It's a nice shot of us. We're all smiling, which must qualify as a miracle. Well, and it's clever how Mindy cropped the photo to cut out Eric. His hand made it in, but that's all right.

"That was a good present," Chris says, leaning back against the wall, plate in hand. "Real thoughtful."

"Make sure you tell Mindy that," I say.

"Will do." He pushes his fork under the last of his cake and lifts it to his mouth.

"Thanks, buddy."

"You better get a piece of cake before your dad eats it all," he says. "Looks like he's getting thirds already."

I glance over just in time to see Linda plop another serving on Dad's plate and him putting his finger to his lips when he catches me watching.

As if I'd tattle on him. The man deserves all the cake he can get into him.

After we leave the facility to let Mom rest, everybody comes over to our place for a bonfire. It's probably the last one we'll have all year. It's a bittersweet realization.

Evie sits on my lap, the fire warming both of us against the chilly night. She's got chocolate and marshmallow stuck to her face from a couple too many s'mores. I know it's more than she should have had—especially after cake and ice cream earlier—but when she asks as nicely as she did, I have a hard time saying no.

"Grandpa?" she asks.

"Yeah?" I say, picking a couple crumbs of graham cracker out of her white-blonde hair.

"Who's that boy with Aunt Holly?" She scrunches up her face. "I saw her kiss him."

"Oh, gross." I grimace.

"It was really gross."

"I imagine it was." I squint my eyes. "Would you believe that's her boyfriend?"

"I guess." She leans forward and glares across the fire at Holly. "Are they gonna get married?"

"Maybe." I put my hand on the top of Evie's head. "That okay with you, squirt?"

"Only if they don't kiss at the end."

She leans back into me and opens her mouth with a long yawn.

"Grandpa?" she asks again.

"What's up?"

"Why's Aunt Holly so much younger than Mommy and Aunt Mindy?" She rubs her eye.

"Well, we thought we were done having kids," I say. "Then Aunt Holly surprised us."

"How?"

"Huh." I squint my eyes at her. And then, trying to change the subject, "What do you want for Christmas?"

"Oh. Aunt Holly surprised you in a grown-up way," Evie says. "I guess I don't want to know anyway."

"Whew." I run a hand across my forehead, wiping away imaginary sweat.

"Faith knows about grown-up things." Evie wrinkles her nose. "Mom told her. She said it's kind of gross."

"Well, I don't know about that."

She shifts her weight and then lies back so that I'm cradling her. It won't be long until she's far too big for this. She's darn well near that point now. I know my arm's going to start tingling soon. I don't mind too much.

"Grandpa?"

"That's me."

"I miss Uncle Eric," she says. "Don't tell Aunt Mindy."

"It'll be between you and me." I wink at her.

She winks back.

The truth is, as much as I'd like to kick the guy for breaking my daughter's heart, there are moments when I miss Eric too. A man can't spend twenty-five years in a family and go without being missed once he's gone.

Evie's breathing deepens and slows. I can't help but smile. My word, she looks like her mama. I draw her up closer to me and wonder how she can sleep with so much sugar in her bloodstream.

Mindy circumvents the fire to stand beside me. Looking down at the snoozing Evie, she puts a hand to her chest and lifts her eyebrows as if to say "how cute."

"You okay?" she asks, whispering. "You want me to take her inside?"

I shake my head. "I got her."

She pulls a camp chair close to me and sits, rubbing her hands near the fire.

"That was a nice present you gave Grammy," I say.

"Oh, it was nothing." She shrugs.

"I thought it was the best thing she got today." I watch the fire for a couple of minutes, mesmerized by the movement of the flames. "Your grandmother . . ."

I stop myself and put a hand over Evie's ear so she can't hear what I'm about to say, even if she is sleeping. It's another of those grown-up things that she's not quite ready to understand yet.

"She wasn't always like this," I say, trying my best at an apologetic smile.

"I know." Mindy pulls the sleeves of her sweatshirt down past her knuckles. "It's all right."

"What's not all right is that you get the brunt of it."

"I'm sort of used to it." She gives a slight shake of the head. "It doesn't bother me as much as it used to."

"You know it's less about you and more about her, don't you?"

"Yeah."

"She wasn't like this before."

"Before what?" Mindy asks.

"Before my brother died." I swallow hard, the sting of losing Dale still as sharp as ever. "It's no excuse, though."

"I know."

"I've let her get away with it so long," I say. "Too long."

"It's all right." She blinks hard. "Seriously, it is."

If it weren't for this pit in my throat, I'd tell Mindy that it isn't all right. Not by a long shot. And it's not fair that my mother has put the full weight of her deepest grief squarely on her shoulders.

I'll never know whose fault it is that my brother died. What I do know, though, is that it wasn't Mindy's.

I want so badly to apologize for tiptoeing around Mom's behavior toward my daughter. We all have. And it's not right. Not even a little.

But before I open my mouth to say I'm sorry, Mindy grabs my hand that's been covering Evie's ear.

"I think you're smushing her," she says with a smile.

Evie nuzzles into me and I glance down, catching her sneak a peek at me with one eye.

She's faking and I don't mind one bit.

CHAPTER Eight

Linda, 1975

The little TV that we kept in the corner of the living room was nearly as old as I was. A castoff from Hilda and Ivan, it only got two stations—three if we pointed the antennae just right. Black and white and all kinds of fuzzy, the picture left much to be desired.

Usually it was fine. The only program we watched with much regularity was the news anyway. Well, and sometimes we'd try for PBS so Sonny could catch *Mister Rogers' Neighborhood*.

It was the cutest thing when she'd see him on the screen. She'd clap her little hands and call him "my friend." If her idea of a friend was what she saw in Fred Rogers, I had all the confidence in the world that she would grow up to be a happy person.

Bruce moved the rabbit ears from one position to the next, adjusting the aluminum foil we'd wrapped around the ends, trying his hardest to get reception so we could watch the news.

"Come on," he said under his breath, as if hoping to convince the antennae to give us a clear picture.

"There, there, there," I said, nearly yelling, once the static cleared. "Perfect."

I patted the floor beside me so Bruce would sit close to me. He sat cross-legged and his knee rested against mine, and I thought it a wonder that being so near to him could still make a pleasant flutter in my tummy.

Dan Rather was in for Walter Cronkite that evening, and I was a tad disappointed. Cronkite was my favorite.

"Good evening," Dan Rather said. "South Vietnam is now under Communist control."

Bruce let out a soft groan and hung his head. I covered my mouth with my hands and leaned forward, my elbows resting on my thighs.

For ten years all we'd heard from our government was that we, as a nation, had the obligation to keep South Vietnam out of the hands of the North. That was why we spent hundreds of billions—*billions*—of dollars fighting that war. And it was why we sent millions of our soldiers—most of them still boys—over there.

Too many came back with wounds that had cut far deeper than skin and muscle and bone. Like Chris.

Far too many never made it back at all. Like Bruce's brother Dale.

Still, despite all of that, the Communists came riding into Saigon on their tanks to accept the surrender of the South Vietnamese. The flag of North Vietnam flew over the presidential palace.

It was over.

Just like that.

I felt sick to my stomach.

I'd spent most of my adult life praying that the war would end.

I protested and wrote songs about peace that I sang in smoky coffee shops to rooms full of hippies that all agreed with me.

It felt like I was really *doing* something.

Hogwash. That was what all my efforts had amounted to. In all that time I hadn't done a single thing to change the world like I'd hoped I could. All I'd accomplished was the making of much noise.

Through the muddy reception of the television, we watched folks running across a rooftop to the open back of a cargo helicopter. We saw the fleet of row boats in the South China Sea, Vietnamese families fleeing somewhere, anywhere they could find safety for just a little while, hoping to end up in a more peaceful place.

"Will they let them come here?" I asked.

"I don't know," Bruce answered.

The scene changed, showing buses with people standing close together, all trying to get on board. A reporter's voice came through the speaker sounding garbled, nearly indecipherable. But one image was clear as could be.

A little boy—I guessed just about two or three years old—traveled along above the heads of the crowd, passed from hand to hand toward one of the buses. He had on a little baseball cap, T-shirt, and shorts. He hardly moved, didn't seem to make a sound as he was pulled up and through a window.

But what about his family? Where were they?

"Families separated . . ." came through. *". . . pleading not to be left behind."*

My heart ached.

Helicopters that had just airlifted evacuees were shoved off the side of an airlift carrier. A few others crash landed into the sea, the pilots jumping out, swimming to safety.

It surprised me how long the helicopters bobbed on top of the water before resigning to sink to the bottom of the ocean.

"Why would they do that?" I asked, shaking my head.

"I don't know," Bruce answered. "But I don't think they need them anymore. They aren't going back to Vietnam."

The news went to commercial. A car pulled a camper down an old road, kicking up a cloud of dust behind it.

"Today," the announcer said, "your getaway car needs all the traction it can muster."

I closed my eyes, annoyed by the jazzy, peppy music of the commercial. The smiling family in that car didn't know anything about needing a getaway. Not really.

For that matter, neither did I.

Dan Rather was back on the television with more heart wearying news.

After having watched coverage of the war every single day for almost half my life, I was fed up. I couldn't do it a moment longer.

I reached over and turned off the television.

Bruce got Sonny to bed that night. From the kitchen I could hear him read a bedtime story and then the two of them singing *This Little Light of Mine*. She made him stay with her while she said her prayers and told him to check the closet for monsters.

She wasn't afraid of them. She didn't even believe in ghosts and goblins and those kinds of things. But she did know how to get her daddy to linger.

Really, though, I didn't think he minded in the least.

I didn't have a window over my kitchen sink, so I was reduced to staring at the wall while I washed the dishes by hand. So I'd made a collage of sorts, pinning a few things that made me think happy thoughts as I did my least favorite chore.

There on the creamy yellow wall I'd tacked a bit of needlework I did shortly after Bruce and I got married of a little Holly Hobby wearing a blue bonnet and holding a sprig of forget-me-nots.

A turkey feather Sonny and I found in the yard in the spring.

A copper Jell-O mold of a fish I got at a garage sale for a nickel that looked exactly like the one my grandmother had.

But most precious was the black-and-white photo of Sonny when she was just barely three years old.

We'd taken her to a petting zoo on what was probably the hottest day of that summer. The humidity encouraged soft curls in the baby-fine ends of her hair.

I didn't know if it had been the heat or if she was just very tired, but Sonny had been skittish, not wanting to touch the bunnies or brush the sheep or feel the coarse hair of the goats. She'd just about thrown an atomic fit when we even suggested that she look at the baby cows.

Exasperated and ready to give up and go home, we walked past one last enclosure.

It was nothing more than a kiddy pool in a chicken wire fence, but Sonny tugged at my hand to get to it. Her bad mood melted, replaced by the most bubbly of dispositions.

What had made her so happy?

Half a dozen giant bullfrogs.

Giant, by the way, was absolutely no exaggeration. The creatures were bigger than my head.

"You wanna touch one?" the man inside the wire fence asked Sonny, unhooking a makeshift gate.

My little girl didn't hesitate a second. She ran right in, grabbed a bullfrog, and hugged it to her, not minding at all when it peed on her.

Glancing back up at the picture, I chuckled at the memory.

"What's so funny?" Bruce asked, opening the fridge and grabbing a bottle of Coke. "When did you buy these?"

"Oh, I was just thinking about Sonny and her bullfrog," I said, rinsing the pot I'd just scrubbed. "And your mother brought them over for you. The Tab is for me."

"Why'd she bring that stuff?" he asked, wrinkling his nose.

"She said it was never too early for a woman to watch her figure." I rolled my eyes.

"She didn't mean anything by it."

"Uh-huh."

"We should take Sonny there again this summer." He nodded at the picture on the wall before popping the top of his Coke. "Although I don't think she'd turn her nose up at a bunny this time."

"You know she'd try to sneak one home with her." I pulled the plug in the sink, letting the dirty dishwater gurgle down the drain. "Your mom offered to have Sonny sleep over after family supper Friday."

"She did?" He raised his eyebrows and lifted one corner of his mouth. "When was the last time she did that?"

"No idea. Something must have gotten into her."

"I'll bet it was Dad's idea," he said. "Anyway, we're taking her up on it, right?"

"Yes, we are," I said. "We could go to a movie. The theater's showing *Monty Python and the Holy Grail*."

"Sure."

I filled the kettle before putting it on to boil.

"It's been forever since we've been out just the two of us," I said, grabbing a tea bag from the cupboard.

"Having a kid will do that," Bruce said. "Just imagine when we have two."

"Well, we won't have to think about that for a very long time." I shrugged and took my favorite mug out of the strainer.

"We won't?" He sidled up to me, putting a hand on the small of my back. "What if I said that I don't want to wait?"

"What do you mean?" I whispered, turning toward him.

"I think it's the right time."

"We can't afford it," I said. "Remember? We talked about this."

"Well . . ."

"Bruce, don't lead me on here." I dropped the tea bag into my mug.

"I'm not, babe," Bruce said. "I had a meeting at work today."

"Yeah?" I asked. "A good meeting?"

"Very good." He kept his eyes on me while he took a sip from his bottle. "They asked if I'd be too sore if they promoted me to Assistant Parks Director for the county."

"For the county?" I asked. "Not just Bear Run?"

He nodded. "It would come with a pretty nice raise."

"What did you say?"

"I told them, nah. I'm happy where I am."

"You did not." Then, second-guessing, "You didn't, right?"

"I told them I wouldn't mind at all."

"Honey," I said, putting a hand on my chest and feeling my heart pounding. "This is great."

"I thought we could call the adoption agency tomorrow," he said. "Get things rolling."

Mug still in hand, I threw my arms around his neck—later I'd be glad I hadn't poured the boiling water into it yet.

"Thank you," I whispered, my voice cracking from the suffocating joy I felt.

When the kettle whistled, Bruce didn't let go of me. Instead, the two of us shuffled across the floor until I could reach the knob and turn off the burner.

I hardly slept a wink that night, my mind cycling through a hundred images and ideas and sound bites.

Whenever I closed my eyes, I saw the little boy in the hat and shorts being passed from hand to hand, eventually being lifted through the bus window and into my arms.

CHAPTER Nine

Sonny, 1988

My life was totally ruined. Somehow everybody found out, like, right away that I'd been abandoned at prom. By Kevin Woods. Yes, *that* Kevin Woods.

I could have sworn that the newspaper had printed a special Saturday night edition with a picture of me on the front page looking like the pathetic loser that I was.

"Dorky Girl Gets Dumped by Local Hero."

What a waste of my fifteen minutes of fame.

By the time Dad and I got home from drinking our milkshakes, I'd already gotten three phone calls—one each from the Jennies and another from some sophomore at school that I hardly knew.

Even the little old ladies at church came up to me after Sunday school to offer their condolences and to tell me about the first time a boy broke their hearts.

For the record, my heart wasn't broken—at least not anymore.

I was just really, really mad. And, like, super embarrassed.

Since my parents wouldn't let me call in sick to school the

following Monday, I seriously considered running away and never showing my face in Bear Run again.

"That's a bit overdramatic," Mom said. "Don't you think?"

"My life is over," I cried, collapsing onto the table in a fit of tears next to my bowl of Cracklin' Oat Bran.

I appreciated that she didn't point out that I was only proving her point.

"Honey," she said, "you did nothing wrong. I want you to walk into the school with your head held high. All right? You have nothing to be ashamed of."

Sometimes I wondered if my mom remembered what it was like to be a teenager.

Mindy didn't rush me, but somehow we still managed to leave the house on time. The El Camino started on the first turn of the key, which hardly ever happened. There was no traffic and we didn't get stuck behind the bus of little kids that stopped a hundred times in one block.

We were, by some miracle, early to school.

And on the one day that I'd rather not be there at all.

"It really stinks," Mindy said as I pulled the car into a parking spot. "But you know what?"

I sighed after I wrestled the gearshift into park. "What?"

"Sonny."

"What?" I didn't even try to tame my annoyance.

"Kevin Woods used you and that was so uncool," she said. "And everybody knows it."

"Yeah, and I'm the dweeb who fell for it." I turned off the engine, leaving the key in the ignition, knowing that nobody would steal that hunk of junk.

"You're not a dweeb. You're the girl that he thought would make his ex insane with jealousy," she said.

"Oh," I said.

"But don't let it go to your head." Mindy pushed her door open and stepped out. Ducking down, she looked in at me. "Are you coming?"

When we walked into school, I tried to hold my head high like Mom had said to, even if breakfast sat heavy in my stomach. I wasn't sure what to expect, but when nobody stopped to stare at me or make fun of me, I was kind of surprised.

"Sonny," Amelia called. "Hold up."

I turned, and she gave me a sympathetic look. She was the only one I'd called to cry to. If there was anyone at that school I could trust not to spill my secrets, it was her.

"Hey," I said, grabbing her hand and dragging her to the girls' bathroom. "Nobody's talking about it?"

She shrugged. "Well, I mean, Mike was talking about it a little bit."

"Figures." I glanced in the mirror to check the height of my bangs, grabbing the comb from my bag to tease them up a little more. "I bet he's the one that told everybody in the first place."

"Sonny, that's not fair."

"He never misses a chance to make me look stupid," I said.

"Did you forget that he got dumped too?" She pushed up her sleeve to look at her swatch. "The bell's about to ring."

"What's he been saying?" I asked.

"I don't know," she said, grabbing me by the wrist. "Nice things."

"Why would he do that?"

"It's because he likes you, Sonny." She rolled her eyes. "I don't know how you can't see that."

"He does not."

"You're so blind," Amelia said. "Come on."

It was her turn to drag me around the halls. On the way to first hour—whoever scheduled a physics class that started at eight in the morning was nothing short of a monster—a few underclassmen girls said my name.

"We heard you looked really pretty at prom," one of them said.

"Who told you that?" I asked, turning and walking backward for a few steps.

"Mike Huisman," she answered with a giggle. "He's telling everybody."

"See," Amelia said, giving my arm a little tug. "Told you so."

During class Mike walked past my desk to sharpen his pencil. On his way, he dropped a note onto my textbook.

"Hey, Sonny," it started. *"Want to hang out at the mall after school? I can pick you up at four. From, Mike."*

I caught his eye as he made his way back to his seat. I shrugged and then nodded.

I'd spent all of my babysitting money on my prom dress, so as soon as I got home from school, I scrounged around for spare change in every couch cushion and junk drawer.

All I managed to come up with were two nickels and a handful of crusty pennies.

It wasn't even enough for a small at Orange Julius.

I even tried under my bed, hoping a couple of quarters had rolled there, dropped from my jeans pockets. No such luck.

I pulled Mike's note from the back pocket of my stonewashed jeans and read it for the hundredth time. "Hang out" didn't necessarily mean "date." "Hang out" meant I needed to pay for my own stuff at the food court.

"I need a job," I muttered to myself, pulling a dust bunny from my bangs and then leaning back against my bed.

That was when I remembered the envelope of cash that Mindy kept in her bedside table. At any given time, the girl had as much as a hundred dollars saved up from allowance or birthday money squirreled away. Every once in a while, she'd pull it out and count it to make sure it was all there like that miser we had to read about in English class.

She didn't like it when I called her Silas Marner for some reason.

I sighed at the idea of going all the way downstairs to ask her if she could lend me five bucks. She'd give me the money. Of course she would. But asking was such a hassle.

Crawling across the floor on hands and knees, I decided that I'd just borrow a few bucks and put it back next week after I babysat my cousins. I'd even add a little in interest.

She'd never have to know.

I reached her bedside table and inched the bottom drawer out, knowing it would creak if I pulled it too fast. I checked behind me to make sure she wasn't coming before I reached in.

Mindy had a little lockbox she'd gotten for Christmas one year where she kept her riches. What she didn't know was that the lock on it was so cheap that all someone had to do was shove the end of a bobby pin in to pop it.

It took me no time to click that sucker open and lift the lid. Turning to look over my shoulder, I reached into the box.

My fingertips landed on something glossy. A picture. Without thinking, I picked it up.

It had been torn out of a magazine. Probably some dusty *National Geographic*. It looked like a painting of a baby holding a really big, totally whacked-out looking chicken.

Mindy was always collecting the weirdest things. Most of the time I wrote it off as her being a geek, but that picture was something different. For one, it didn't have anything to do with *Star Trek*, at least not that I could tell. And for another, she'd put it in her lockbox and I wondered why she would hide something like that.

The caption at the bottom of the page didn't help at all.

Dong Ho folk woodcut painting, Bac Ninh Province.

I turned the page over to see if the other side might help me understand. But it was just an ad for Polaroid cameras.

"What are you doing?"

I jumped at the sound of Mindy's voice and sprang to my feet so fast I got stars in my eyes.

"Can I borrow some money?" I asked, putting my hands behind my back, the picture pinched between finger and thumb. "I can pay you back later."

She rushed across the room, eyes narrowed at me. "Why?"

"I'm going to the mall." I cleared my throat. "I'd only need a few dollars. Five dollars max."

"No. I mean, why are you digging through my stuff?"

The look in her eyes made me feel like the worst person in the world. She glanced at the drawer and the lockbox with its open lid, and I didn't resist her when she pulled on my arm and snatched the picture from my hands. I watched her eyes blink fast. It was what she always did when she was annoyed or upset.

She laid the magazine picture back in the lockbox with all the care in the world, and I felt so guilty for violating her privacy. I closed my eyes, trying to think of a way to apologize.

"What's the picture from?" I asked instead.

"Nothing," she said under her breath.

"Is it from . . ." I was going to say Vietnam, but she cut me off.

"I said it's nothing." She stood up and put a ten-dollar bill in my hand. "Have fun."

"I'm sorry," I said.

Nudging me aside, she pulled out her desk chair and sat down, pulling the cover off her typewriter and rolling a fresh piece of paper in through the top.

"Mins," I said.

She didn't acknowledge me.

I walked away as soon as she started her clicky-clacky on the keys—harder and faster than usual.

Mike dropped me off around eight o'clock and even walked me to the door. He didn't kiss me, though, which was both a relief and a disappointment at the same time.

Dad was in the kitchen, loading the dishwasher and wearing his "Best Dad" apron we'd gotten him the year before for Father's Day.

"How was the mall?" he asked, running a plate under the water.

"Good," I answered. "Is Mom home?"

"Yeah." His eyebrows lowered. "She's in bed already."

"This early?"

"Being pregnant's exhausting, I guess." He dropped a handful of silverware into the basket of the dishwasher.

"You're doing that wrong," I said.

"Oh?"

"Mom always puts the forks and knives pointy side down."

"Well, my mom taught me to put them pointing up," he said. "You want to call your grammy and tell her she's wrong?"

"No way." I reached down and flipped all the silverware so they'd be the right way. "She'd probably disown me."

"Oh, I don't know about that. She might write you out of the will, though." Dad scrubbed at the bottom of a pan with a Brillo pad. "You and Mike have a good time?"

"I guess so," I said. "He's fun."

He nodded, keeping his eyes on whatever gunk was stuck to the pan.

"Does this mean that the two of you are . . ."

"You know what, I think I'll go see what Mindy's doing," I cut him off and grabbed an apple from the fruit bowl on the counter.

"Aren't you hungry? I mean for real food?" He turned off the water. "You need me to warm something up for you?"

"No thanks," I said. "I had some pizza at the food court."

Mike had ended up paying after all. When I tried to protest, he told me that the guy always pays on a date. So, that settled it.

When I left the kitchen, Dad called after me not to leave my apple core in my room.

"Okay," I yelled, headed upstairs.

Mindy was sitting on her bed, reading some forever-long Stephen King book that she'd checked out of the public library. If the Bible teacher at school knew that she read such things, he would probably fail her.

Then again, if he knew I listened to Madonna, he might pass out.

"What's that one about?" I asked, flopping down at the foot of her bed.

"Um. There's this, like, really bad flu or something that kills almost everybody on earth," she said, putting her finger in between the pages to keep her spot. "The people who survive have this war to decide who gets to take over what's left of the world."

"Huh."

"You probably wouldn't like it."

"Maybe I would."

She tilted her head to one side and frowned at me. "I don't think so."

"Is it creepy?"

She pointed to Stephen King's name on the cover. "Yup."

I reached into the coin pocket of my jeans and pulled out the money she'd given me, dropping it on her bedspread.

"I didn't spend it," I said.

Mindy shrugged and opened her book again.

"Listen, I'm sorry," I went on. "I shouldn't have been snooping."

"With an intent to steal." She didn't lift her eyes from the page.

"Yeah. I know." I rolled my eyes. "I shouldn't have done that either."

"I forgive you."

When she smiled, I knew she was over it.

She was done talking, that was obvious by the way she turned her body from me and went back to reading. I got up off her bed and changed into my pajamas, tossing my jeans and shirt on the back of my desk chair, if for no other reason than to see if she'd say anything about it. She really hated when I left my clothes all over the place.

"So, are you and Mike going out now or what?" she asked.

Her book was closed and she'd moved to the end of her bed.

"I don't know," I answered, hopping onto my bed, glad that she wasn't done talking after all.

"I heard he told everybody at school that you were the prettiest girl at prom," she said. "He definitely likes you."

"Maybe." I grabbed my pillow and held it against my stomach. "I just don't know. What if I get to college and realize I'm not good at long-distance relationships?"

"You won't know if you don't try."

"Or what if I meet somebody else?"

She just shrugged and pulled the scrunchie out of her hair, fitting it on her wrist.

If we'd been in an after-school special we would have moved on to talk about the picture Mindy had hidden in her lockbox. She would have told me that she just wanted to know more about where she came from or that it was hard being adopted.

She would have cried. I would have hugged her. Then we both would have gone downstairs for ice cream with our perfect little family, all of us smiling and happy and loved.

And all of that with cheesy music playing in the background.

Instead, she went back to reading about the end of the world and I took a shower.

CHAPTER Ten

Bruce, 2013

My three girls only lived under the same roof for a month before Sonny left for college. Aside from the times when she came home on a weekend to do laundry or for a holiday break, she missed the first few years of Holly's life.

Then, right after Holly turned two, it was Mindy's turn to head out.

Holly's earliest memories are from life with just Linda and me in the house. It was almost like we were raising an only child in those days. Every once in a while I lament all she missed by not having her sisters closer when she was growing up.

So tonight, with the family room set up for a sister sleepover—air mattresses inflated and sleeping bags rolled out—well, it's giving me a nice, warm feeling.

Earlier today Mindy had a phone conversation with Eric that didn't go so well. I guess it was naive of me to think that once the ink was dry on the divorce papers that it would be the end of the struggles for them.

Unfortunately, that's just not so. Not yet, at least.

Anyway, the call upset Mindy, and the minute Linda heard about it she sent a text message to Sonny and Holly, declaring a state of emergency and telling them their sister needed them.

"BRING CHOCOLATE!" she tagged on to the end of it.

We ordered pizzas, made sure the fridge was stocked with pop, and I ran to the store to get the fixings so I can make them a big breakfast tomorrow morning.

I'm letting the ladies have some time to themselves while I noodle around a little on my guitar in the music room. There's a song that I've been meaning to write. This seems like the perfect time.

But I hardly get into tune before Holly peeks in at me. "Hey, Mom got out all the old photo albums. Wanna look at them with us?"

Well, I'd be a fool to say no to something like that.

The five of us sit around the dining room table, passing albums back and forth, taking our time over the old family pictures of birthdays and vacations and band concerts. Of course there are the shots from assorted church pageants in which our girls played sheep or angels or slapped on a yarn beard to be a disciple.

"Aw, look at this," Sonny says, pointing at a square and yellowing picture. "Mindy's kindergarten graduation."

"You were so tiny." Holly looks over Sonny's shoulder.

"Can you believe I was a year older than everybody else?" Mindy says. "Mom wouldn't let me start kindergarten until I learned enough English."

"Okay," Holly said, completely uninterested in the timeline of Mindy's early education. She points at the picture, finger resting on the bell-bottoms Mindy had on under her little robe. "But what's with those pants?"

"It was the seventies, honey." Linda reaches across the table for a cookie. "Everybody had at least one pair of plaid pants."

"Even Dad." Mindy flips through an album. "See?"

"Hey now," I say, squinting to see the picture she's holding up. "Those pants were cool."

"I liked them," Linda says, lifting her eyebrows at me.

"Ew, Mom." Holly cringes.

"Well, this is an oldie," I say, turning my album so they can see. "Your Uncle Chris and Aunt Dana's wedding."

"Back when Uncle Chris still had hair," Sonny says. "And check out that beard."

"Aunt Dana's so pretty." Mindy smiles.

"Grammy and I made all the dresses," Linda says.

"Hol, aren't you impressed that they made those bridesmaid dresses out of curtains?" Sonny asks.

"They did?" Holly pushes her lips to one side of her face. "Why would they do that?"

"We did not," Linda says. "That was just the style back then. I think they're pretty."

"The seventies were weird." Holly grabs a different album, and a loose photo falls out.

"What's this one?" she asks, holding it up. "Is this Sonny?"

"How about that," I say. "I haven't seen that in years."

"What is this monster?" Holly wrinkles up her nose. "And why does she have it in a choke hold?"

"It's a bullfrog, silly," Sonny says, taking the picture. "I was hugging it. Can't you see how it's smiling?"

"Hey, didn't you used to have that on the wall above the sink?" Mindy asks Linda.

"Oh, that's right. I did," Linda says. "Bruce, do you remember how Mindy would stand in the kitchen and stare at it when she first came home to us?"

"Yup." The memory makes me smile. "We kept finding her up on the countertop so she could get a better look at it."

"Why?" Holly asks.

"I was a weird kid," Mindy answers.

"You know what I just remembered?" Sonny says. "Mindy, you know when I got into your drawer to borrow money before my first date with Mike?"

"You mean you were going to steal money, right?"

"Details." Sonny rolls her eyes. "Anyway, there was a picture from some magazine. You know what I'm talking about? A baby holding a bird or something."

"Oh yeah." Mindy nods. "It was a chicken."

"Where did you find a picture like that?" Linda asks.

"It was in a *National Geographic* in Grammy and Grumpy's attic. I was looking through one about Vietnam—I was just really curious, you know—and saw it. Something about it triggered a memory for me."

"Really?" I ask.

"Yeah. It was like I'd seen that kind of picture before."

"I have no idea what any of you are talking about," Holly said, turning her head and squinting at her big sisters.

"Sorry, Hol." Mindy grabbed her phone, typing on the screen with her thumbs. "So, there's this village in Vietnam where they make these woodcut paintings."

"Of kids holding chickens?"

"Well, sometimes." Mindy holds up her phone. "See?"

I have to put on my cheaters to see the picture on her screen. The artist used bold colors when painting the bald-headed baby holding an enormous yellow fish. Mindy flicks through to show one where the child is holding a chicken, then one with a duck, even one with a lumpy-looking frog.

"Weird," Holly says.

"They aren't weird, Holly," Sonny says. "They're just different from what you're used to."

Holly rolls her eyes, and I have to bite my tongue so I don't scold her. She's an adult. Sometimes I have to remind myself of that.

"Anyway," Mindy says, "I did a little research on them a while back."

"Nerd," Sonny says.

"Yup. And proud of it." Mindy smiles. "They're supposed to bring good luck and prosperity. From what I understand, the people of that town have been making these paintings since the eleventh century or something."

"Where did you find out about this?" I ask.

"Google." Mindy lifts one shoulder. "It's kind of near Da Nang. On the coast. There was an American military base there. So, the orphanage was pretty full."

"Oh," Linda said, putting one hand to her cheek.

"What does that mean?" Holly asks.

She's a smart girl. Valedictorian of her high school class and summa cum laude in college. See? Smart. But though she's rich in brains, she's a little lacking in common sense.

"Well," Sonny says, "I think Mindy's saying that some of the American soldiers hooked up with Vietnamese women and got them pregnant."

"Ah." Holly's eyes go wide. "Do you think your birth dad was an American?"

"No clue," Mindy says. "I'd have to take a DNA test to find out. It's possible, though."

"Maybe if you find your mom you could ask her." Holly unwraps a chocolate and pops it in her mouth.

"*Mom* is my mom," Mindy says, voice soft. She swallows hard.

"Well, you know what I mean."

"The woman in Vietnam is my *birth* mother," Mindy says. "And I'm not even sure she's alive."

"Okay." Holly looks down. "I'm sorry. I should be more careful with my words."

"It's all right."

Linda catches my eye and pulls her mouth into a cringe. I nod.

I try to think of something to say that might defuse the situation, or at least ease the tension. I can tell Linda is doing the same. I don't know about her, but I'm coming up with a big, fat nothing.

"Oh my word, Mom," Sonny says out of the blue, holding up one of the albums. "Why did you keep this picture?"

Linda lowers her reading glasses from the top of her head and leans forward to see. Her shoulders relax and so do mine.

"Because you looked so pretty," Linda says, smiling.

"But this is the prom I got dumped at." Sonny rolls her eyes.

"Oh my gosh," Mindy says, grabbing the picture. "I can't believe we all thought that guy was so cool."

"That mullet, right?"

Holly, who's never heard the story, insists that we tell her right this moment. In the middle of the telling, I'm sure I see Mindy mouth the words "thank you" to Sonny, who answers with a wink.

I left the ladies to it when they put in *An Affair to Remember.* Not because I don't like the movie. I do a whole lot. It's just that it gets the waterworks going as soon as Cary Grant and Deborah Kerr first meet. And they don't let up until the credits roll.

My heart was already tender as it was after looking at all those old pictures. The last thing I needed was a tearjerker movie on top of it.

So, I went to bed with the intention of reading a little Wendell Berry. I couldn't tell you how many times I've read *Hannah Coulter*, but I know I'll give it as many readings as I can. It's a beauty of a novel.

But, intentions being what they are, I end up jolting awake, the book open on my lap, and Linda apologizing for startling me. A quick glance at the clock tells me it's well past one in the morning.

"I was just going to sneak into bed," she whispers, adjusting her pillow.

"It's all right." I blink hard, my eyes feeling so dry. "I didn't mean to fall asleep."

She takes my book, making sure to save my place with a scrap of paper.

"Your neck's going to be sore tomorrow." She gives me a sympathetic frown. "Honey, you're too old to fall asleep in that position."

"Don't I know it." I tilt my head back and forth, feeling an ache that's settled into my muscles. "How was the movie?"

"Good," she answers. "Of course."

I wait until she's in bed before I roll over and reach for the light switch.

From downstairs comes a loud laugh and then a shushing sound.

It reminds me of a line from *Hannah Coulter* about love

being the thing that carries us. That, even in the dark, love is always there.

In my bed, the lights off and the house mostly still, I wonder at that idea. As I sink into the warmth of falling back to sleep, I can't help but feel deep gratitude for this family I've been given.

It's nice to have them here tonight.

CHAPTER Eleven

Linda, 1975

Bruce and I stood on either side of Sonny where she sat on her brand-new, lemon-yellow Schwinn. We each had ahold of a handlebar and the back of the banana seat.

"Ready?" Bruce asked.

Sonny shook her head no, making her pigtails flutter. She had her little jaw clenched, and her knuckles were white from holding on so hard.

"What's wrong, honey?" I asked, leaning down to her level.

"I don't wanna fall," she answered, keeping her face trained straight ahead as if turning her head might end up tipping her over.

"Daddy won't let you fall."

"What if he does?"

"Well, what's the worst thing that would happen?" I tilted my head. "You might get a skinned knee. That's all."

"I don't like getting skinned knees."

"Well, I don't think anybody does," I said. "Hey, remember

when you went to the playground with me last week? What did you like the most there?"

"The balance thing."

"Yup. The balance beam." I pushed a few wisps of stray hair out of her face. "This is a lot like that. You've just got to figure out how to balance, that's all there is to it. Once you've got that, you'll be surprised how easy peasy it is."

Bruce crouched down so he could look her in the eye, a wide smile on his face. "Tell you what, you pedal down to the end of our driveway and back with me holding on, and I'll take you out for an ice cream cone."

That little girl sat up straighter, let her jaw relax, and nodded. Anything for ice cream.

"Okay."

"What kind do you want?" Bruce asked, standing and getting himself ready to guide her.

"Pink and brown and white."

She meant Neapolitan. Her favorite. She thought she was getting three times as much ice cream when she had it.

"All righty." Bruce nodded at me to let go. "Ready now?"

"Yup."

I watched them go and she got started right off, pedaling her feet and pumping her legs up and down as Bruce trotted alongside her. About halfway down the drive, he took his hand off the seat. Then let go of the handle, all the while keeping his arms outstretched and ready should she wobble.

When she did, he steadied her with a hand on the back of the seat and she kept going.

"I'm such a big girl," she yelled.

I hoped he would get her a double scoop. She deserved it.

From inside the house, the telephone rang. I thought about

letting it go. If it was important, whoever it was would call back. But, as much as I wanted to stay there and watch Sonny on her bike, I had a feeling that I needed to see who was calling.

I sometimes had an intuition about things like that.

I got to the phone on the fifth ring.

"Mrs. Matthews?" the voice on the other end of the line asked.

"That's me," I answered.

"Hi. This is Jan from Northern Michigan Family Services. I'm sorry for calling on a Saturday."

"That's all right." I swallowed hard.

I'd been waiting on that call for a little over a week. It was the one where they'd tell me there was a baby boy in need of a home. We'd all hop into the car to meet him at whichever hospital he'd just been born at.

We'd even put together a list of names we liked, waiting to pick the exactly perfect one until after we held our son for the first time. I turned toward the refrigerator where we'd hung the list. Bruce had marked a star next to the name Jason. I'd circled the name Andrew.

At the bottom of the page in red crayon was Sonny's pick.

Matt. She thought Matt Matthews had a nice ring to it.

I lifted a hand, placing it over my racing heart. This was it. We were going to meet our baby boy, give him a name, bring him home. He'd be ours and we'd be his.

I forced myself to take a deep and very slow breath in and out to calm myself so I wouldn't scream from excitement. There would be time for that after I hung up the phone.

"I'm calling because we have a bit of an unusual situation and I wondered if you might be willing to help," Jan said. "Do you have a few minutes to chat?"

"Sure."

Unusual? I was certain my heart had skipped a beat at that word.

I stood in the doorway between the kitchen and the living room, the telephone cord pulled taut. From there I could see Bruce and Sonny. He helped her turn around at the end of the driveway, keeping her steady for the ride back toward the house.

"We have your paperwork here," she said.

"Oh, is everything all right with it?" I asked. "If we made a mistake . . ."

"No, this isn't about anything like that. Everything looks good," she said. "I'm sure by now you've heard about the Babylift out of Vietnam."

"Yes, I'm familiar with it." I cleared my throat.

Outside, Bruce took his hands off the bike, and Sonny panicked. The handlebars weeble-wobbled, and she fell down. My stomach dropped. He didn't hesitate to scoop her up, putting her on her feet so he could check her knees and elbows. Dusting her off, he said something that made her nod and wipe what I imagined was a tear from under her eye. When he noticed me watching, he gave a big thumbs-up. Sonny turned and did the same, adding a wide grin.

"We've had a few of the children come to Michigan," Jan said. "Placing them with families has been relatively easy."

"I'm glad to hear that."

"But there's one . . ."

She hesitated, and the line went silent.

"Are you still there?" I asked, worried that our call had been disconnected.

"Yes. I'm sorry." She cleared her throat. "One of the adoptions fell through."

"What does that mean?"

"Well, in this case it means that the adoptive parents decided not to, well, adopt the child."

"Why not?" I asked.

"They said that they didn't want her."

For the second time in as many minutes, my stomach dropped.

"Why not?" I asked again.

"Well, this little girl has some impetigo on her face."

"And?"

"The family said they didn't expect it," Jan said. "They declined."

"But it's treatable, isn't it? It's just a rash. Didn't they know that?"

"She's been on penicillin since she arrived in the States." She sighed and it came through very clear over the line. "We tried explaining that it would clear up soon but they . . . you know, some people are just like that."

"I simply can't imagine."

"Me either. Anyway, I'm calling to see if you'd be interested in adopting her." She paused. "I know that you requested a baby boy, but we thought it couldn't hurt to ask."

"What's her name?" I asked.

"Minh," she answered.

"Minh," I said, trying the word out. "How is that spelled?"

I grabbed a piece of scrap paper from the junk drawer, writing the name out.

Minh.

"And how old is she?"

"We believe she's between four and five years old," Jan said.

"You don't know?"

"There's not a whole lot of paperwork from the orphanage."

"Really?" I said. "How can that be?"

"From what I understand, they left Vietnam as fast as they could. Some kids' files got left behind or mixed up with another child." She cleared her throat. "It's sort of lucky that Minh has any paperwork at all. It's been a bit of a nightmare for those of us who like order."

"I imagine it has."

I closed my eyes, seeing the images from the news of people running through the streets of Saigon, the clogged traffic, the women handing babies up into the arms of strangers. That little boy in the baseball cap. Then the pictures in the paper of children sitting on the floor of a cargo plane or babies in boxes strapped in rows of seats.

Then I thought of the bassinet we'd bought at a garage sale the day after filing our paperwork and the hand-me-downs from baby Teddy that Dana had offered.

Another little girl wasn't in the plan. We'd had our hearts set on a Jason or Andrew or Matt.

I turned, looking at the scrap of paper on the kitchen counter, running my finger under the name I'd written across the top. Minh.

"I met her just a little bit ago," Jan said. "She's a sweet girl. We all just want the very best for her."

"Can I talk it over with my husband?" I cradled the receiver between my cheek and shoulder and picked up the pencil so I could draw a heart next to the name.

"Sure."

"When do we need to let you know?"

"As soon as you can."

She gave me all the details she could, which weren't many, and I jotted them down along with the phone number where I could reach her over the weekend before letting her go and hanging up the phone.

When I looked back out the window, Sonny was riding without any help.

CHAPTER Twelve

Sonny, 1988

G raduation lasted forever. I was sure I was going to sweat to
  death wearing that mustard yellow gown, which, by the
way, did nothing to complement my skin tone. Fanning myself
with a program, I wondered how anybody had thought it was
a good idea to jam hundreds of people into a school gym that
had no air-conditioning.

Somehow in my class of thirty-eight we'd ended up with a
four-way tie for valedictorian, and each of them got to deliver
a speech. Add to that the special academic awards the principal
acknowledged and the choir's mini-concert and a sermon from
the superintendent, etc., etc.—I thought we were all going to
die in that stuffy gym.

The only thing that made it bearable was that I knew that
at the end of the ceremony—whenever it came—I would be a
high school graduate and well on my way to actual adulthood.
Well, that and Mike was in the row ahead of me and kept half
turning to smile at me.

When it was finally time for us to go up and receive our diplomas, I stood with the rest of my class, asking the kid next to me if my hair looked okay.

"I don't know," he said. "I guess."

It would have to do.

I adjusted the gold braided cords that hung from my neck, making sure they were even, and waited for my name to be called.

When it was, I stepped up onto the stage, careful in the heels I'd worn to what had become known as my ill-fated prom— they weren't cheap, and I decided I might as well get at least one more use out of them even if they did clash with the yellow gown.

Mr. Shepherd, the principal, handed me my diploma with a smile and a handshake, and I turned to see my family. They occupied an entire row. Uncle Chris and Aunt Dana were there with Teddy, who just glared at me as if I was the cause for all the misery in his life. Grumpy yelled out a very loud "Way to go, Sonny!" and Grammy elbowed him.

It only made him shout it again, and with more volume.

Then there were Mom and Dad and Mindy. Dad gave me a thumbs-up and a smile, but I could tell he was trying really hard not to cry. Mom, on the other hand, wasn't trying to hold it back. Not even a little. And I was sure that I could hear her sniffling all the way across the room.

Mindy, though, gave me her biggest, cheesiest smile and waved like a madwoman. What a weirdo.

Mom lifted her camera to her face and I held my diploma like one of Barker's Beauties showing off a fabulous prize on *The Price Is Right*.

But then Mr. Shepherd made a coughing sound in my

direction, and I remembered that I was supposed to move off the stage so I wouldn't hold everything up.

In the next five minutes all of us high school seniors would move the black-and-yellow tassels from one side of our hats to the other and we would be announced as the graduating class of 1988. The band played "Pomp and Circumstance" again, and it was over.

As I walked back down the aisle, arms linked with Nick Minnaar, I suddenly felt way too young to be almost on my own.

My plan was to go out with my friends after graduation. Pizza Hut and mini-golf and then a bonfire at Alissa Durrow's house. It was supposed to be one last party with everybody together.

But my family had something else in mind.

"You're only going to miss the pizza," Mom said. "You can meet up with everybody for golf."

"It's mini-golf," I said, pouting in the back of her station wagon, my bundled-up gown on the seat between Mindy and me.

"Grammy's been cooking all day." She looked back at me. "You can go as soon as we're done eating."

"Linda, if she wants to be with her friends, I think we should let her," Dad said, inching forward in the line of cars waiting to leave the school parking lot. "She's an adult now."

"But your mother . . ."

"My mother should have asked before making plans for everyone," he said, interrupting her. He looked at me in the rearview mirror. "If you really want, we can drop you off at Pizza Hut."

"Why do you get to make that decision?" Mom threw her hands up.

"I'm not," Dad said. "We're letting Sonny make it."

"Do you know who your mother will blame if she's not there?" Mom pointed at herself. "Me, Bruce. I'm always the one she blames."

"Come on, that's not true."

I glanced at Mindy. She had her eyes closed as she breathed in and out slowly.

"I'll go to Grammy's," I said. "Just stop fighting."

Dad glanced at me again. I looked away.

"We aren't fighting," he said, rubbing the back of his neck. "We're just disagreeing."

"Well, could you please disagree without yelling? You're stressing me out."

I picked up the graduation program, flipping through it and feeling sufficiently sorry for myself.

"I'm sorry, honey," Mom said, half turning in her seat to look at me. She reached back for my hand, the way she did when I was little.

I ignore her and pretended to read the list of my classmates.

Out of the corner of my eye I saw Mindy lift her hand to Mom's so as to not leave her hanging.

It was no fair, making me feel guilty right after my high school graduation.

Not only did I miss out on pizza, I was so late for mini-golf that all my friends were on the seventeenth hole by the time I got there. It was enough to make me want to cry my eyes out.

I didn't, of course. Instead, I faked excitement when Amelia got a hole-in-one on the last green and went with her to get her free fountain drink that she'd won.

"Mike asked where you were," she said, waiting for the kid behind the counter to get her pop.

"He did?" I asked. "That's weird."

"He asked, like, a hundred times." She rolled her eyes. "It was annoying. And cute."

"Annoying and cute," I said. "The perfect words for Mike."

"Uh, I need to tell you something." She looked over my shoulder. "He's coming. But you have something in your teeth."

I panicked and tried to feel for it with my tongue. "Did I get it?"

"It's right there. Yeah." She cringed. "Almost."

"Is it gone?"

"Just stick your fingernail in there." She pointed at her own mouth. "Okay. Okay! You got it."

And just in time.

"Hey, where were you?" Mike asked, leaning into me and nudging me with his shoulder.

"At my grandma's," I said.

"Oh. Cool." He scratched the back of his neck. "Did you drive here?"

I shook my head. "My dad dropped me off."

"I could give you a ride to the bonfire." He lifted his eyebrows.

"Well, I was going to ride over with Amelia . . ."

"Nope. Sorry. I just remembered," Amelia said, grabbing her Coke from the counter and jabbing a straw through the lid. "I've got the Jennies and one of the Kellies already riding with me. I won't have space."

"Yes, you will."

"No. I won't." She grabbed my hand and squeezed it. "Ride with Mike."

And, with that, she walked away, leaving me and Mike alone

with the kid behind the counter. He looked between us, arms straight on either side of him.

"Ready?" Mike asked, pulling the keys out of his pocket.

"I guess so."

It was a fifteen-minute drive to Alissa's house and, about half-way there, Mike reached over and held my hand.

CHAPTER Thirteen

Bruce, 2013

It's a lazy Saturday morning. The kind where you move slower, take smaller sips of coffee, and by eleven o'clock wonder where the day went. It's the kind of morning I get very little done and don't feel the least bit sorry about it.

I'm stepping into the house from the garage, feeling good about at least raking up a pile of leaves and filling all the bird feeders, when I hear music. After making quick work of washing my hands and grabbing a cup of coffee, I head to the living room to see who's playing the piano.

Linda and Mindy share the bench. Linda's got the middle and bottom notes and Mindy's playing the top melody with her right hand. They both nod their heads along with the rhythm, laughing whenever they hit a wrong note.

Even when they mess up, they don't get derailed. They just keep right on playing.

When it's over, Linda wraps her arms around Mindy and kisses her cheek.

Such joy, I almost can't take it.

"Not too shabby," Linda says. "Gosh, we haven't played that one in, what, thirty years?"

"You're making me feel old, Mom," Mindy says.

They don't know I'm standing here, watching them. That's fine by me.

"Let's do it again," Mindy says, setting her fingers on the keys.

I pull the phone out of my pants pocket and snap a picture just as Linda turns to beam at our girl.

After lunch Mindy and I take off for a hike on the trail nearby. This afternoon the sun shines just bright enough. The air's crisp, but not biting. The sun's bright, but not blinding. And the busiest crowds in the woods are of the feathered variety.

We take an easy pace, neither of us having anywhere to go or anything pressing we've got to do. Every once in a while we stop to identify a bird call or to wonder over some sort of animal track.

Of my three, Mindy's the only one who ever really enjoyed hiking. Sonny was more inclined toward the water and Holly, well, Holly enjoyed nature only in doses she got while walking around a city. The bigger the better.

I won't be surprised if she moves away, swapping small-town comfort for busy streets and tall buildings. Holly likes to go a hundred miles an hour, which is hard when Bear Run has a speed limit of thirty-five at the fastest.

Mindy, though, always loved being surrounded by trees with a trail ahead of her and lots of time to explore.

We've hiked this one so many times over the years that we don't have to think too hard about which way to go or when there's going to be a turn in the path. Still, somehow, it never gets boring.

"You know, I used to bring you out here when you were little," I say. "Just the two of us."

"I remember," Mindy answers.

"If you were having a rough day, I'd get you out of the house and we'd take a little walk." I breathe in the fresh smells of the woods. "Even in the winter. I'd just bundle you up so you wouldn't get too cold."

"It's settling out here," she says. "There's something special about it."

A squirrel scampers up the trunk of a spruce, stopping on a branch just above our heads, his tail twitching. He chatters at us so we know of his great displeasure.

"It's all right, fella," I say. "We'll be outta your hair soon."

As we go, we hear the laugh of a nuthatch, the cheep-cheep of a chickadee, a couple of screeching starlings. The leaves clap against each other in the breeze and the ancient tree branches creak as they sway.

I almost say something about how all of creation calls out songs to the Creator, but from the way Mindy has her head tilted back, smile on her face, I can tell she's got thoughts of her own about this good place, and I don't want to interrupt them with my own.

We reach a fork in the trail and stop.

"Which way?" I ask.

"You pick," she says.

I nod to the path on the left, knowing from years of hiking how it has a few more turns in the trail and roots and rocks to hazard. It is, without a doubt, the one less traveled of the two.

The trail's tough, but the view it supplies over the apple orchard—especially with its changing leaves this time of year—is well worth every effort.

"Can I ask you a question?" she says.

"Sure thing," I say, holding a branch out of her way.

"What made you and Mom decide to adopt me?" She adjusts the strap of her pack on her shoulder. "I know you guys wanted a baby boy, so I must have been a little outside the plan."

"Who told you we wanted a baby boy?"

"Sonny." She rolled her eyes. "It was when we were kids. She was mad at me about something and told me."

"She didn't always fight fair, huh?" I step over a root.

Mindy shrugs and smiles. "I got my digs in too now and then."

We walk in silence for a minute or so while I let the memories loose in my mind. That day, the first day we ever heard about Mindy, is a vivid one. I can remember the crunch of the gravel driveway under the wheels of Sonny's bicycle and the way Linda's eyes glistened with tears when she told me about the little girl from Vietnam. The mug of coffee warmed my cupped hands as we sat at the table to hash it all out.

Strongest of all is the memory of how scared I was at the idea of adopting Minh. It had more to do with my insecurities than anything, even if I couldn't admit it back then.

"I know we haven't talked about this much." She clears her throat. "And I'm sorry if you feel blindsided. We can just drop it if you want."

"I don't mind talking about it." I stop in the middle of the trail so I can face her. "Mindy, I'm not sure if you know this about me or not, but I was a bit of a hippie."

She laughs and nods. "Everybody knows that, Dad."

"They do?"

"Have you seen the pictures of you from the sixties?"

"Fair enough." I start walking again. "Your mom and I spent

a lot of our early twenties protesting the war. We even marched in Washington, if you can believe it."

"I bet Grammy loved that," she says.

"Oh no. She didn't." I chuckle. "My dad didn't like it much himself. But I think he understood my reasons for doing it."

"Which were?"

"Well, it's complicated. On one hand, I wanted our boys home." I stop again and take in a good breath. "Every day we'd hear about the death count of American GIs on the news and it drove me nuts to think they all could've been spared."

"Especially Uncle Dale?" she asks.

"Yep." I blow out a stream of breath that turns to steam in front of me. "More than that, though, were the kids over there who were getting caught in the crossfire."

I shove my hand into my pocket, pulling out my hanky and rubbing under my nose.

"At the time we were getting lots of pictures from the war," I go on. "On the news, in the papers, magazines. Some of those images were impossible to shake."

One picture in particular is still as clear in my mind's eye as it was the day I saw it for the first time. A man holds the body of a very small boy after a firefight between US troops and Vietcong guerillas. There was no story written up about the lives of the man and child, no clue as to which side they were on in the war. It little mattered.

It was a glimpse into tragedy, and it woke up something inside me that I couldn't ignore.

"I guess I protested out of some idealistic notion that I could help make the world a better and safer place," I say. "Your mom and I marched for the kids over in Vietnam."

I nod toward the trail so she knows I'm ready to walk again.

"Well, eventually the fire cooled and we gave up hope of making any kind of difference," I go on. "We settled down and had Sonny and sort of forgot about why we protested."

"But then you got the phone call."

"Yup." I blink against a sting of tears. "It was scary, I have to admit. But once we made the decision, there was no turning back."

We round a bend that leads to a clearing. There's a small lake here with a dock that was built years ago as part of a boy's Eagle Scout project. It's got some loose boards, and termites have taken up residence in the bench. Still, it's a good place to stand and try to catch sight of a heron or to be quiet to hear the bloop, bloop of fish surfacing to eat a water bug.

Mindy rests her head on my shoulder. "I'm glad you said yes to being my dad."

"Me too, Mindy," I say. "What I want you to understand, though, is that adopting you wasn't some act of resistance or altruism. We didn't adopt you to protest the war. It was nothing like that."

I pause for a beat or two, resting a hand on the rough wooden slat of the deck.

"Back in my marching days I was absolutely sure it was a good thing I was doing," I go on. "But when you came along, everything changed. I realized that none of it was about me or what I was doing after all. The moment I saw you, I realized that the only thing that I could do that made a lick of a difference was to love you and Sonny and your mom. And to let you three love me back. Getting the chance to be your dad is one of the best things in my life. I hope you know that."

"You're going to make me cry," Mindy says.

"Well, I didn't mean to do that."

"It's okay." She turns her body to face me, leaning one hip against the deck. "Can I ask you something else?"

"Of course."

"Did you ever think about me looking for my birth mom?"

"Is that something you want to do?" I ask.

She nods.

I look at my feet, trying to think of how to say exactly what's on my mind. When I was a younger man I might have just blurted it out. But now I'm older and know the weight of words. I measure them a minute or two before opening my mouth.

The fact is, before we called the agency to let them know we were willing to adopt Minh, Linda and I made an agreement. We said that if ever Minh wanted to reunite with her family in Vietnam, we'd put up no fight. We would give our blessing and help in any way we could.

When we shook on it, it seemed an easy thing to do. A no-brainer.

But then, over time we forgot about our agreement. Eventually, I even stopped expecting that Mindy would ever want to learn about her life before us.

I'd gotten selfish with her, wanting to hold her close. For years I convinced myself that it was because I wanted so badly to shield her from anything that could hurt her. That may have been part of it, I guess. But another share of it was the fear that if I let her go, I'd lose her.

Turns out that small birds are going to fly whether we like it or not. It's no different for our kids.

And, whether I'm always aware of it or not, it's the nature of God to see every dip and dive and lift, to glory at the triumphs and grieve when they fall.

It's time I loosen my grip.

I've held her so tight for so long, it hurts to let her go.

"Listen," I say. "If you want to look for your birth mom, you've got my blessing. If you want to fly to Vietnam, I'll help pay for the plane ticket."

"Thanks, Dad," she says.

"And no matter what, we're always here for you, your mom and me."

We come to a steep incline on the trail, one that I used to be able to climb without a thought. These days it takes a little more effort, and I hope Mindy doesn't notice my huffing and puffing.

At the top of the hill is a view that's more than worth it, and when I reach the peak, I'm glad we picked this less traveled path. Looking out over the tops of trees at their most vibrant color is something I'll never grow tired of.

CHAPTER Fourteen

Linda, 1975

Hilda made her coffee strong and served it without cream or sugar. She was of the mind that if someone wanted to drink coffee, they should have it as it was. Anyone who doctored it up didn't really like the flavor of it and was, therefore, unworthy to drink it.

I, on the other hand, was the kind who liked her coffee more on the beige side and sweet enough to count as dessert. But for all the years since meeting Hilda, I never told her my preference because I thought it might make her think less of me.

So, at Hilda's house, I drank my coffee black and tried my very hardest not to grimace with each swallow.

That day she poured four cups, one for each of us, and told us that we'd drink it in the parlor.

As soon as Hilda turned her back, Ivan cracked open a cupboard and reached his hand in, pulling out a fistful of sugar cubes that he dumped into his coffee. When he noticed me watching him, he froze like a little boy caught doing something naughty.

I lifted my cup and raised my eyebrows. "I won't tell if you let me have a few," I whispered.

He nodded and kept his eyes on Hilda. Covering for me, I guessed.

"After you," Ivan said, nodding toward the parlor and then following me down the hallway.

There wasn't a sign on the door or velvet rope to ban admittance; still, Bruce had grown up understanding that the parlor in his mother's house was off-limits to children. That room contained the best furniture in the house. Antiques either purchased at a flea market or passed down by some dead relative. That was where Hilda hung the finest art and an old, gilded mirror that she claimed someone had brought with them all the way from Germany.

Years ago, I'd risked a look at the back of the mirror to find "Made in the U.S.A." stamped on the back.

Whenever I thought about it, I ended up with a bout of the giggles.

Bruce patted the seat beside him, and Hilda eyed me the whole time I crossed the room. I was already nervous enough; her scrutiny only made my hands shake more.

Hilda lifted her chin at me as I sat down, and it seemed like she was willing me to spill just one drop of coffee on her rugs. Rugs that had, no doubt, received a thorough beating recently at her hand.

Bruce always told me that she wasn't much of a hitter when he was a kid. Just a few spankings that he said were well deserved. And even those hadn't carried too much of a sting. According to him, she let loose her wrath on the various rugs around the house. He'd once told me that it wasn't altogether uncommon for her to break a carpet beater.

I let out a sigh of relief when I got my bumper into the chair without so much as a slosh.

"So, what brings you two over?" Ivan asked before slurping his coffee. "And where's my Sonny-Bunny?"

Hilda cleared her throat in his direction, and he looked into his cup as if something very interesting was at the bottom of it.

Sugar cube sludge, if I was to guess.

"She's with a friend from school," I said. "We thought we'd come just the two of us this time."

"You have something to tell us?" Hilda asked.

"Yes, actually," Bruce started.

He took a sip of his coffee before putting the cup on the table in front of him. I nearly gasped when I noticed he hadn't used a coaster. From the way Hilda's eyebrow jutted up, I didn't think it had escaped her notice.

I leaned forward and slid one under his cup in hopes of keeping the conversation as smooth as possible.

"Well, Linda and I have been talking about adding another little one to our family," Bruce continued.

Hilda wasn't a woman prone to displays of emotion. But there was a certain warmth that glowed behind her deep brown eyes whenever something greatly pleased her. The corners of her lips turned up and she sat straighter in her chair.

She gave me the same look she had on her face when we told her we were expecting Sonny.

"Are you in a family way?" she whispered.

Bruce turned toward me and put his hand on my knee, and I nodded for him to go on.

"Well, Mom," he said. "We decided to adopt this time."

Hilda held her smile a little too long. Instead of bright and happy, it was dull and uncertain, her eyes darting between Bruce and me.

"Is there something wrong with having one of your own?" she asked through her teeth.

I grabbed Bruce's hand.

"No. There's not," he said. "But remember how we were working at getting pregnant a few years ago?"

Hilda cringed at the word *pregnant* and lifted a hand to finger the hairline at the nape of her neck. I could almost hear her internal scream of "Well, I never!"

"Working at it?" Ivan asked, chuckling. "I never thought it was work. Did I, Hildie?"

"Ivan," she gasped.

All traces of a smile dropped from her face and I thought for certain that she would have slugged Ivan right in the arm if we weren't sitting in the parlor. She angled her shoulders from him and set her jaw.

"Anyway," she said, prompting us to go on.

"Uh," Bruce said, rubbing at his beard. "Well, we filled out all the paperwork and went to a couple of meetings with the adoption agency."

He stopped to take a breath, and I wanted to fill the void with my pleas for Hilda to soften her gaze. I desperately wanted to beg her to stop looking at him as if he was a boy in need of a stiff scolding and being sent to bed without supper.

Bruce had told me more than a dozen times that she wasn't so stern and cold when he was little. I wasn't entirely convinced of it, though. In my opinion, it would do the woman some good to have someone give her what-for every once in a while.

Tightening my hold on Bruce's hand, I thought of all the

things I would say to Hilda if only I was a bolder woman and not quite so afraid of her.

When she fixed her eyes on me with her most withering gaze, I knew I'd do no such thing.

"And?" Hilda prompted, lifting her chin.

"The short of it is that we got a call from the adoption agency a few hours ago." He lifted his eyebrows. "We get to meet our second child tomorrow."

"Hot dog!" Ivan slapped hands to thighs and stood up, reaching across the coffee table to shake Bruce's hand. "Congratulations, son."

"Thanks, Dad." Bruce cupped both hands around his father's.

"Hilda, isn't that something?" Ivan asked, turning toward his wife. "Bet you didn't expect this news when you got up today."

"I did not." Hilda pulled her lips into a smile. "I'm very happy."

"Boy or girl?" Ivan asked, sitting back down and resting his arms on his thighs.

"A little girl," I said.

"A baby?"

"No. She's between four and five years old."

"Between?" Ivan asked, squinting. "You don't know?"

"Why don't they just ask her?" Hilda asked, putting her half-full cup of coffee on a coaster. "She might know how old she is."

"She doesn't speak English," I said. "Not yet, at least."

Hilda turned her head and looked at me out of the corner of her eye.

"What does she speak?" Ivan asked.

Panic zipped through me, starting behind my sternum, and I put a hand to my chest, taking in a sharp breath in hope of clearing it. But that only added dread to the anxiety.

"Vietnamese," Bruce said. "She's from Vietnam."

Hilda got out of her chair, smoothing the front of her smock-shirt.

"I don't know what to say," she said.

"Mom." Bruce moved to the edge of his seat and dropped my hand. "Say that you're happy for us. Please."

"No." She put her palm up as if to hold him back from her. "Think of your brother. What would Dale say about such a thing?"

"I don't know."

"They killed him, Bruce." Her voice caught as if she was near to breaking. "And now you want to bring one of them here? Into our family?"

"Mom."

"No," she said again. "What will happen when Chris sees her? Don't you know that he has nightmares still? And you want him to play uncle to one of their children."

"Now, Hilda," Ivan said.

"I will not have one of them in this house." She set her jaw. "That child won't be welcome here."

"She's just a little girl," I said, trying so hard to keep my voice calm.

"Don't you think I've heard the stories of what they make children do there?" Hilda's eyes sliced right through the heart of me. "They turn them into soldiers and make them kill our people."

"That's enough of that." Ivan tugged on the hem of her skirt. "Sit down, dear."

"I will not sit down!"

Her voice filled the room and spilled out into the hallways, up the stairs, soaking into the floorboards. It was rage and grief and hopelessness all mingled together.

The thickness of emotion paralyzed me past even shaking.

"Mom, we don't need your blessing," Bruce said, his deep voice soft. "It would be nice to have, but I won't beg for it."

Hilda drew back her shoulders and looked down her nose at us. From where I sat, I felt like a little child who had been caught doing something bad.

"She needs a family," I said, choking on the lump in my throat.

"Then let her be with some other people," Hilda said. Then she walked out of the room.

"Now, see here," Ivan called after her.

But she didn't turn back to us. Her footsteps got quieter as she went toward the kitchen.

Bruce dropped his head into his hands, pushing his fingers through his hair. I still didn't move, not knowing what I could do to ease the tension in that house.

As for Ivan, he slung back the last of his coffee as if he was hoping it was something even stronger. Then he looked up at Bruce and me.

"Does my new granddaughter have a name?" he asked.

"Her name's Minh," Bruce answered.

Ivan touched his ear. "Minnie?"

"Just Minh."

"When will she be here?"

"Tomorrow," Bruce said. "Three in the afternoon."

"That fast, huh?" Ivan nodded. "I'd have thought it would be a longer flight from Vietnam."

"Well, she's already in the States. She's coming in from Lansing," Bruce said. "Maybe you could come over and meet her on Monday. If you want to."

"I'd like that." Ivan cleared his throat.

I finally took a sip of coffee, wishing I'd stirred the sugar into it, knowing it was all settling at the bottom.

Ivan got up from his seat, lowering his cup to the side table as careful as could be. Not bothering to use the coaster seemed more an act of defiance than absentmindedness.

"Your mother'll come around," he said. "Just give her a little time."

Patting his son on the shoulder a few times, he sighed.

"I'm sure proud of you," he said.

Bruce reached up and covered his dad's hand with his own.

We sat in our lawn chairs in the backyard after Sonny was in bed. It had been a long day and we were both beat.

Not so tired that we wanted to go to bed, though.

"She wasn't always such a hard woman," Bruce said, resting his head against the back of his chair and shutting his eyes. "Losing Dale broke her heart."

"I'm sure it did." I wanted to add that she didn't have to be mean to everybody else, but I didn't.

Bruce already knew that and didn't need me stirring the pot for him.

"He was her favorite." He crossed his arms. "But that didn't mean he got special treatment. It just meant she was tougher on him."

The light was beginning to fade from the sky. A couple of bats zipped here and there, and I silently cheered them on, hoping they'd thin the mosquitoes so we'd have a less buggy summer.

"I was at Michigan State, protesting the war, when they got the news about Dale," Bruce said, opening his eyes. "They didn't know how to get ahold of me, so I didn't find out until five days later when I came home to do my laundry."

He lifted a hand to cover his eyes, and his shoulders shook.

I got up and put both hands on his shoulders. Pulling me to him, he pressed his face into my stomach and wrapped his arms around my waist.

"You couldn't have known," I said, rubbing the back of his neck. "It's not your fault."

"I miss him."

"I know."

I held him like that until he let go. He tipped his head back and looked up into my face, his shaggy hair a mess.

"You need to make a trip to the barber," I said, pushing his bangs to one side.

"Yeah," he said. "We're doing the right thing, aren't we?"

I nodded.

"I'm sort of scared."

"Me too," I said. "But I can't hardly wait to meet her."

The sky was clear that night and I was glad to live far enough away from the streetlights of Bear Run so that nothing dimmed the bright twinkling of the stars.

CHAPTER Fifteen

Sonny, 1988

We usually went to church on the other side of town from the one that Grammy and Grumpy attended. Apparently, somebody said something that really offended my mom a long time ago and that's why we switched.

Whatever.

At least a lot of kids from school were in my youth group. That was, like, all that really mattered to me.

But the Sunday after my graduation, my cousin Teddy was getting baptized, so we all had to go to First Baptist Church and stay for the potluck after the service. Grammy said so.

It wasn't too different from our church. We sang three hymns, passed the offering plates while some lady did her very best Sandi Patty impersonation along with taped accompaniment, prayed, then listened to a sermon. Teddy got baptized in the tank behind the altar and we all cheered, singing "Now I Belong to Jesus."

After the service we joined the long line for the potluck. Somebody had already invited Mom to get first crack at the food, scooting her all the way to the front, claiming that pregnant women should never have to wait to eat. When Mindy and I tried to join her, Grammy gave us the evil eye, telling us to wait our turn.

That was all right, I guessed. It wasn't like I was in a hurry to see how many gross ways people in that church had of making tuna casserole.

"Good heavens," Grammy said under her breath. "Here comes Winifred."

Out of the corner of my eye I saw the smallest woman I'd ever seen coming toward us with the speed of a mall walker. She had the brightest carrot-orange dye job and didn't seem to care that it was fooling no one.

"Oh, Hilda, Ivan, you have visitors this week," she said in a trembling voice. "Who are these beauties?"

"These are Bruce and Linda's girls," Grammy said, touching my arm. "Sonny and then Mindy, who they adopted from Vietnam."

Mindy put her hands into the pockets of her skirt and turned her eyes to the tiled floor. She always got shy like that whenever somebody mentioned that she was from Vietnam.

"Yup," Grumpy said. "These are our granddaughters and we are so proud of them."

Mindy tilted her head and leaned toward him, nudging his arm with her shoulder.

Leave it to Grumpy to ease her bashfulness.

"I bet you are." The tiny woman smiled up into our faces. "Mindy and Sonny, I am glad to meet the two of you. I'm Mrs. Winifred Olds."

She offered her thin hand and I took it, surprised by how firm her grip was. Then she took Mindy's hand.

"It's nice to meet you too," Mindy said.

"Now, tell me, girls," Mrs. Olds said. "Are you hard workers?"

Mindy and I met eyes before nodding.

"And do either or both of you need a job?" Mrs. Olds shifted her eyes back and forth between Mindy and my faces. "Just for the summer, of course."

"Um, I guess so," Mindy said.

"Good. Here's why I'm asking," Mrs. Olds said. "I'm turning the old Huebert house into a museum. I need quite a bit of help."

"Well, I . . ." I started, trying to decline politely so that Grammy wouldn't be embarrassed.

"Tell you what." Mrs. Olds squeezed my hand, and I had to stifle a grimace. She really clamped down on my fingers. "How about you two stop by tomorrow after lunch? I'll show you around and you can decide then. All right?"

I didn't answer because I was too busy trying to slide my hand out of her hold. Once she let go, I crossed my arms so she couldn't grab it again.

"Sure," Mindy said. "We'll be there. Is one o'clock okay?"

"Of course," Mrs. Olds answered.

I tried giving my sister the hairy eyeball, but she didn't notice. She was too busy beaming at the little old lady.

It was the first official day of summer and my only plan was to do a whole lot of nothing all day long. I spent the morning watching reruns of *The Partridge Family* and *The Brady Bunch* before going upstairs to do my nails and blast my Madonna tape in my boombox.

I didn't hear Mindy come into our room, so when she tapped me on the shoulder I jumped, wrecking two of my nails.

"Sorry," she said, covering her mouth in a lame effort to hide her laugh.

I sighed and turned down the volume on "Papa Don't Preach." "What do you want?"

"Remember we're supposed to go see Mrs. Olds today." She shrugged. "We said we would."

"Nope. You said we would. I never agreed to anything." I grabbed my nail polish remover and a tissue to try to fix my nails. "I'm going to look for jobs with Amelia tomorrow."

"Sonny, come on."

"Why?"

"The least we can do is go and see what the job's like," she said. "It could be fun."

"Go ahead without me," I said. "Nobody's stopping you."

"Well, I need a ride, and Mom's taking a nap, so . . ."

I made a really big show of rolling my eyes and sighing before saying, "Fine."

I had to make quick work of taking the polish off all my nails.

❧

Every year the fourth graders at Bear Run Christian School performed a play about the history of our town. There were catchy little songs about chopping down trees and a few about women making butter on the porch.

It wasn't exactly Broadway, but it was fun for the kids who got to play in it.

In the background of each performance was a board of plywood cut out to look like an old house with spires and a purple paint job, and pink and teal trim around the peaks and windows.

When Amelia and I were in fourth grade, I got the part of

Eliza Huebert, wife of the old lumber baron himself. I stood in front of the purple cutout building and delivered my lines, wearing a dress that had been worn by other lucky ten-year-old girls for over twenty years. Unfortunately, it was held together by safety pins and smelled like mothballs.

Even all those years later, I still remembered my lines.

"My husband, Johannes Huebert, built this house for me and our eight children," I'd recited. "There were also servants' quarters for our butler, maid, cook, and nanny."

That was it. Hardly worth the half hour it took for Mom to get my stage makeup on.

I thought of the Hueberts with their eight children and servants as I pulled my car into the driveway next to that old mansion, its purple paint peeling away from the wooden siding. I parked in front of the sloping porch and looked up at the arched doorway.

It was going to take an awful lot of work to get that place in shape for people to want to come visit.

"Good luck," I said.

"Aren't you coming in?" Mindy asked.

"Nope. I'm going to wait out here."

"Oh." Mindy released her seat belt and half turned toward me. "I thought you were just going to come in and check it out."

"Mins . . ."

"It won't take long, I promise." Her shoulders tensed almost up to her ears and she clenched her jaw.

"Listen, I need a real job," I said. "I want to have some money saved up before I leave for college."

"This is a real job."

"You know what I mean."

She shifted in her seat, pushing the passenger side door open and getting out. Before she closed it, she bent at the waist and looked in at me.

"Please, Sonny," she said. "Just come in with me. If you hate it, we can leave."

Over the years my sister had perfected the most pathetic puppy-dog-eyed look when she wanted something. I knew I should avert my gaze as soon as she lifted her brows and lowered the corners of her mouth. But I didn't. I met her dark eyes and knew I was a goner.

It was totally bogus for her to play me like that, and she knew it.

"Fine. You win." I pushed open my door. "But if I get any Bat Motel vibes from the place, I'm out."

"I think you mean Bates Motel."

"Whatever."

Taking the steps up the front porch, Mindy gave me a half smile. "Thanks."

She hesitated and breathed in deeply before knocking on the door.

"Come in," Mrs. Olds called from inside.

Mindy pushed open the door, and I wrinkled my nose at the dusty, musty air. The floorboards in the foyer creaked when we stepped inside. Nobody had lived there for a long time, and I doubted that anyone had swept the place for years. Huge cardboard boxes were stacked up against all the walls.

"It stinks in here," I whispered, wondering what kind of beast—raccoon, maybe—had made it his home for any number of decades.

Mindy didn't act like she'd heard me. Instead she pulled a slip of paper from her purse.

"What's that?" I asked.

"My resume," she answered.

"Geek."

"Girls, hello. Hello," Mrs. Olds said, coming our way with arms spread. "I'm glad you made it."

She reached for Mindy first, pulling her in for a hug before moving on to me. It wasn't a creepy hug like I thought it would be. It was actually kind of nice. Her arms were strong for as little as she was, and she smelled like brown sugar and cinnamon.

"Let's take a tour of the place, huh?" she said once she let go of me. "Then we'll have a cookie and talk about details."

"Cookies?" I said, perking up like I was a six-year-old.

I would have been embarrassed if anybody other than Mindy was there.

"I made them this morning," Mrs. Olds said. "My mother's recipe. But for now, let's look around."

We followed her from room to room, boxes and tarp-covered furniture crowding each and every one. Using her gnarly index finger, she pointed at the walls, telling us what she imagined ending up there. Each room would have a theme from the various artifacts that people around Bear Run had donated.

I had to admit that it seemed like it was going to be pretty cool.

We ended up in the kitchen, the one completely spic-and-span room in the mansion. Mrs. Olds had us sit at the drop-leaf table while she got a jug of milk from the refrigerator.

"Help yourselves, girls," she said. "I made plenty."

They were, without question, the best cookies I'd ever had. Like, ever. They were even better than Grammy's. Not like I would ever have said that out loud though. Grammy was one to hold grudges.

"Now, did you know that I taught your father when he was in

kindergarten?" she asked, pouring three glasses of whole milk. "Your uncle too."

"I didn't know that," Mindy said.

"Well, it was a hundred years ago." Mrs. Olds carried all three glasses to the table without spilling a drop. "I was heartbroken over Dale's death. He was such a kind boy."

"We never met him." I shrugged my shoulders.

"I suppose not." She took a seat. "It is a pity."

"Yeah."

I never knew what to say when somebody mentioned Uncle Dale. They'd want to offer condolences or tell me that he was a hero. I thought they wanted to see me tear up about him. But he died three years before I was born. If anything, it made me sad to think about him because of Dad. I couldn't imagine how awful it would be if Mindy died.

It would be the worst.

I grabbed another cookie, breaking it in half before taking a bite.

"Well, I suppose we should talk about the job," Mrs. Olds said before taking a drink of milk. "I'd need you here at eight o'clock sharp, Monday through Friday. You'd work until noon."

I let a mouthful of cookie melt on my tongue, thinking that everything about this job sounded good. That was the trick, wasn't it? She'd lure us in with cookies so we couldn't refuse the job!

Well, it was working.

"The wage is $5.50 an hour," she went on.

I nearly spit out the sip of milk I'd just taken.

$5.50 an hour? I quick did the math. That was $2.15 over the minimum wage. There was no way I would make that much working at Dairy Queen or some store in the mall.

"What do you think?" From the old lady's grin, I could tell she enjoyed shocking us. "Shall we have another cookie to celebrate your new employment?"

When we finally said our goodbyes, Mrs. Olds told us to extend her apologies to Mom for ruining our suppers. Then she reminded us to wear clothes we didn't mind getting dirty in.

"This is going to be grimy work, my girls," she said. "But it will be worth it in the end."

She stood on the sloping porch and waved at us as we drove away.

CHAPTER Sixteen

Bruce, 2013

The view outside my parents' apartment is of a marshy area. Tall grasses and cattails edge the wetland, and lily pads float on the surface of the water. A pair of wood ducks have claimed the spot as their own. As I stand looking out the window, I see a perfect place for a nest box.

It wouldn't do to put it in now. The ducks need to migrate soon. But they'll be back come spring, and I do believe they'll make good use of that box I plan to make for them.

Early summer we might just see the mama swimming with her chicks.

Man, it's something when those little critters jump out of the box, their still-flightless wings held out at their sides. Then with a plop they land in the water, swimming by instinct to keep up with their mother.

It's been a tough month for my folks. Mom's getting better, despite her grumbling and groaning through every physical therapy session. She's not well enough, however, to go back to taking care of the big house she's kept since I was a boy.

Somehow we've managed to whittle down their stuff from sixty-seven years of marriage to what we could fit in the one-bedroom apartment in this retirement home. The rest we've either split up among the family, sold, or put in storage.

Dana told me that Mom pitched a fit when she told her. I don't doubt it for a second.

That woman has been in charge of nearly everything she's touched for most of her life. All of a sudden she doesn't get to decide what she eats or when she does therapy or even where she's going to live.

Letting go of that kind of control must be hard for her.

Behind me Mom's talking at Linda about my brother Dale, and I wish I would have taken Dad up on his offer to join him for his first woodworking class.

Some days I'm all right to talk about Dale, and I'm able to laugh at some goofball thing he did when we were kids.

Today's not one of those days.

My brother's been dead for nearly fifty years and still, every once in a while, I get twin stabs of guilt and grief when I think about him.

But Mom feels like talking about him today, so I indulge her even if it is hard on me.

Linda, bless her, has heard all this from Mom at least half a dozen times over the years. But sweet soul that she is, she's sitting there, listening to it all over again as if it was the first time.

Most people who know my mom now think of her as being a hard-nosed, stiff-upper-lipped, difficult-to-love woman. From what I remember of her from my childhood, though, she wasn't this way. She didn't let us kids get away with much, but she was kind. There was a softness to her. Back then she laughed more than she yelled and smiled more than she scowled.

She didn't understand me, not even then. I guess I've always been more like my dad. We'd argue, but there was a spark in her eye when we did.

When Dale died it took a toll on all of us. We all had to carry on in our own ways.

For a couple years after, my mother kept his room just as he'd left it. She even went so far as to rumple the bedclothes to look like he'd just been sitting on top of them, and she set his shoes by the door in a less-than-perfect line.

His careless housekeeping had always irked her, but when he was gone, it was one of the things she could hold on to of him.

Right around the time Sonny was born, Mom cleaned out the room.

I never found out what she did with all his things. They were just gone, and nobody had the nerve to ask her about it.

"I need to get another cup of coffee," Mom says after a lull in conversation.

"I can get you some," I say, turning from the window.

"I've got a new jar of Nescafé up there." She points at the cupboard over the sink in her small galley kitchen. "Make yourself a cup too if you want."

Instant coffee. I try not to pull a grimace.

"No thanks," I say, getting a mug out for her.

"I was proud of my son when he enlisted," Mom goes on, glancing at Linda as if she expects her to pull out a sign and stage a war protest right there in the living room. Once a hippie, always a hippie in my mother's book, I suppose.

"Dale was always a patriotic boy," she says. "He knew they'd send him to . . ."

She stops and looks from Linda, not speaking the word *Vietnam*, as if it is a swear she doesn't want to get caught saying.

I draw water from the sink into the cup before popping it into the microwave and tapping a couple buttons to get it started.

"Vietnam?" Linda offers.

Even from across the room I can see that Mom's closed her eyes.

"I was more proud of him than I'd ever been of anybody else in my life," she says. "But I was scared every day for him."

"I bet you were." Linda rests her elbow on the arm of the loveseat. "Did you watch the news coverage of the war while he was gone?"

Mom nods.

What she doesn't say is that Dad refused to watch it. That he'd find some task to do that would take him out of the house. Mowing or weeding in the warm months turned to raking in fall and shoveling in winter.

And she doesn't tell Linda how, when I was home from school, I would pontificate about the injustices of the war after each report of how many GIs had lost their lives in the war that day.

Poor Dana tried to keep the peace between us, but it hardly ever worked.

The microwave dings and I measure the instant coffee into the hot water, hoping I put in the right amount. If not, Mom will send me back to fix it.

"Thank you," she says when I hand her the cup.

"Babe, you want a cup?" I ask. "It's decaf."

"No," Linda says, widening her eyes to let me know she thinks I'm nuts for asking. "Thanks."

I wink to tell her I'm teasing her.

Mom takes a sip. "That's good, Bruce."

I sit beside Linda on the loveseat. A group of people make

noise in the hallway outside the apartment, but Mom doesn't seem to notice. Either because she's growing accustomed to it or because her hearing has dulled that much.

Just another thing to ask her doctor about.

"Didn't Mindy want to come see us today?" she asks after a few minutes of looking out the window.

"She's at work," Linda says. "Remember, she's at the newspaper now."

"Ah."

Dad shuffles in, a fresh bandage on his pointer finger. He smirks when he notices me looking at it, proud of his battle wound.

"Don't tell your mother," he whispers.

"Wouldn't dare," I whisper back.

"Well, since you're both here," Linda says, nodding and taking my hand, "Bruce and I have something we need to tell you."

"Everything okay?" Dad asks, a shadow of worry darkening his eyes.

"Oh yes," Linda says. "In fact, everything seems to be really good. It's about Mindy. She's started to look for . . ."

"A new husband?" Dad says. "Hope he's better than that good for nothing—"

"Hush, Ivan," Mom interrupts him. "What's she looking for?"

"Bruce, maybe you better," Linda says.

"Mindy's looking to reunite with some of her family in Vietnam," I say as simply as I can, but it still sounds complicated to my ears.

There are a lot of layers of complicated to all this.

"Why?" Mom's eyebrows tense.

I should have anticipated that question, should have planned an easy, one-sentence answer. It might not have mattered anyway. My mother had the interrogation skills of a hardened FBI agent. Even at sixtysomething years old, I still got intimidated when she got started on a line of questioning.

"What does it matter why?" Dad asks. "It's none of our business."

"Well, I think it is." She widens her eyes at him. "She's our granddaughter."

"Yup. She is. And so we'll be happy for her and support her."

"Linda, how do you feel about this?" Mom asks.

"I think it's good," Linda answers.

"I knew this would happen." Mom points at an afghan in a basket beside her chair. "Linda, would you get that for me? I'm suddenly chilly."

Linda does as she's asked, even tucking the blanket around Mom's legs.

"There you go," she says. "Now, what did you mean that you knew this would happen?"

"That the girl would never be happy here. I knew she wouldn't like being away from her own people."

"Now, Hildie," Dad says. "We're her own people."

"You know what I mean." She smooths the afghan and picks a few lint balls from the top of it. "It's why I didn't come see her at first. I didn't want to get attached just so she could leave us in the end."

Back on the loveseat beside me Linda droops just slightly. Like a little bit of air let out of a balloon.

"That's not why, Mom," I say.

"It most certainly is."

"No." I swallow hard. "It's not."

My folks raised me to believe that children ought to honor and respect their parents. I still hold to that belief. Always will.

Even with all her faults, my mother deserves a measure of esteem.

I want to honor her.

But, doggone it, sometimes the most honoring thing is to hold our elders to account when they're wrong minded and hurtful.

It makes my stomach clench and the bile try to creep up my throat. But I shake my head and honor her with the truth.

"Mom, you didn't come see Mindy when she first came because she was Vietnamese," I say. "You were ready to disown me and Linda over it."

"Well . . ." she starts.

"Now, I don't have a grudge over it," I go on. "Because I love you and I've forgiven you. But I'll be darned if I let you gloss over how you acted back then."

"You always chose them over your brother," Mom says. "Always."

"Who?" Linda asks.

"Those Vietnamese," she answers. "Your brother went off to war and what do you do? You protest against him and for them. When he died, where were you? Off gallivanting across the country with your greasy hair and peace signs."

"I'm sorry about all that," I say. "I still wish I would have done things differently. But I will never regret bringing Mindy into this family. Never."

"Well," Mom says, but so quietly I hardly hear her. Her face is turned away from me, but I can see that her lips are quivering.

"She's not going to leave us," Linda says. "Hilda, did you hear me?"

My mother nods but doesn't turn her head toward us.

"Good," Linda goes on. "She needs us all to support her right now. It's a really scary thing she's trying to do."

"Don't know what I can do to help," Dad says. "But whatever it is, you can count on me."

"Thanks, Dad," I say.

We don't stay much longer. The mood's gone quite icy and I fear we've already overstayed our welcome. When we announce that we're heading out Mom doesn't budge, not even when I kiss her goodbye.

Seventeen

Linda, 1975

W hen I was pregnant with Sonny we had the better part
of a year to get ready for her arrival. Dana threw a baby
shower for me in the church basement, and the ladies of the
congregation brought all sorts of green and yellow baby things
for us.

Bruce put together the crib and I washed the bedding and we
two dreamed about the little one that was coming, speculating
over whether it would be a boy or a girl.

We took all the time in the world getting our little nest ready,
and it was so much fun.

For Minh we had from Saturday afternoon to Sunday at
three. Just over twenty-four hours.

Ready, set, go!

Bruce happened to find a twin bed frame at a garage sale for
a couple bucks, and Ivan bought a brand-new mattress for it at
Sears, something we were to keep a secret from Hilda for the
time being. A neighbor lent us an old dresser they no longer

needed, and a couple from church filled our fridge and pantry with groceries.

Sweet mercies every one of them.

Sweetest yet, Sonny was staying over at Amelia's house until Monday after school. That way little Minh could dip her toe in the water of our family before being plunged into the deep end.

It took some doing, but we managed to arrange and rearrange Sonny's bedroom to make space for Minh, setting up the beds toe-to-toe along the far wall and dressers on either side of the closet. It was tight, but it would work.

When we were done, Bruce and I stood in the doorway, dreaming of the little girl we were about to meet. It was much the same way we had in the days before Sonny was born.

In that moment I felt no anxiety, no hesitation, no question about what in the world we thought we were doing.

"Are you ready to be a daddy to another little girl?" I asked, leaning my head against Bruce's shoulder.

"Can't hardly wait," he answered, tightening his arm around me.

My heart felt full to bursting.

Over the past few months I'd seen more than a dozen news stories about Babylift families meeting for the first time. Every one of them showed a man and woman in a crowded airport terminal with flashing cameras and far too many people looking on.

The poor children seemed overwhelmed by all the hustle and bustle, not knowing where to look. Then the stranger that was to become his or her mother or father scooped them up, holding them tight.

Just the thought of meeting Minh that way made my palms sweaty and my head spin.

Fortunately, we'd arranged with the adoption agency to meet them at our house. They were driving up from Lansing; it was hardly worth taking an airplane.

What a relief.

Bruce and I started out waiting for them in the house, but being confined only made both of us anxious. So we put lawn chairs in the shade of our maple to wait.

Bruce stayed in his chair for less than a minute before getting up to deadhead the morning glories in the lattice by the front door and check on his tomatoes in the backyard garden. He found half a dozen things to do, which I supposed made the wait more bearable for him.

As for me, his constant movement only made me more nervous, and I wished he'd just sit next to me and hold my hand.

All the calm from before had dissipated, leaving behind trembling hands, shallow breaths, and a thumping heartbeat.

When a car came down the road, turning its blinker on well before our driveway, I stood, holding my hand at my brow line to block the sun from my eyes.

"Bruce," I called.

"Is she here?" he asked, rushing to my side.

We waited there together, the two of us, the seconds feeling like little eternities.

But the car stopped on the road, parking just north of our driveway. A man got out, the car's only occupant, a camera around his neck. A minute later two more vehicles trundled along, kicking up dust behind the tires. Then another. And another.

Out of one van a man hauled a television camera.

"Reporters?" I asked. "How did they find out?"

"No," Bruce said. Then louder, so they could hear him from where they gathered at the end of the driveway, "Nope. Not happening."

"Come on, man," one of the reporters called, jerking his head so his long hair flipped out of his eyes. "Just a couple pictures."

"No thanks."

"But we got a press release," another said.

"That's not an invitation to come to my house." Bruce put his hands on his hips.

"We'll stay off your property," said the first one that had shown up. "Honest."

"Don't you all have enough stories on this?" Bruce asked, shaking his head.

I could tell he had more to say, but there was no time to get it out. A dark-colored Lincoln was making its way toward our house. It slowed as it neared the drive, waiting for a few reporters to step out of the way so it could turn in.

"Can you ignore all those people?" I whispered. "Pretend they aren't here. Okay?"

"I'll try," he answered, huffing out a lungful of air.

"We're about to meet our girl," I said, grabbing his hand. "Are you excited?"

His grin was all the answer I needed.

The very first I saw of Minh was through the windshield of the Lincoln. She sat on the lap of a woman in the passenger seat, eyes wide and face completely stoic. I could tell two things about her, even through the windshield. First, that she was so much smaller than I'd expected, and I worried that all the clothes we had for her would be far too big. Second, she wasn't missing a thing, the way she looked all around her with those big eyes.

"Would you look at her," Bruce said, rubbing his thumb over my knuckles.

I couldn't have taken my eyes off her if I tried.

Car doors opened and the people inside stepped out. The woman from the passenger side slipped Minh up and onto her hip like she weighed nothing at all before pushing the door closed.

"Hi, Linda?" the woman asked, extending her left hand to me, her right being occupied in holding Minh. "I'm Jan. We spoke on the phone."

"Of course, hello." I took a step toward her, taking her hand. "This is my husband, Bruce."

"Nice to meet you both."

"You too."

"And this," Jan started, turning her face toward the little girl. "This is Minh."

At the sound of her name, Minh perked up and glanced at Jan.

Her dark, shiny hair was cut just to her jawline, and she wore a pretty pink dress with ruffles down the front of it. Her shoes looked brand new, patent leather and without so much as a single scuff on them. She even had on fancy socks with a lace trim.

She wrapped both arms around the middle of a blond-headed baby doll, tapping the fingers of one hand against the doll's back as if to comfort it.

Jan let go of my hand and then bent down to set Minh's feet on the ground. Minh was quick to lean into Jan's leg, pressing her face into the fabric of her skirt.

"It's all right," Jan said, her voice even soothing *me* a little bit. "Come meet Mommy and Daddy."

She coaxed Minh out and kept a hand on her shoulder.

"Hi," I said, lowering down to my haunches. "Hi there, Minh."

Bruce reached out for her as if asking for the hand of a princess. "Hello," he said, his voice soft as velvet.

She didn't take his hand, so he let it fall to his side. But he kept a winning smile on his face.

Jan bent at the waist to whisper in Minh's ear. "Mommy and Daddy."

Minh nodded as if she understood, but her eyes still looked confused, frightened.

"Minh," I said in a soft voice, hoping that I was saying it right.

She turned her eyes to mine for a second before lowering them to my nose.

"It's okay," I said, ducking my head so she'd look into my eyes again.

She did, but only for the flash of a second.

After Jan was gone and the reporters at the end of the driveway dispersed—likely very disappointed—Bruce, Minh, and I stood in the living room. She still held her baby doll and Bruce had the envelope that contained what few documents she'd come with. I held a bundle of nerves in the pit of my chest.

We showed her around the house—kitchen, bathroom, bedrooms. Bruce carried her from room to room, pointing to different things—piano, bookcase, toilet—keeping his voice gentle and low.

She'd blink at him, watching his mouth move but betraying no emotion.

"So serious," I whispered.

"It's a lot to take in." Bruce turned toward Minh. "Isn't it?"

She nodded, but I doubted she understood what he'd said.

"What now?" I said when the tour was over after only a couple of minutes.

"No idea," Bruce answered.

That was when the phone rang.

The suddenness of it made Minh flinch and make the slightest whimpering sound.

"Oh, sweet pea," I said. "It's just the telephone. It's okay."

Bruce handed her to me and went to answer it, his back to me and hand on his hip. Minh kept her eyes on him, watching as he talked to whomever was on the other end of the line. When he moved his hand, she watched it. When he turned toward us and smiled at her, she cocked her head to one side as if trying to figure him out.

"Daddy's silly, isn't he?" I asked.

At the sound of my voice, she turned and looked up into my face as if surprised that I was there.

"I wonder what you're thinking about all this," I whispered. "This must be so confusing for you."

"Yup," Bruce said to the person on the other end of the line. "Thanks for understanding. Bye, now."

He hung up and turned around.

"Who was that?" I asked.

He opened his mouth to tell me but couldn't get it out before the phone rang again. It went on like that for a full hour, people wanting to drop over to meet Minh. How did they already know about her?

It was a good thing Bruce was the one to answer the calls because he didn't flinch when he had to tell them "not today."

"It's hard to keep secrets in a town this size, I guess," Bruce said, shaking his head as the phone rang again.

Eventually he took it off the hook.

"There," he said. "Now, how about we read a couple books to her?"

He squatted beside the shelf next to the TV and pulled out a few Berenstain Bears and another few by Dr. Seuss.

We sat on the couch, Minh between us, and took turns reading aloud, pointing things out in the pictures like the fishbowl balanced on the end of the rake or the bee hovering around the daisy in Mama Bear's hat.

All the while my chest felt tight, and sitting still like that was near agonizing. I felt ready to jump right up out of my skin.

I looked at the clock, watching the second hand make its spasmodic circle past the numbers. In thirty minutes, I would start dinner. In an hour, we'd eat. Then I'd get Minh in the bath, and we'd read her another story. In three hours, she'd be in bed.

In the morning we'd get up and move our way through the day, half an hour at a time.

The ticking of the clock sounded louder than usual and made the tightness in my chest close to crushing.

Forcing myself to look away, I turned my eyes on Minh. Her mouth was open, just slightly, as she watched Bruce's finger move along under the words as he read them. He stumbled as he went, tongue-tied by *Fox in Socks*.

I took in a breath that seemed to reach all the way to the soles of my feet.

The tightness was still there, but it was easing as what felt like a warm rush spread all the way through me.

I wanted that moment to last. I didn't want to shoo it away.

CHAPTER Eighteen

Sonny, 1988

The first few days of working with Mrs. Olds were dusty, exhausting, and like super sweaty. Before doing anything else we had to scrub every window, wipe down every cupboard and shelf, sweep and mop every floor in every room. One morning we even took old toothbrushes to the most stubborn stains on the tile floors in the bathroom.

One thing I learned about old houses was that they had lots of places for dirt and grime to build up. Another thing I learned was that ancient houses had a way of collecting grody things over the years like mouse turds, cobwebs, and other assorted creepy-crawlies. And I only got a little embarrassed that I'd scream when happening upon such things that totally barfed me out.

On the third day we rubbed oil into all the woodwork, then went back through to wipe it clean. Banisters and trim and floorboards and doors. From all the wood in the place I wondered how many forests Old Mr. Huebert had chopped down just to build his own house.

By noon each day Mindy and I dragged ourselves to the car. Filthy, exhausted, and sore, we'd go home and take a nap after lunch like a couple of toddlers.

Who wasn't wiped out every day after work? Mrs. Olds. That little old lady did every job we did in those four hours. Only she did it faster, better, and with a smile on her wrinkly face. She had to have been at least seventy-five years old. Maybe even older. But I was pretty sure she was going to outlive Mins and me by a couple of decades.

"You girls did such a good job," she said on Friday, writing out a check to each of us in the pretty penmanship that all women her age had. "Same time on Monday, all right?"

"Yes," Mindy said, folding her check and slipping it into the pocket of her jeans. "Thank you."

"I'll walk you out." She straightened up, passing my paycheck to me before heading to the foyer and out the front door. "Next week we'll begin to unpack the artifacts."

"Sounds interesting," I said, and I totally meant it.

Looking at treasures was way more exciting than sweeping up petrified spider carcasses.

"Ah yes." She pointed back inside. "Those boxes are full of them. This and that from the citizens of Bear Run and a few things from other places in Michigan. Some of them even older than I am, if you can believe it."

"Oh, I can believe it," Mindy said.

I resisted the strong urge to roll my eyes at my sister's blatant attempt to earn brownie points with the boss. Instead, I made my way off the steps and onto the gravel walkway.

Mrs. Olds took one last step on the porch, one of the boards creaking under her foot.

"Did you hear that?" she asked, eyes wide behind her wire-rimmed glasses. She moved her foot, causing the old wood to groan again. "Do you know what that is?"

I shook my head, no idea how to answer her question.

"It's history," Mrs. Olds said. "Saying 'thank you, girls.'"

I glanced at Mindy, thinking that maybe our boss was a few artifacts short of a museum.

"You're welcome, history," Mindy said, cupping her hand to her mouth.

Mrs. Olds clapped once and grinned. Mindy laughed.

I was working with a couple of lunatics.

Mindy hated going to the mall. But we both had a pocket full of money to spend after cashing our checks and I had no one to go shopping with, so I dragged her there with me. That was, after we both cleaned up and changed into cool clothes.

The parking lot was so full I had to drive around looking for a space for the old El Camino that wasn't in the wing where Casual Corner and Hickory Farms was. I gave up after a while and parked near Sears, telling Mindy that she had to remember which entrance we came in.

"Granny bras," she said when we stepped in through the automatic doors. "That shouldn't be too hard to remember."

"Oh my goodness," I said, walking past a rack of exceptionally sized brassieres. "Do you remember when Teddy snooped in Grammy's underwear drawer?"

Mindy threw her head back in a laugh. "Yes. The little booger."

We'd all been at Grammy and Grumpy's for someone's birthday and Teddy wandered off, which wasn't unusual for him. He was four years old at the most and always getting into something. Uncle Chris found him in Grammy's room with one of her bras on his head like a hat.

"I'll never forget the look on Grammy's face when Uncle Chris brought him out to show us all," Mindy said.

"Yeah, who knew she could ever be embarrassed."

I wondered if anybody'd gotten a picture of him like that. It would have made for some pretty righteous blackmail material if they had.

The undies section eased into the ladies' wear section, which led us to the opening of the mall. Stores lined every wall with neon lights over their doors. One way was the food court with every kind of greasy snack you could ever want. The other way was the theater with movie posters for *Big* and *Willow*. The smell of buttered popcorn made my mouth water. People filled every nook and cranny of the mall, some of them carrying bags of what they'd bought, and others just milled around, window shopping. "Time After Time" played over the loudspeaker, and I had to really try not to sing along with Cyndi Lauper.

Not that anyone would have noticed or cared. It was Friday afternoon and the whole place was buzzing with people from the whole Tri-County area with plenty of money to spend.

Oh my gosh, I loved the mall.

I promised Mindy that if she went to Deb with me and didn't complain while I tried stuff on that I would go to Waldenbooks with her. After waiting outside the fitting room while I tried on a hundred pairs of jeans, she'd totally earned a little time browsing the fiction section.

"Wanna play a game?" Mindy asked when we stepped into the bookstore. "It's kind of nerdy."

"Sure," I said. "Maybe."

"I get to pick out a book for you and you get to pick out a book for me," she said. "Like, we try to find the very most perfect book for each other."

"Okay."

"We only get ten minutes." She raised her eyebrows at me. "Ready?"

"Yup."

"Go."

Mindy went to one end of the store and I went to the other. I knew within two minutes which book I'd pick for her, so the last eight, I pretended to be rummaging about for her sake. I checked my watch, making my way to our meeting spot, the book hidden behind my back.

But always-on-time Mindy wasn't there. I thought maybe her own challenge was harder for her than she'd expected. I decided to give her another minute, but when she still hadn't come back after that time, I went looking for her. She was backed into a corner, a woman about our mom's age holding a book out to her.

"The reason I ask," the woman was saying when I walked toward them, "is because my book club is looking for an author from China. You see, we're trying to read a book from each of the continents."

"Well," Mindy said, "I don't think Pearl S. Buck was Chinese."

"Oh, really?"

Mindy shook her head.

"Then why would she write a book about the Chinese?" The woman pursed her lips. "It doesn't make sense."

"I don't know."

"Well, I'll just have to find something else." The woman

dumped *The Good Earth* on a shelf, far from where it belonged. "Do you know any Chinese authors?"

"Uh, I don't think so."

"That's interesting. What do you read, then?"

Mindy shrugged.

"A Chinese girl who doesn't read Chinese books. How funny."

Mindy didn't say anything. She just blinked her eyes really fast. I could tell she was super upset.

"You are from China, aren't you?" the woman asked.

"Actually, I'm from Bear Run."

"Of course. I figured that out," the woman said. "But China's where you're *really* from, right?"

I waited for Mindy to correct the woman, to say that she was from Vietnam, but she didn't open her mouth. The girl was going to have to learn how to stand up for herself. I wouldn't always be there to swoop in and rescue her.

Lucky for her, though, I was there that day. Even luckier for that woman, I was working overtime to keep my temper at bay.

"Hey, Mindy." I made my way between the woman and my sister. "We should get going."

"Sorry I couldn't help you," Mindy said to the woman.

I took my sister's hand and pulled her toward the children's section and far away from that woman. We ended up next to the shelf with all the Beverly Cleary books and I had to remind myself not to be distracted by Ramona Quimby.

"What was that all about?" I asked in a half whisper. "What was with that woman?"

"I don't know." Mindy rolled her eyes.

"Why didn't you just tell her that you're from Vietnam?"

"Because it wouldn't have mattered. She probably thinks

all Asian countries are the same." She turned her eyes toward the floor. "Why can't I just be from Bear Run like everybody else?"

"Being from Vietnam is special, Mins."

"I'd rather not be special."

"You're so weird."

It wasn't the right thing to say and I knew it as soon as the words were out of my mouth and Mindy flinched.

"I didn't mean it like that," I whispered. "I'm sorry."

"It's all right," she said. "Can we just go?"

"What about the books we picked out?"

"Oh yeah," she said, holding up the one she'd picked for me. "You don't have to buy this if you don't want to."

I took it from her, feeling the gloss of the cover. *The Glass Menagerie* was something that we were supposed to read for sophomore English, but it got bumped my year when a parent complained about certain swear words in it or something.

As if teens—even Christian school teens—had never heard a cuss word before.

"It's a play," Mindy said.

"Right," I said before handing over the bright green book I'd chosen for her. "I think this might be a little expensive."

"Oh my goodness." She smiled. "I've wanted to read this book for forever."

There was a dragon on the cover and the name Stephen King. I knew I couldn't have gone wrong.

"I hope it isn't too scary," I said.

"This is different." She turned it over and looked at the back. "*The Eyes of the Dragon* is more like a fairy tale, I guess. You might even like it."

"As long as it doesn't give me nightmares."

I looked over the shelves, watching the woman leave the store, a bag dangling from her hand.

Even though it was a Friday night and I could have been hanging out with my friends, I decided to stay home. Dad had ordered pizzas and rented a tape of *The Princess Bride*. Besides, I was tired and didn't feel up to being social if I didn't have to.

After the movie was over, Mindy and I went to our room to read our new books in bed.

Our lamps didn't turn off until late night became early morning, both of us completely absorbed in the stories.

As soon as I read about Laura's glass unicorn breaking, making it nothing but a regular old horse, I stopped reading and looked over the top of the book at my sister.

"What?" she asked when she caught me staring.

"Nothing," I answered. "My eyes just got tired."

"Do you like it?"

"Yeah. It's really good." I smiled. "How about yours?"

"It's the best."

She went back to reading and so did I. When I finished and turned off my light, I lay in bed not able to sleep for a long time.

CHAPTER Nineteen

Bruce, 2013

I t's the kind of day when I'm aware of how, as Elizabeth Barrett Browning said, "earth's crammed with heaven." The kind of day when the sacred is at my fingertips as I hunt for the prettiest of the fallen leaves in our yard to bring inside for Linda to press between layers of wax paper when Sonny and her girls come by later.

Days like these, I would be happy to stay outside to enjoy the cathedrals of creation, but when the youngest daughter's boyfriend texts, asking to meet up for coffee, I must go.

I have a pretty good idea what he wants to talk about, and I intend to give the kid my blessing. Not, however, before making him promise to be good to my girl and give her the best life he can manage.

Once I've got a good collection of leaves, I take them in. But not before checking to make sure they're free of slugs or other slimy critters.

"Oh, these are pretty, hon," Linda says, spreading them out on the kitchen counter. "Perfect."

"Wish I could stick around to help you and the girls," I say. "Zach just asked me out for coffee."

"He did, huh?" Her eyes widen, brighten. "Do you think . . ."

"Yup."

"How wonderful!" She claps her hands and does a little bouncy dance.

"He's a good kid."

"You'll be nice to him, won't you?" She starts arranging the leaves by color, reds and yellows and oranges. "Don't scare him too much, all right."

"I won't."

I give her a kiss and then grab the keys to my truck. "Better scoot."

"Thanks for these," she says, nodding at the leaves.

They're pretty. But they don't hold a candle to her. Not by a long shot.

When Zach asked me to meet, I told him to pick the place. He wondered if I'd ever heard of Bear Town Beanery on Huebert and Lane and if I'd like to meet up there.

Well, I know that place pretty well. In my day it was where the beatniks had their poetry readings and folk bands went to sing their renditions of Bob Dylan songs. Of course, back then it wasn't called anything but the Coffeehouse. There wasn't a sign over the door and there weren't comfy chairs in the corners. It hadn't been well lit back then and it was always smoggy from all the things the kids smoked in there—cigarette and otherwise.

I don't tell him all that when he greets me at the door and shakes my hand.

He's not here to listen to an old hippie jabber on about the past.

"You order yet?" I ask, nodding at the extensive menu written in chalk on the wall.

Back in my day, it was just coffee. If we were lucky, the half and half wasn't expired and the sugar wasn't rock hard in the dispenser.

"Not yet," Zach says, shoving his hands into the pockets of his jeans that are so tight I wonder if he didn't accidentally get them from the women's department. "Whatever you want. My treat."

"Well, you don't have to do that."

"Sure I do. I invited you, I pay." He smiles.

That smile is what must have made Holly fall for him. If nothing else, it was how he caught her eye.

I fight the temptation to think he's spent a lot of time practicing that smile in the mirror.

He's a good kid. I need to keep that up front in my mind.

We order, both of us opting for something warm to take the chill off the cool day. The guy behind the counter says he'll bring them to us once they're done.

Zach starts in on what he wants to say before we've even taken a seat.

"Mr. Matthews," he says.

"Bruce is fine." I smile and squint my eyes so he knows it's a friendly correction.

"All right, Bruce." He lets me sit first before he pulls out a wicker-backed chair across from me. "I really love your daughter."

"Which one?"

His face drops.

"I'm joking, Zach."

"Oh. Right."

Linda would have kicked me under the table for that, and I feel bad for derailing him.

"Sorry," I say. "Go on. You love Holly."

"More than anything."

He's off to a good start despite me.

"I was going to wait until Christmas to do this, but I can't."

Oh, I know that feeling. I've never been one to believe in love at first sight. Still, somehow I knew I wanted to marry Linda after the first week of knowing her. Again, I don't lay that on the kid. It's his time to talk. Not mine.

"See . . ." he starts.

But the barista brings our drinks, interrupting him with a "Hey, don't I know you, man?"

"Uh, maybe," Zach says, glancing at me.

"From seminary," the guy says. Then, pointing at his chest, "Alexander."

"Oh, right." Zach swallows hard. "How's it going, Alex?"

"It's Alexander."

"Sorry."

Alexander goes on to tell Zach exactly how he is and in full detail. And how is Alexander? Busy. By the time another couple customers come in, pulling the guy back behind the coffee bar, I know more about him than I know about myself, including his stance on several theological debates that we never covered in my Sunday school classes.

"Sorry," Zach says. "He's a nice guy, but he really likes to talk."

"It's all right, son." I take a sip of my coffee, careful not to get too much whipped cream in my mustache. "You were saying?"

"Well." He clears his throat. "I got offered a position at a church."

"Okay?"

"It's just outside of Cleveland. You know, in Ohio."

"Yup. I've heard of it."

"But they only want to hire me if I'm married."

"Are you asking me for my daughter's hand just so you can get a job?" I lean forward, resting an elbow on the table.

"Yes. Well, no." His Adam's apple bobs up and down. "What I mean to say is, we were planning on getting married next spring anyway. This is just a little bit earlier than we'd expected."

"How much earlier are you thinking?"

"Soon. Before Thanksgiving," he says. "We're not sure which day yet."

"Huh. That's pretty quick," I say. "You sure Holly's okay with that?"

"I think so."

"Son, she's been dreaming of her wedding day since she was a flower girl when Mike and Sonny got married." I give him what I hope looks like a sympathetic smile. "I'm worried that she won't be happy about having to rush."

He lowers his eyes and runs a hand through his hair.

"I'm not saying you can't marry her, Zach," I say. "I'd be proud to have you for a son-in-law. But I . . ."

"Mr. Matthews." He takes a breath. "Bruce. I've never met anybody like Holly. I love her so much. She's smart and funny and kind."

The boy didn't mention how pretty she is—and she's real pretty. She looks so much like her mama. More than once have I seen the way he looks at her, him definitely noticing her beauty. But him not mentioning her looks as a reason for his love deepens my respect for him a whole lot.

"I want to spend every day with her," he goes on. "This earlier start just gives me more time for that."

He takes a bolstering drink of his coffee.

"And as for the quick wedding," he says. "We've talked about it a lot, Holly and me. She's okay with it. I promise, she is."

I nod. "If this is really what the two of you want."

"Life with her is what I want."

If I'm not mistaken, his eyes are as watery as mine are.

"Well, I can't argue with that." I get out of my seat, walk around to his side, and give him a hug, slapping him on the back. "Linda's going to be thrilled."

"I was so nervous," he says once I've returned to my spot.

"I don't blame you, son." I take another sip of my overly sweet coffee. Then I point to the far corner of the coffee shop. "You know, I was sitting right over there the first time I saw Linda."

"Really?" Zach's carrot-colored eyebrows go up. "I didn't realize this place has been around that long."

I don't react to that. He meant nothing by it. Besides, I've been around longer than this old coffee shop.

Instead, I tell him the story. It's nothing spectacular. I was there to see some band that'd been scheduled to play, and she walked in, guitar case in hand. There weren't any seats open except for the one across from me, and I was more than happy to let her borrow it while she waited for the rest of her crew to get there.

When it was time for the band to play, she got up and sang a handful of songs. No matter how I tried, I couldn't manage to take my eyes off her.

That's it. That's the story. Fireworks didn't go off over our heads and I didn't fall out of my seat. It wouldn't make the cut in a romance novel. But, then again, I wasn't much interested in that kind of thing in the first place.

He listens politely even though I have an idea that he's not all that interested. That's all right. I wouldn't have been at his age either.

The kid doesn't waste any time in getting that diamond on Holly's finger. Within an hour of my returning home, Holly calls to tell us the news. Within two hours she's put it up on Facebook. After three she's at the house with Zach in tow, a pile of bridal magazines in her arms.

Linda, true to form, wraps her arms around Holly, magazines and all.

"We'd better start planning, huh?" she says, putting both hands on our youngest's face. "You will be such a beautiful bride."

"Thanks, Mom," Holly says, handing the stack to Zach.

"Let's see the ring," I say.

Holly holds up her left hand, showing a ring that I'm certain cost more than a month of the kid's salary. Especially a kid working in the ministry.

"It was my grandma's," he says.

I wonder if he read my expression.

"How sweet," Linda says. "Let's take all of these magazines to the family room. Mindy just put a pan of brownies into the oven."

"Mom, I'm going to have to fit into a wedding dress soon," Holly says.

"Oh, one brownie won't bust the seams." Linda shakes her head.

That's when Mindy emerges from the kitchen, one of Linda's aprons tied around her waist. She gushes over Holly, ooohs over the ring, agrees without hesitation to be a bridesmaid.

"How many attendants are you planning on?" Linda asks.

"Just Mindy and Sonny," Holly says. "I mean, I kind of planned on having ten bridesmaids and a couple of flower girls. But there's kind of no time for that. This is better, I think. Simpler."

"Simple will need to be the name of the game." Linda winks at her. "But we can do it. Right, honey?"

I realize she's talking to me and I nod, feeling just a little bit out of my element.

The girls head into the family room, Zach trailing along behind them.

"This is going to be a whirlwind, isn't it?" I say before pushing out a stream of air. "Never thought Holly'd settle for a quick wedding."

"Oh, I don't think she's settling for anything," Linda whispers, only for me to hear. "You saw how thrilled she is, didn't you?"

I can't deny that.

"Are you ready to give away another daughter?" Linda asks.

"Don't know," I answer.

Is there a way to be ready for such a thing?

CHAPTER Twenty

Linda, 1975

I had to stack a few phone books on a chair for Minh so she could reach her plate at the table. When she saw the grilled cheese, cut into quarters, her eyes narrowed, and I wondered if she'd ever seen such a thing before.

Then I worried if such unfamiliar food might upset her tummy. Just one more thing on a running list of questions I should have asked before the adoption agency people got back in their car and drove away.

I decided to see if the library had a Vietnamese cookbook, not having even the faintest idea what kinds of things she might have eaten over there.

She sat still, hands in her lap, and stared at her plate.

"Minh," Bruce said. "Look here."

He waited for her to give him her attention. Then he picked up the sandwich from his plate and took a bite, chewing it slowly.

"Mm. That's good," he said. Then he pointed at her plate. "Now you take a bite."

Serious as could be, Minh picked up one of her squares of sandwich, extending it to Bruce.

"She thinks you want her food," I said.

"Thank you." He took it from her, holding it near to her mouth. "But this is for you."

She nodded and took a tiny bite, mushing it slowly between her teeth. .

Bruce waited until she swallowed.

"Another?" he asked.

She nodded and took another bite.

And then another.

He showed her the green grapes, popping one into his own mouth before offering her one.

The way her poor little mouth puckered made me think she'd gotten a sour one. Still, she chewed and swallowed it before taking another off her plate.

"You don't have to eat them if you don't want to," I said.

She answered me by stuffing another in her mouth, both cheeks round with grapes, looking like a little chipmunk.

"I think we might get this figured out," Bruce said, shaking a few red dots of hot sauce onto his plate and dipping his sandwich into it.

Minh caught his eye and then nodded at the bottle of Tabasco.

"Oh, honey," I said. "I don't think you'd like that. It's spicy."

She put her hands back in her lap and nodded at the bottle again.

"Maybe just a little bit," Bruce said, tipping the bottle over her plate.

Minh picked up a square of sandwich and dabbed up the sauce, taking a bite and nodding as she chewed.

"More?" Bruce held up the bottle.

She kept nodding, so he shook out more for her.

"I'm worried she'll get a sore stomach," I said.

"I don't know, Linda. I think she likes it."

By the time she was done, she'd eaten three of the four pieces of sandwich and left only a few grapes.

Not too shabby.

By seven that night, Minh's eyelids had grown heavy and she yawned, hardly able to stay awake for the end of the story Bruce read to her on the couch. I didn't think she'd even stay awake if we put her in the bath, so we decided to hold off on that until the next day.

I found an old nightie that Sonny had just grown out of and turned down the covers of her bed. While helping Minh out of her dress and into her jammies, I saw the hint of impetigo on her face, nearly healed up.

I wondered that there were people in the world who would reject a child over such a small thing as a rash. What mercy that this precious little girl didn't end up in that home.

Bruce and I were far from perfect, the Lord was well aware of that. Possibly he was more acquainted with our faults than even we were. But we would love Minh past our imperfections. We would love her and cherish her.

Kneeling there on the girls' bedroom floor, the shag carpeting scratchy against my bare knees, I gave my thanks to the God who cared enough to sometimes use a rash for the good of one of his dear ones.

"We love you, Minh," I whispered, smoothing down her hair that got tousled when I pulled the nightie over her head. "Now let's go brush those chompers, okay?"

I got her teeth clean—finding that her top front teeth were worn down nearly to nubs—and had her use the potty before calling for Bruce to help me tuck her in.

She looked so small in the bed, her hair so dark on the white pillowcase. I pulled the silky trimmed blanket up to her shoulders when she shivered and wondered how much hotter Vietnam was than Bear Run.

"Don't forget your baby," Bruce said, handing her the doll.

She nodded and kissed the yellow head of it. Then she peeked at us, as if unsure what we would make of such a thing.

I put my hand on her forehead, moving the bangs that someone had trimmed recently to one side.

"I'm so glad you're here," I whispered, smiling at her. "Sleep tight, sweet girl."

Bruce woke me in the morning with a cup of coffee, setting it on the bedside table before pushing the curtains open, letting the sunshine into the room.

"Good morning," I said.

He put a finger to his lips. "She's still sleeping," he whispered.

"Did you check on her?" I asked, sitting up before taking a sip of coffee.

Just the right amount of cream and sugar. The man loved me so well.

He shook his head. "Didn't want to disturb her. I thought she needed the sleep after yesterday. It was a big day for her."

"She slept through the night, didn't she?" I said. "I didn't hear her at all."

"I think she did."

He climbed into bed, grabbing a book and leaning back against the headboard.

It was Monday and his boss had given him the day off. I was grateful that he was there; still, I tried not to think of what a day without pay would do to our budget. I tried—unsuccessfully—not to tally up the cost of taking Minh to the doctor for a checkup and the dentist for an examination, let alone if we decided to enroll Minh in school for the coming fall. Just thinking about paying two tuitions made my head swimmy, especially knowing we couldn't rely on Hilda helping us.

Not anymore.

I wondered if she'd ever forgive us for going against her will. As much as I wanted not to care what my mother-in-law thought of me, I just couldn't calm the panic that pressed hard on my chest when I knew I'd displeased her.

Blinking hard, I tried to shoo away those thoughts. We'd be okay. With or without Hilda's approval.

"I can't wait for Sonny to meet her," I said, forcing myself to think about something else. "What will she think of Minh, I wonder."

"No idea." He put the book on his lap. "I think I'm more worried about what Minh will think of her."

"They might be good for each other."

I finished that first cup of coffee and got up, deciding that I should probably get some breakfast made. I didn't think I should let Minh sleep all day or she wouldn't ever sleep that night.

Still in my nightie, I peeked into the girls' room on my way to the kitchen.

"Rise and shine," I sang through the doorway.

Minh wasn't in her bed. The covers were rustled, like they'd been pushed off, and there was still a divot from where her head had been on the pillow. But she wasn't there.

"Minh?" I called into the room.

I checked the bathroom. Empty. The living room and kitchen. Both empty. Then went back to my bedroom to find Bruce, nose in his book.

"Did she come in here?" I asked.

It took him too long to respond, so absorbed was he in what he was reading.

"Bruce." I said his name in a half shout so he'd come to attention.

"Yup?" he asked, looking up. "What's wrong?"

"Minh isn't in her room. I can't find her."

He about jumped out of bed and I turned, rushing toward the back door to make sure it was still locked. It was. So was the front door.

The house just wasn't that big. I couldn't for the life of me figure out where she could have gone.

Then I heard Bruce's voice, gentle and deep, from the girls' room.

"Well, what are you doing under there?" he asked.

My heart still pounding far harder than was comfortable, I went to the doorway. Bruce was on hands and knees, the skirt around Minh's bed frame pulled up. Underneath, two very large, very dark eyes peeked out.

"Did you sleep down there last night?" Bruce asked. "Is that more comfortable for you?"

She pushed the baby doll from under the bed first and then shimmied out, the back of her hair in snarls.

I leaned on the dresser, my legs a very wobbly form of jelly.

"I'll get breakfast started," Bruce said.

I shut the door behind him, taking a deep breath in and out before turning back toward Minh.

"Let's get you dressed," I said.

I pulled open the bottom drawer of her dresser for a pair of overalls. There, with the hand-me-downs from Sonny, was a square of grilled cheese and a handful of grapes—leftovers from dinner the day before.

"Oh, sweetheart," I whispered, looking at her over my shoulder.

She was so small, so thin. And her eyes were so frightened.

"It's okay."

I closed the drawer.

Twenty-One

Sonny, 1988

When I was in middle school, I got up early every day in the summer so I could have breakfast with my dad before he went to work. We even had a whole routine where he'd make the coffee and I'd scramble the eggs. I got out the jam for the toast he made. We would sit at the kitchen table, keeping our voices low so we wouldn't wake up Mom and Mindy.

He was being considerate of them.

I, on the other hand, didn't want them crashing the party.

It was probably super selfish of me, but I liked having that time with him all to myself.

At some point I'd stopped getting up early on summer mornings. It wasn't like I did it on purpose or anything. It just slipped my mind.

I wondered if he missed those mornings. I wondered if it hurt his feelings that I didn't get up with him anymore.

So, since it was my last summer at home, I thought maybe I'd try and get up a few times to have breakfast with him again.

Not every day, though. The man got up ridiculously early and I was in desperate need of my beauty sleep.

On a Tuesday morning my alarm went off half an hour before Mindy's was set to, and I got up, tiptoeing down the stairs so I could surprise him.

Once I got to the bottom of the steps, I heard the running of water in the kitchen. He was already making coffee. I picked up the pace, making it to the swinging door before I heard Mom's voice.

Bummer.

It wasn't like her to be up that early. Then again, she wasn't really acting like herself much these days.

I was about to slump my way into the kitchen for a bowl of Cheerios but then stopped, deciding that maybe I should eavesdrop a little first.

"This baby does not want to let me sleep," Mom said.

"It's just getting you ready for two a.m. feedings," Dad said.

I almost let out a huge sigh of relief that I would miss all of that newborn stuff while I was away at college. Sure, I'd miss all the snuggles and baby smiles and stuff. But changing poopy diapers and waking up to a screaming infant at all hours of the night were not my idea of fun.

"It's too early to be up," Mom said. "I need a cup of coffee."

"Didn't the doctor say you're not supposed to have any? It's not good for the baby."

"Oh, who cares what that old fuddy-duddy said? My mother drank a beer every week when she was pregnant with me, and I'm fine!"

There was a tinkling sound that I guessed was mugs tapping each other.

"Linda," Dad said.

"I'm only going to have half a cup," Mom said. "And it will be mostly cream and sugar. I promise, it won't hurt the baby. Remember, I drank four cups of coffee a day when I was pregnant with Sonny. She's fine."

"Well, that's debatable."

I rolled my eyes. So rude.

"She's a wonderful young woman and you know it, Bruce," she said. Then, "After this baby's born, I'm going to drink a whole pot of coffee by myself."

"I have a hunch you'll need to," Dad said. "I think this one is going to put us through the drills."

"Oh, I know it."

"And too bad Sonny won't be here," he said. "You know how she likes to run the show."

My mouth dropped open and I wanted to shriek an extra loud "as if" in Dad's direction. It wasn't the first time somebody had implied that I was bossy, and I doubted that it would be the last.

Still, it bugged me.

It wasn't my fault that I knew how things should be done.

They didn't talk for a few minutes. The only sounds from the other side of the door were of slurps—gag me—the clearing of a throat, and dishes being put into the sink.

Ugh. Parents could be so boring.

"I can't believe Sonny's almost out of the house," Mom said. Then her voice started to warble like she was crying. "It just . . . she grew up too fast."

Dad said, "Babe, I know."

"I'm going to miss her so much."

I pressed the palm of my hand against the door and was about to push it open when Mom started sobbing. Not just crying. She let out full boo-hoos and wails.

Over me.

I clenched down on the spot in my throat where the bawling threatened to erupt and blinked hard against the stinging that always came right before I started crying.

"I've just really loved being her mom."

"It's hard to let go, isn't it?" Dad asked.

Mom said something that was so garbled I couldn't understand it.

"She's going to be all right, Lin." His voice was so gentle it made my heart hurt a little. "We've got to let her go. She can't stay in our nest forever."

I took my hand off the door and leaned back against the wall.

For years I'd been looking forward to moving away to college. I'd visited a couple of different schools, hoping to find the very best one for me, and dreamed of the classes I could take. In the middle drawer of my desk, I even had a diagram of how I wanted to set up my dorm room. I'd colored it in and everything.

It was my chance to start over without anyone having expectations for me.

I might have considered telling everyone to call me my real name, Sondra. But then I worried that I wouldn't respond to it. I'd decided to just go by Sonny.

It was easier that way.

But for all my excitement, I hadn't even taken a second to think of how hard it would be to leave everybody behind.

❧

Mrs. Olds met us at the door, tugging a little red wagon behind her. She had on a pair of overalls that she wore when she expected the work to be extra grimy, and her hands were covered by a pair of garden gloves.

"Oh man," I whispered to Mindy. "Is it going to be a day for champions? I don't think I'm up for that."

Over the past few weeks I'd come to learn that when Mrs. Olds declared it a day for champions that it really meant it was a day in which we were going to get our butts kicked. On our first day for champions we had to carry a hundred-million boxes of books from the attic to the study only to carry as many boxes filled with tools from the study to the basement.

On the second, Mindy and I took turns mowing the yard. It wouldn't have been so bad if we'd had something other than an old rusty push mower that somebody donated.

I seriously didn't want to know what it could be that day.

"Good morning, girls," Mrs. Olds said, beaming at us from the doorway as we climbed up to the porch. "Today is . . ."

"Don't say it," I said under my breath.

". . . a day for champions."

Darn.

"Someone was"—she cleared her throat—"kind enough to donate a large amount of rocks."

"Rocks?" Mindy asked.

"Yes." Mrs. Olds smiled and widened her eyes. "A large amount of them."

Double darn.

"Are they inside?" Mindy tilted her head to see around Mrs. Olds.

"Oh no. They're in the backyard." She relaxed her shoulders. "But they need to be moved because they're currently right where I'd planned to plant a Victory Garden next summer."

"What's a Victory Garden?" I asked.

"What *are* they teaching in schools these days?" She shook

her head and stepped out onto the porch, pulling the wagon behind her. "Never you mind, dear. I shall tell you. But first, kindly help me get this down the steps."

Mrs. Olds hadn't been joking when she said there was a large amount of rocks in the backyard. I was glad she'd thought to drop two pairs of work gloves into the wagon, otherwise Mindy and I were going to have blisters for days.

I wasn't too stoked about the totally lame tan lines I was going to have, though.

"Let's cart these to the far end of the yard," Mrs. Olds said, pointing forever far away where the grass gave way to wildflowers. "We can build our own Robert Frost wall."

"Oh, 'Mending Wall.' I like that poem," Mindy said, picking up a rock in each hand and dropping them into the wagon. "I memorized it in ninth grade."

I rolled my eyes. Such a teacher's pet.

"Good for you," Mrs. Olds said.

"Well, I memorized 'Nothing Gold Can Stay,'" I said, shrugging.

"That was my father's favorite." Mrs. Olds winked at me.

I didn't tell her that the only reason I ever heard of that poem or of Robert Frost was because I'd watched *The Outsiders* at least a dozen times with Amelia. Even just thinking of Johnny telling Ponyboy to stay gold made my eyes sting.

"Would you girls believe that I got married when I was sixteen years old?" Mrs. Olds said. "It's true."

"Wow," Mindy said, squatting down to get her arms around a rock as big as her head. "That's really young."

"Too young." Mrs. Olds pointed at us. "Don't even think of getting married that early."

I didn't remind her that I was already eighteen.

"But you must have been really in love," I said, giving Mindy a hand with the giant boulder.

"I was in something." Mrs. Olds shook her head. "More like deep doo-doo than love, though."

Mindy and I both laughed.

"Take no offense, but sixteen-year-olds aren't ready to make vows that are meant for the rest of their lives." She nodded at the wagon. "It's full enough."

Mindy pulled the handle, and I pushed the back side of it, lifting it when it got stuck in the ruts of flattened molehills. Mrs. Olds walked alongside us, carrying a rock like it was a baby.

"Well, after about a year, he took off," she went on. "I had no choice but to move back with my mother and dad. I read that poem—'Nothing Gold Can Stay'—every day. Let me tell you, it was no comfort to me then."

"Why did you read it?" Mindy asked, giving the wagon a tug.

"Everyone around me wanted me to put my chin up and get over the abandonment. They expected me to carry on as if nothing was amiss. But that poem, it allowed me to be sad for what I lost." She stopped walking. "Right here, I think."

We unloaded that bunch of rocks, making a neat pile for whoever Mrs. Olds would get to come and build her wall. Apparently, it took a certain amount of know-how to do it right, and I was totally cool with not having that skill.

"I'm an old woman," she said on our trip back. "Seventy-eight years old, if you'd believe it."

"You don't look it," Mindy said.

"Thank you, sweetie. I feel it in my bones some days more than others." She nodded. "In my life, I've learned that the golden things usually fade. Often you find that they weren't real gold in the first place."

She put out her hand to stop us in the middle of the yard.

"When life changes, and it does on the regular, we can be sad," she said. "But pay attention, lovelies. Oh, pay attention. Because the ending of one thing almost always means the beginning of something else."

Her eyes were watery, and it surprised me to see a tear fall down her cheek.

"God is so kind," she said. "And he's always up to something."

She brushed the tear off her face and turned back toward the large number of rocks still to be moved.

"Let's keep at it," she said.

That night I sat on the back patio to watch the sunset. When Mom noticed me out there, she joined me on the glider. We went back and forth at an easy pace, and she held my hand on her stomach where the baby was kicking.

The whole time we kept our eyes on the fire-red sky that darkened to a deep blue with each minute that passed.

When it was finally over, the sun completely sunk, I sighed.

"Everything okay?" Mom asked.

"Yeah. I just wish sunsets would last longer," I answered.

"Me too." She turned her head and kissed my cheek.

Twenty-Two

Bruce, 2013

The breeze is just strong enough this morning that it sends a flutter through the leaves, breaking some of them loose, and the big old clouds move slow and lazy across the sky. A blue jay announced my arrival when I first got to the river, jeered a loud warning to all the other critters in the woods.

Apparently the fish took heed of his alarm. I can't get a single one of them to bite.

That's all right, though. I don't mind standing here in my waders, the river moving around my knees and the sun keeping me warm.

Linda knows well enough after all these years that every once in a while I need to get out in the water by myself, even if I don't bring a single fish home for supper. It's good for my soul, being in the woods, in the river, in creation.

If a man walks long enough on this earth, he's bound to have seen his share of change. Some of it he chooses, but most of it chooses him. He weathers some of it with grace and joy and wisdom. Other times he pouts about it for a little while, which is a lot better than pitching a temper tantrum.

I'll be the first to admit that I've reacted badly more than a couple of times when change came along that I didn't want.

But I'm a fortunate man who has witnessed God's new mercies coming every morning whether I deserve them or not.

More often than not, I've needed Linda to point them out to me. She's always on the lookout for the goodness of God.

My life would have been so much different without her in it.

We've done a lot of living together, her and I, in the years since we first met. In that living we've had our share of ups—grandbabies and retirement and more beautiful days than I can count—and plenty of downs—financial hiccups and Mindy's divorce and troubles getting along with my mother. Mixed in with the good and bad is a whole lot of stuff that was just normal, everyday living.

Isn't that life, though? So much all jumbled together.

Shakespeare said something about our life being a web of mingled yarn. The good and bad is twined together.

That's a paraphrase. He, of course, said it better.

When I was a younger man I thought if I worked hard, cared deeply, and read my Bible every day that life would be happy, without any bumps in the road.

How naive, huh?

I reel in my line, readying it for another casting. Pausing a moment before I do, I turn my face upward, closing my eyes against the sun.

Man alive, it's a great day to be outside.

Really, though, any day is.

Rain or sun, storm or calm; nature is good, full of glimmers of God's glory.

Opening my eyes, I cast my line, knowing full well that I might not get anything for my efforts. Knowing there's even a chance I'll get an old boot or a rusty tin can. Then again, I might get something big and tasty.

It's a risk.

There's just no way of knowing.

What I know is this, that mingled yarn of Shakespeare's? It's stronger than a thread of good, bad, or normal could ever be on its own. There's no morning without night.

And there's no need of overcoming if in this world we don't have trouble.

How's all that for a little navel-gazing?

I throw out my line one more time.

***

The only fish I bring home is the kind that's deep fried and comes packed up in a Styrofoam box from a restaurant in town. I can tell Linda's relieved when she realizes she won't have to worry about me cleaning my catch here at the house.

Mindy comes downstairs, bleary eyed and yawning, rotating her hands to loosen up her wrists.

"You feeling all right?" I ask, handing her a plate.

"Yeah. I'm fine." She pulls out her chair at the dining room table and sits. "I brought work home so I could redline some articles before they have to go to print tomorrow. The sportswriter pushes back on every edit I make."

"That must be frustrating," Linda says. "Do you want iced tea?"

"Yes, please," Mindy answers. "Thank you."

"Anything we can help with?" I ask.

"Aside from coffee delivery?" Mindy smiles. "I don't know. I keep thinking I'm not tough enough for this job."

"Sure you are, honey," Linda says.

"The worst part?" She pauses to take a sip of tea. "I don't think he'd fight me if I weren't a woman."

"Probably not," I say.

I've known the sportswriter—a guy named Jim Rogers— most of my life. We went to school together, and he was a bully then. But only to the girls, if I remember right. I never knocked his block off, but that doesn't mean I didn't want to.

If he doesn't ease up on my daughter, though, I might take a chance. I may be in my sixties, but I've still got a little fight in me yet.

"Anyway, he's retiring next year," Mindy says. "So I'll be rid of him soon enough."

"That's the spirit." Linda plops a dollop of tartar sauce on her plate.

"I'm a little frustrated, though." Mindy grabs a hush puppy from her plate, dipping it in a puddle of hot sauce. "I haven't had much time to look into the Vietnam stuff."

"Well, I could help a little," Linda says, then points a thick-cut French fry at me. "Bruce, don't we have a folder of paperwork from the adoption agency somewhere?"

"We sure do." I rub my palms together. "Upstairs in the safe."

"What kind of paperwork?" Mindy asks around a mouthful.

"You know, I haven't even thought about it in years," Linda says. "Once the adoption was final, we stuck it in the safe and all but forgot about it."

I push away from the table and place my napkin next to my plate. "I'll go get it."

"No, eat your dinner," Mindy says. "You don't want it to get cold."

"It won't take me but a minute," I say. "And I'll pop this in the microwave if need be."

I take the stairs, the ache in my knees reminding me of my age. It won't be long before I'm not able to stand all day in a river and expect to go up and down the steps.

Linda and I have talked a little bit about finding a smaller place sometime, one without a second floor. She's even got her dream house picked out. A cute Arts and Crafts home in town that probably won't be up for sale any time in the near future.

But I let my Linda have her dreams. And I add a few of my own too.

I get the safe cracked and locate the manila envelope in a jiffy. When I pull it out from the stack of forms and files and such, a couple old newspaper clippings come with it, dropping onto the carpet. I bend at the knees to pick them up.

One has a grainy picture of the four of us—Linda, Sonny, Mindy, and me—standing on the front stoop of our old house a week or two after Mindy came. We're holding hands, the girls between me and Linda.

The headline reads "Bear Run's Own Babylift Delivery." I shake my head. It's still a hokey line, as far as I'm concerned.

Boy, though. Looking at that picture of us brings up some pretty good feelings. We were scared, sure. We had no clue what we were doing. But, man, we were happy.

I look at the other clipping. Wouldn't you know it, it's Dale's obituary.

After putting that particular paper back into the safe, I shut the door and turn the lock.

Good and bad together.

The fish is still warm enough when I get back to it.

CHAPTER Twenty-Three

Linda, 1975

Bruce sat on the couch, guitar resting on his knee, finger picking a little ditty for Minh. She stood no less than two feet from him, her hair still damp from her bath. One of the straps of her overalls had slid off her shoulder, but I didn't dare reach out to fix it for fear of making her jump. She was still unsure of us—me especially—and I tried not to let that get to me.

It would take her some time to grow accustomed to all the new people and places in her life. Lucky for us, we weren't in any hurry.

As she listened to Bruce, she swayed back and forth, just barely. I imagined if Sonny was there, she'd have been turning pirouettes until she fell down dizzy.

I glanced at the clock on the wall, wishing that lunchtime would come sooner so Sonny could come home and meet her sister. Some strong urge in the pit of me couldn't wait for my girls to be together.

Minh took a few shuffling steps closer to Bruce, gripping her

baby doll tighter as she did. I lowered the basket of dirty laundry
to the floor and leaned into the frame of my bedroom door.

She'd been home with us for less than a full day, but I already
knew that she found a certain calm with Bruce. He eased her
in a way that I doubted I'd be able to. I batted away the seed of
jealousy that wanted to plant itself in my heart. That wouldn't
do any good for anybody. Instead, I let a deeper love for my
husband take root.

When I was a girl, my mother told me once to only fall for
a man who had money. And a lot of it. I knew she'd said it out
of concern for me, only wanting for me what she'd never hoped
to have. My mother hadn't known there were better things in
the world than social rank or large houses.

Maybe if she'd had the chance to meet Bruce she could have
known it was possible to be just making it money wise, but to
be happier than a lark. For me, happiness was a man who loved
my children.

It hurt my heart that my mother had never known that sort
of goodness.

I blinked away thoughts of my past and refocused my eyes
on Bruce and Minh, wishing I had a camera so I could capture
the moment. My memory would have to do.

He sang "Blackbird," somehow keeping his voice steady and
deep. I could never make it through that song without my voice
cracking with emotion. There was just something about those
lyrics.

As the song went on, Minh inched little by little to Bruce
until she was right beside him, her hip against the couch cushion. She stood there until the very end of the song, her eyes
moving from the fingers of his left hand as they picked the guitar
strings to his face as he sang.

Through the open window I heard the crunch of car tires in our driveway and saw the flash of green that was Ivan's Chevy.

Bruce lifted his head when the car door slammed.

Minh, though, jumped at the sharp noise, holding the baby doll tight against her neck.

"It's okay. It's just Grumpy," he said, pointing out the window. "Can you see him?"

Minh nodded, not looking outside. Her bottom lip pushed out into a pout and her chin quivered.

"He'll be nice to you." He propped the guitar against the couch and put out his hand to Minh.

She looked at it but didn't reach for it.

Ivan tapped on the screen door, coming in when I told him to. In his hand he had a brand-new teddy bear. A pink one with a purple bow around its neck.

"Hey, Dad," Bruce said, getting up to greet him.

Ivan extended his hand and shook Bruce's, something that always made me want to yell, "Just hug each other already!"

I didn't, though. It would have embarrassed them too much.

"Did Mom come?" Bruce asked, looking out the door toward Ivan's car.

Ivan dropped his head and gave it a small shake. "Not this time, son."

"Oh." Bruce blinked twice, hard.

"I'll keep working on it," Ivan said. "She'll come to her senses sooner than later."

"Yeah. Well, I'm glad you're here at least. Come meet Minh," Bruce said, stepping aside to let his dad pass.

"Hey there, girlie," Ivan said, stooping with the bear extended toward Minh. "This is for you. You like pink?"

Minh nodded her head but didn't take the stuffed animal.

"Go on, honey." Ivan put it on the arm of the couch. "It's for you. Don't let that sister of yours steal it, all right?"

He moved it just a tiny bit closer to her and she reached out, taking it by the paw and gathering it in her arms next to the baby doll. She nuzzled it against her cheek. It did look soft.

"You and me are going to get in all kinds of trouble together." Ivan cleared his throat. "You just wait and see."

He reached out to bop her on the nose, but she flinched and took a step back. Her little chin trembled.

"Minh," Bruce said, going on one knee beside her. "It's all right. It's okay."

"Oh, golly," Ivan said, nodding at him. "Did I scare her? I didn't mean to."

"It's fine. She'll be just fine," I said, nodding at him. "She's overwhelmed, that's all."

"You sure?"

"I am."

I put an arm around him, leading him to the couch to have a seat. In the seven years that I'd known him, I'd never seen him so flustered. It made me love him even more than I already did. How gentle of him, to care so deeply about the feelings of my little girl.

"Turn toward me, okay?" I said.

He did and I bopped him on the nose with my fingertip and he smiled, catching my drift. He tapped the tip of my nose in response. It was so ridiculous that I laughed, which got Ivan going too.

Minh stood beside Bruce, watching the two of us. She straightened, allowing a hint of a smile to tug at the corners of her mouth. Then she pointed her finger, touching the end of her own nose.

"There you go," Bruce said, then took her hand in his, having her touch his nose.

That was when we heard her laugh for the first time. It was small, but it was beautiful. I would have cheered for the pure joy of it, but I didn't want to startle her.

I offered Ivan a cup of coffee, making sure he got all the sugar he wanted.

CHAPTER Twenty-Four

Sonny, 1988

The first time I heard of Clinton Montgomery was at church camp when I was just starting middle school. The counselors had let us stay up late on the last night and we sat around the bonfire, swatting at mosquitoes and singing cutesy little Sunday school songs. Amelia and I shared a bench near a couple of boys we'd been too afraid of to talk to all week.

They hadn't talked to us either, so I thought they were kind of scared too.

One of the camp counselors started telling ghost stories. Every one of them about Clinton Montgomery—otherwise known as the Bear Run Boogeyman. Each of them more terrifying than the last.

Amelia and I huddled together, trying to act cool so the boys nearby wouldn't think we were total losers. I thought about getting up and going back to my cabin so I wouldn't hear any more, but I was too frightened to walk through the dark woods.

When told in the daylight, any story about his mangled hand

or half-melted face didn't seem so bad. But in the dark, with all the sounds of the woods snapping and creaking, they were horrifying.

The next year at the last bonfire of camp was the same thing, only that time Mindy was on a bench across the pit from me, sitting with her friend Becky. For as many Stephen King novels as my sister read, I wouldn't have thought that those ghost stories would have bothered her. But they had. A whole lot.

She never admitted to having had any nightmares of the Bear Run Boogeyman, but I was sure she did. How could she not?

So, when Mrs. Olds told us that we were setting up the collection from the Clinton Montgomery estate, Mindy and I met eyes, our mouths hanging open.

"I know what you're thinking," she said, turning toward us. "But he was not a monster."

"It's just that we heard stories," I said.

"Oh, I know you have." She wagged her finger at us. "Follow me."

Mrs. Olds made her way to what had been the parlor where Mrs. Huebert had served her teas. There, leaning against the wall and split into four stacks, were at least a dozen fancy picture frames—the kind used in an art museum. A shoebox sat on the windowsill nearby, and Mrs. Olds reached into it, lifting out a few photographs.

"Oh, the poor man," she said and then made a tsking sound. "Mr. Montgomery fought in the Great War."

"Didn't he die in one of the battles?" Mindy asked.

"He did not, dear," Mrs. Olds said. "He survived the war. But he came home looking like this."

She held up an old picture that was so gross and so shocking

I knew that I'd never, ever forget it. Mindy grabbed my hand, and out of the corner of my eye, I saw her lift her other hand to cover her mouth.

"The fighting in France was brutal," Mrs. Olds said. "Like General Sherman said, 'War is hell.'"

I jerked my eyes from the picture to Mrs. Olds's face. Never in my life had I heard an old lady swear. I didn't think it was possible.

"What happened to him?" Mindy asked, seemingly unfazed by the curse word.

"Oh, it appears he was shot in the face."

Mrs. Olds said it as if it was an ordinary, everyday thing to happen. Like, "Oh, I guess he went to the store," or "Huh, I think he got caught in the rain."

When she turned the picture around and took another look at it, she shook her head.

"You know, they didn't have the same medical care as we do now," she said.

"Then what happened to him?" I asked.

"He became somewhat of a recluse, Clinton did, as you might imagine," Mrs. Olds went on. "From what I understand, folks in town weren't so welcoming, even if he was a war hero."

"Why not?" I asked.

"I suppose it was hard to look at him. Wouldn't you think?"

"That's so sad," Mindy said.

"Indeed." Mrs. Olds shook her head. "He took to living in an old logger's cabin deep in the woods. Well, they bulldozed that forest years ago, but in the twenties it was still quite overgrown. Wild. He didn't venture into town except late at night. And only then to visit his mother, who lived by herself in an apartment over the barber shop."

"Did those belong to him?" I asked, nodding at the art against the wall.

"My dear," Mrs. Olds said, a sparkle in her eye. "He painted them."

"Really?" I whispered, stepping toward the frames and squatting down to see them. "Wow."

"Did he stop painting after he came back from the war?" Mindy asked.

"Oh no. That was when he started."

I expected the paintings to be dark. Like, of death and war and bombs and blood. But to my surprise they were all pretty, with bright colors. Daisies in a vase and fruit in a bowl kind of art. And not bad. Like, I could imagine them in a gallery, that was how nice they were.

Mrs. Olds showed us where to put the hooks and which painting she wanted on which wall. She had us carry a few benches upstairs from the basement so that when people came, they could rest and spend time looking at the Clinton Montgomery masterpieces.

Last, we hung a framed photograph of the artist on the wall. Mrs. Olds had found one of him from before the war, his face whole. He was actually sort of cute back then.

"How about we put this other away," Mrs. Olds said, looking once more at the photo of his damaged face. "I've known my share of monsters. Mr. Montgomery wasn't one of them."

I wanted to ask what monsters she could have known, but she turned and walked from the room, still looking at that picture.

❧

"How do you think he died?" Mindy asked once we were in the car and on our way home.

"Who? Clinton Montgomery?"

She nodded.

"I don't know," I said, stopping at an intersection and hoping the engine wouldn't stall out.

The last thing I needed was to be stuck in the middle of nowhere on a day as hot as that. Heat waves ribboned up from the hood of the El, and I got nervous about the old beast overheating.

"The sign under his picture said that he died in 1922," she said. "That was only four years after the war ended."

"Huh." I held my left foot on the brake and gave the engine a little gas with my right.

"I bet everybody felt badly about how they treated him."

"I think you give people too much credit." I drove past the stop sign once the way was clear, relieved that the car went without too much shaking.

"It must have been hard for him to be so different from everybody else," she said.

"I guess." I pointed at the Dairy Queen up ahead. "Let's get ice cream."

"But we haven't had lunch yet."

"It's too hot for lunch," I said.

"Okay then."

I pulled into the parking lot just before the El Camino sputtered out. Coasting into a space, I worried that I'd never get the darn thing started again. Good thing the Dairy Queen had seating in the air-conditioning and I had Uncle Chris's phone number memorized.

"Can I tell you something?" Mindy asked before we got out.

"Can you tell me in there?" I asked, nodding at the building. "It's so hot out here."

"I'd rather not," she said. "It's personal."

"Fine."

"I'm switching schools next year."

"What?" I asked. "Why? I mean, are you talking about going to public school?"

"Yeah . . ."

"Mins, you don't know anyone there." I half turned in my seat. "Listen, it's so different from Christian school."

"That's exactly why I want to go there."

I dropped my jaw and stared at her, not knowing if it was better to tell her she was stupid or to try and see things her way. Neither seemed like a good option in the moment, so I went with what was more reasonable.

"Mom and Dad won't let you do that," I said.

"Well, actually, they told me it was fine."

"What?"

It came out louder than I'd wanted it to, and a couple of cute boys glanced over from a picnic bench. I smiled and pretended that everything was totally cool.

"Aren't you even interested in why I want to switch?" Mindy asked, completely unaware that the boys were looking at—and admiring—the two of us.

"Sorry. Yeah. I want to know."

It was no small thing, but I gave her my full attention and tried to forget about the guys.

"I think it'll be good for me." She looked down at the footwell. "It might be nice to be somewhere that I'm not the only person who isn't white."

"Mindy," I said, lowering my voice, "I don't think that's a very good thing to say."

"But it's true." She shrugged. "In case you haven't noticed, I'm not Caucasian."

"Well, duh. I know that."

"It's just that I get tired of being different."

"You aren't different."

"Um, yes, I am."

I took the keys out of the ignition and dropped them into my little purse.

"So, what, do you feel like you don't belong in our family?" I asked.

"I'm not saying that."

Using the tip of my pointer finger, I wiped a line into the dust on the dashboard. I jerked my hand back, it was so hot.

"I'm just not like you," she said. "You're white and I'm Asian."

"I never think of you that way," I said. "I don't think of myself as white, either. I'm just Sonny. And you're just Mindy. That's it."

"Well, I think of myself as Asian every day. It's who I am." She shrugged. "I'm Vietnamese even if I don't really know what that means."

"It means you were born in Vietnam. Right?"

"Yeah. But culturally I have no idea what it is."

"So, I'm like part German and English and Dutch and whatever else," I said. "I really don't know anything about those cultures either."

"It's different."

"Is it?"

She wiped under her eye. Shoot. She was crying.

I checked and, luckily, the boys had lost interest. I wouldn't have wanted them playing lookie-loo at my sister while she was so upset.

"Hey," I said, softening the tone of my voice. "What is it?"

"I have never fit in at our school," she said. "Being Sonny Matthews's adopted sister from Vietnam gets old fast."

"That's not all you are."

"To some people, yeah, that's it."

"They're horrible, then." I cupped my hand around her upper arm. "Mins, seriously. You're so awesome. And if anybody doesn't realize that, then they aren't worth your time."

"Thanks," she said, the space between her eyebrows creasing with a new wave of crying.

"Do you need me to hug you?" I asked.

She shook her head.

"Good," I said. "Because it's too stinkin' hot for that kind of nonsense."

That got a little bit of a laugh out of her.

I grabbed a handful of McDonald's napkins from the glove compartment and handed them to her to wipe her face on. Because I'm a good sister, I pretended to be totally grossed out when she blew her nose, even though I wasn't really.

"If you want to switch schools, I'll support you, I guess," I said.

"You guess?"

"Yeah."

"Maybe at public school I won't stand out like a sore thumb. Maybe I can blend in a little."

"I don't understand why you'd want to blend in."

"Son, you get to choose if you want to stand out or be like everybody else," she said. "I don't. I hate being different for something I have absolutely no control over. It's exhausting."

"I don't understand," I said again. "I'm really sorry that I don't."

"You don't have to," she said. "I just need you to know that's how I feel."

"Okay." I nodded.

She looked at the wadded-up napkins in her hands. "I'm going to be smelling French fries for the rest of the day."

"There are worse things," I said.

"Yeah, like your feet." She laughed at her own joke. Of course she did. "Sorry for crying."

"It's all right."

I opened my mouth to say something else but thought better of it and closed it again.

"What?" Mindy asked.

Swallowing hard, I thought through what I was going to say, wanting it to come out just right.

"I don't want you to get hurt," I said.

"I might," she said. "It's a risk I'm okay with."

"But if you do, I won't be here."

"You can't always take care of me." She grabbed my hand. "I mean, it's nice that you care, but I'm not fragile."

"I've never thought you were fragile."

She squinted at that, and I knew she didn't believe me.

Man, I hated it when she was right. Mom, Dad, and I moved around Mindy like we were afraid she'd shatter.

Really, though, she was the strongest of all of us.

CHAPTER Twenty-Five

Bruce, 2013

Halloween was my favorite holiday when I was a kid. Of course, I never gave that answer when they asked us our favorite in Sunday school. My mother was the teacher and there were four right answers and only four in that class. Easter, Christmas, Thanksgiving, and Fourth of July. Oh, Lord help the child who dared to give a different answer. He was bound to get a stern look from Mom.

Still, Halloween was the best, as far as I was concerned.

On what other day of the year did a kid get to wear a costume that let him be a superhero or cowboy or lion? Not only that, but to come home with a pillowcase full of candy for a reward? Now, how could any Easter Bunny beat that?

I still look forward to Halloween every year. The costumes have changed a whole lot since I was trick-or-treating. In recent years the kids that stop by are either Captain America or Rapunzel. Sometimes we get a spooky one come through and it makes me chuckle to have a zombie thank me for an extra Kit Kat.

Every year Linda takes one of my old flannels and a pair of

Dad's worn-out jeans. Stuffing them with straw, she makes herself a pretty creepy scarecrow to sit on the bench on the front porch. Suspenders hold his body together, and his head is one of those plastic jack-o'-lantern buckets.

Living in the pinkie knuckle of Michigan usually means kids have to fit their winter coats under their costumes or over. Some of the braver ones go without, shivering all the way. This year, though, it's just over sixty when we turn on the porch light and welcome the candy seekers.

There's not a hint of rain on the air, and that's inspired all the kids around our block to come out, running up and down the sidewalks with their slower-moving parents ambling along behind.

It's a good thing too.

Linda's bought enough candy to keep them all sugared up until Christmas.

At eight o'clock, sharp, we draw the curtains closed and switch off the porch light. The scarecrow we leave to be disassembled after the weekend. We're having Sonny's family over tomorrow night for a little party of our own. They'll wear their costumes and we'll have chili. Then we'll eat popcorn and watch *The Princess Bride*.

It still boggles the mind when I think that Sonny's girls haven't seen that one yet.

Linda and I take the candy bowl, with just a couple Twizzlers and a Charleston Chew left in the bottom, to the kitchen. Mindy's at the table, her laptop open. She pushes a button and pulls her earbuds out when she sees us.

"Did you have lots of kids?" she asks.

"Yup." I nod. "I'd say a hundred maybe?"

Linda lifts her hands as if to say "your guess is as good as mine." "They sure were cute, though."

"What're you working on?" I ask, holding out the bowl for Mindy.

"Oh, I found a documentary on YouTube." She takes the chocolate. "It's about a woman from the Babylift who got reconnected with her birth mother."

"Is it okay?" Linda asks. "I mean, is it encouraging to you?"

"I kind of thought it would be." Mindy shakes her head. "But I'm not so sure I'm ready for this. I just started it."

"Take your time, honey," I say. "If it's gonna upset you . . ."

"It's not that, Dad," she says. She points at the computer screen. "This woman had it so much different than I do. Her adopted mother was horrible."

I nod. One thing we've learned about the Babylift over the past few weeks is that some folks who couldn't get approval to adopt in normal circumstances were allowed to adopt one of the babies from Vietnam. Mindy's shown me some of the stories from the adult children on the websites she frequents. They write about being abused and neglected. Some of them were made to feel like they were less worthwhile than the other kids in their American families.

At first the stories got my Irish up and I regretted that we hadn't been better advocates for these kids. Then I realized that we'd made our share of mistakes in raising Mindy. It was enough to keep me up a whole night, chewing on my regret.

One of the most humbling things a man can do is go to his kids for forgiveness.

But, when they forgive and that burden is lifted—whew—it's what I imagine heaven to feel like.

"I guess her story reminds me of how good I have it," Mindy says. "You guys never made me feel unloved or like I wasn't wanted."

Well, hearing that doesn't hurt either.

"If you're going to watch it," I say, nodding at the seat beside her, "would you mind a little company?"

Mindy's eyes go watery and she smiles. "Thanks, Dad."

"Oh, me too," Linda says. "Should I boil some water for tea?"

"That would be nice," Mindy answers.

I sit on one side of her, and she scoots her chair a little so I can get in closer to the laptop. I think about suggesting we watch it on the computer in the study that has a larger monitor, but by the time I'm about to open my mouth, Linda's asked us what kind of tea we'd like and delivered a plate of store-bought cookies.

The three of us sit as close together as we can manage, and Mindy starts the documentary back at the beginning.

The woman in the film—Paula—smiles easily in the first scene while someone on the crew clips a lapel mic onto the collar of her red polo shirt. Sitting on the edge of a plaid couch, she rubs her hands against the thighs of her light-blue jeans.

"You got it?" she asks, and I'm surprised by her sweet Southern accent. "Where do y'all want me to start?"

A mumbled voice off camera asks her to tell a little bit about herself. This movie's in that casual style most documentaries have these days. Less polish makes it feel more real to me, as if we're sitting on the other side of the room, waiting for this woman to tell us her story.

"Well, I'm Paula and I live just outside Louisville," she says. Then, with a shy smile, "I'm not used to talking about myself so much. Y'all stop me if I'm boring you."

She talks for maybe a minute about her family—husband, a couple of kids—and what they like doing, the camera cutting to a clip of her pushing a little boy on a swing and another of her catching a small girl at the end of a slide.

"I'm just a normal housewife, I guess," she says. "I like my life now. It's good."

"What about your mom?" the off-camera voice asks.

"You mean my adopted mom?" Paula asks. "Oh, we don't get along too good. I haven't talked to her in a while."

"Why not?"

"Well . . ." Paula looks to the right. "She disowned me a couple years ago, so I don't think she wants to hear from me. It's okay. She never did right by me."

The scene changes to several short clips of old footage from Vietnam. Choppers and soldiers and people running along a street. A close-up of a little boy crying.

Mindy clenches her fists, and Linda puts an arm around her.

A woman speaking Vietnamese cuts in, subtitles appearing at the bottom of the screen to translate.

I was frightened, the subtitles read. *I didn't want to send her away, but we all heard that the Communists would come and slaughter the babies of the Americans. Chau was from an affair I had with an American soldier, so I had to let her go. I couldn't keep her safe, so I had to let the orphanage have her. I knew she'd have a good life in America. I could do nothing for her here.*

The close-up face of a woman fills the screen. She's crying, mouth open and eyes shut. Her wails reach right into the heart of me. The angle widens to show a girl rush across the room to the crying woman, using her entire hand to wipe the tears from the old woman's face, her tiny voice cooing.

Grandmother, Grandmother, the subtitles say. *Don't cry. It's okay.*

"I don't like to remember that day too much," Paula's voice comes in. "I wanted to stay with my birth mother, but the people from the orphanage picked me up and forced me to let go of her hand."

Now it's Paula's face in the picture. She's not crying, but her eyes shift with each blink.

"Sometimes I wonder how my life would've been different if I'd stayed there," she says. "I've never felt like I belonged here, you know?"

"Is that why you want to meet your birth mother?" the voice off camera asks.

Paula nods.

Back to the Vietnamese mother, her face dry and her jaw set.

It's time for my daughter to come home, the subtitles read. *It's time for her to come home and take care of her mother. It's been so long since she's been where she belongs.*

Mindy rests her head on my shoulder and takes Linda's hand. I put my arm around her.

Back to Paula, sitting on her plush couch.

"I don't know what to expect," she says. "I'm kind of scared, really."

"Why?" the interviewer asks.

"I don't know." She plasters that smile back on her face. "It could be good or bad. I won't know until I get there. It's scary."

"Do you have anyone who can make the trip with you?" asks the interviewer.

Paula shakes her head.

That's when she starts to cry.

"I'm sorry," she says, hiding her eyes behind her hand. "Can y'all stop for a second?"

Mindy presses the palm of her hand into the center of her chest.

Mindy's on the porch, sharing the bench with the scarecrow. I bring her a warmup on her tea. She thanks me and I lean back against the railing.

Paula's story didn't end well.

That's not to say there weren't good moments, hopeful moments. Boy, when Paula hugged her birth mother for the first time it unraveled me, and I was glad Linda had a box of tissues at the ready.

I would have cried through my hanky, I'm sure of it.

The woman held her long-lost daughter so tight, not wanting to let go even when Paula tried pulling away.

It was the pulling away that might have been a little clue as to how it would all go down.

And how it went down was fast and devastating.

"They keep expecting me to be this Chau," Paula said, trying to form her mouth around the word. "I can't even say the name of the little girl they want me to be."

Three days after she landed in Vietnam, Paula found that she regretted it.

"I never should have come here," Paula cried before pulling the microphone off her top.

She left on the next available flight, promising to never look back.

"I wish I hadn't watched that," Mindy says.

I nod in answer because I have no idea what to say.

"Maybe it's better if I don't try to find her." She looks into her cup, the tea bag floating at the top of the water. "My life is really good. Maybe I should just be content with how it is."

The space between my eyebrows tenses, and I think about the scenes from Vietnam. Paula's birth family didn't have a whole lot by way of material things and admitted to struggling to get by.

Even in our leanest years, Linda and I never knew poverty. We were always able to pay our bills on time.

It's tempting to think that Mindy wouldn't have had as good a life if she'd stayed with her birth mom. My ego wants to believe it's true.

My heart, though, suspects it isn't.

Having all you need and most of what you want does not a good life make. There's a lot more to it.

"What do you think I should do?" Mindy asks before lifting the cup of tea to her lips.

I sigh, sorting my thoughts—which are coming at me fast—hoping to offer the very thing my daughter needs to hear.

"Well, if I went with my gut, I'd tell you to do the safe thing," I say.

"Which is?"

"Not to look for her." I rub my jaw, feeling two days of stubble poking out from my skin. "It's a risk. Right? 'Cause you don't know how it will go. You can't predict it."

"Yeah."

"But my gut's been wrong more than a couple of times." I let my arms drop to my sides. "And I think it's wrong today."

She takes another sip of her tea, eyebrows flinching as she swallows.

"Honey, that Paula has a different story than you do," I say.

"For most of her life, she didn't have anybody, not really. So when things got hard, she was on her own to deal with it."

"I don't think she knew how to be loved." The corners of her mouth turn down. "It makes me sad for her and it makes me sad for her birth family."

"Can you imagine living like that?"

Mindy shakes her head and wipes a piece of stray hay off the bench beside her.

"Let's not quit yet," I say. "All right?"

Linda peeks out the window behind Mindy's head, catching my eye. She puts her thumb up with a questioning look on her face.

I give her a slight nod.

Yeah. We're going to be okay.

Twenty-Six

Linda, 1975

Noon came before we were ready for it, and Sonny's ride home from school pulled into the driveway shortly after. I sent Bruce out to offer our thanks and collect whatever overnight stuff Sonny had shoved into her bag.

I just knew that if I'd gone out there I would have been stuck talking to Amelia's mom and probably would have ended up having to invite her in to meet Minh when what I really wanted was a quiet afternoon to watch my two daughters become acquainted.

Well, perhaps *quiet* wasn't the word for any afternoon spent with Sonny. Still, I wanted some time for just the four of us to get used to being a family.

Sonny, true to form, came tearing into the house, screen door slamming behind her.

"Where is she?" she asked, dropping her backpack on the floor.

"Over here," I said, getting on my knees and reaching for Sonny. "Be gentle with her, okay?"

"Why?"

"Because this is all new and very confusing for her."

Sonny did not approach her new sister gently. She came barreling in like a Mack truck, rushing forward and throwing her arms around Minh's neck.

"Hi, Mindy," she yelled with all the voice she had.

"It's Minh, remember?" I said.

"She likes being called Mindy," Sonny said, letting go. "Don't you?"

Minh nodded, her eyes the biggest I'd seen them yet. The poor thing. She must not have known what to make of Sonny.

"Is she wearing my overalls?" Sonny asked, eyes boring into me with every bit of her kindergarten fierceness.

"Yes. They're too small for you, don't you remember?" I lifted my eyebrows. "Besides, you're going to need to learn how to share."

"For the rest of my life?" Her face went blank.

"Or until you leave for college."

Sonny tilted her head back and sighed.

Minh took a step away from her.

"How's it going?" Bruce asked when he came in through the front door.

I nodded in the direction of Sonny as she moaned and groaned about how it would be forever before she could move away to college and Minh stood by and watched, as if she'd never, ever seen anything like this creature before her.

"About how I expected," he said.

*

Sonny talked Minh's ear off all through lunch, and I had to remind her at least a dozen times to chew and swallow before yammering on. Minh, on the other hand, didn't make a peep as she tried to navigate using a fork on her macaroni and cheese.

"Maybe a spoon would be easier?" I asked, getting up for one.

"Mindy, do you have forks where you're from?" Sonny asked around a wad of pasta.

"For Pete's sake, Sonny," I said. "Stop talking with food in your mouth."

I returned to the table with the spoon, feeling lousy for speaking harshly to Sonny and a little unsure of how to make it right.

But when Sonny swallowed her food and started right back, jabbering on again, I realized she remained unfazed by my tone of voice.

"Mindy, we have a sandbox in the backyard," she said. "We can play in it. I only have one shovel, but I'll let you use it first. Okay, Mindy?"

Minh didn't react. She used the spoon to heave a big bite of macaroni into her mouth.

"Why doesn't Mindy talk to me?" Sonny asked Bruce.

"Maybe because you keep calling her Mindy," he answered. "Her name's Minh."

"And she doesn't speak English yet," I said. "She'll need to learn."

"It's going to take forever, isn't it?" Sonny slumped in her seat and stabbed a green bean with her fork, frowning at it.

"It'll take a while." I motioned with my hand to let her know she should sit up straight. "We'll figure it out."

"Uncle Chris told me how to say hi in Vietnam," Sonny said. "*Chào.*"

I was certain her pronunciation was off—it sounded more like she said "chow" than anything. Still, Minh sat up straighter, her eyes becoming more alert. She looked at Sonny and swallowed before letting words fly, a hundred miles per hour, out of her mouth. Her tiny voice was high pitched and moved along like a song. The expression on her face as she spoke nearly broke my heart.

It was like a crack splintered its way through the dam and it finally shattered.

Then, she said one word over and over, her mouth turned down and her eyes pleading.

"Mà, mà, mà."

It sounded almost like "may."

It didn't take a genius to know that she was asking for her mother.

Not me. Her first mother.

I thought in my mind, *Her real mother*. It stung.

My feelings weren't the ones I needed to worry about in that moment, though. With a mighty shove, I moved them out of the way and tried to focus on Minh. I knelt beside her and put my hands on her upper arms.

"Minh," I whispered. "Minh. It's all right, honey."

I'd never in my life seen a child so small with such a broken heart.

After getting the girls in bed that night, Bruce and I looked in the manila envelope the adoption agency left with us. We pulled the papers out, spreading them across the kitchen table.

On one was the information for the adoption agency—phone numbers and contact names and such. Another had a list of the immunizations she'd gotten when she arrived in California and when her boosters would come due. I moved my finger on the page, relieved that she was mostly up to date on the big ones at least.

Bruce held up a list of Vietnamese words and phrases, their pronunciations, and translations, and I could have just kicked myself for not having found it sooner.

"This might help a little," he said, handing it to me.

"Oh, thank goodness," I said.

I turned and put that page on the fridge using a handful of daisy magnets. We sounded a few of the words out according to the transliteration. We tried out the words for hungry and tired, sick and sad. Mother, father, sister, brother. I'm sorry. I love you. I'm okay.

"Ah, but look at this." Bruce pointed to a separate sheet of paper, the sentence all in uppercase letters.

PLEASE SPEAK ENGLISH TO YOUR CHILD AS MUCH AS POSSIBLE! IT IS THE ONLY WAY HE WILL LEARN!

"Well, all right," I said, tapping the vocabulary list. "But we'll keep this here for now. Just in case."

We sorted through the rest of the papers, pulling out what we could toss and holding on to what looked important.

"Do we have any ice cream?" Bruce asked before getting up and going to the fridge.

"I think so," I answered, lifting my eyes from the paperwork. "Oh, look."

I nodded toward the doorway.

Two little girls stood there, holding hands.

They were my little girls. My daughters. My very most precious ones.

"What are you two doing up?" Bruce asked, his face lighting up with that smile of his.

"We can't sleep," Sonny said, charging her way into the kitchen, pulling Minh along behind her. "We're hungry."

"Oh, you are?" I asked, fitting the papers back into their envelope. "And what would make you not hungry?"

"Um." Sonny made her eyes dart from one side to the other. "Maybe a little bowl of ice cream?"

"You think so?"

"Mindy likes ice cream," Sonny said.

I met eyes with my husband, who lifted both hands and gave me his why-not face.

I leaned forward, closer to Sonny. "Only because today is very special."

Bruce wasn't stingy with the scoops and I found a little jar of sprinkles in the back of the cupboard. I knew I might regret the late-night ice cream social if Sonny couldn't fall asleep from the sugar rush or if Minh's tummy couldn't tolerate so much dairy.

But when Sonny looked at Minh, her jaw dropped in awe that her sneaky little plan had worked, my heart skipped a beat.

I grabbed the envelope off the table to keep it safe from any melty spills and noticed a smaller paper that we'd missed. Thinking it was just another note instructing on some particulars of food or behavior or whatnot, I turned it over.

"Oh," I said. "Honey, look at this."

Bruce set the dishes of ice cream in front of the girls first, forming Minh's fingers around the handle of the spoon and helping her get a little of the vanilla into her mouth.

"That's good, huh?" he said. "Go ahead."

She made a tiny "mm" sound and I couldn't help but tear up just a little bit.

I held in my hand a photograph of Minh standing against a

concrete wall in white shorts and shirt, holding a sign that read "Pham-Quyen-Minh."

The expression on her face in that picture made me want to weep. I'd never in my life seen a child so young so frightened and sad. It made me want to scoop her up and hold her close so that she'd know she was safe.

She wasn't ready for me to do that, though. Maybe in time she'd trust me enough.

"What's that?" Bruce asked, looking over my shoulder at the picture. "Where did you get it?"

"It was in the envelope," I said.

"We'll need to keep that in a safe place." He wrapped his arms around my waist from behind, kissing my temple. "But for now, look at our girls."

I did as he said to see the two of them enjoying their treat. Sonny, I noticed, held her spoon in her left hand, and I narrowed my eyes to watch her struggle to balance it. She wasn't a lefty. I wondered what she was up to.

"What's she doing?" I whispered.

"Look down a little," he said.

Lowering my eyes I saw that, under the table, Sonny and Minh were still holding hands.

Twenty-Seven

Sonny, 1988

It was Mom's idea to invite Mike to Grammy and Grumpy's for dinner that Friday night. Honestly, I was surprised that she brought it up, especially without asking Grammy if it was all right.

"We always have more than enough food," Mom said. "Just call him. We can pick him up on the way there."

"But he's not even officially my boyfriend," I said.

"Use the phone in my room if you want some privacy." She went back to reading her magazine on the couch.

Going into my parents' bedroom was like stepping back into my childhood. Everything was so totally seventies that it made my eyes hurt. My mom even had not one but two macramé plant holders hanging from the ceiling.

So gross.

I sat on Mom's side of the bed and dialed Mike's number, which, of course, I had memorized.

While it rang and I waited for somebody to pick up, I noticed that there was a stack of papers on the end of the bed. I picked through them to see if there was anything interesting. An old manila envelope caught my eye, "Minh" written at the top in black marker. I grabbed it just as Mrs. Huisman answered the phone.

"Hi," I said. "Is Mike there?"

"Well, no," she said. "He's out with a few of the guys. Can I tell him who called?"

"Oh. This is Sonny Matthews." I dropped the envelope into my lap. "Do you happen to know when he'll be home?"

"You know, I don't. I'm sorry."

"That's all right," I said. "I'll call another time."

When I messed with one of the metal clasps on the envelope, it broke off.

"I'm sure Michael will be happy to hear from you," she said. "He certainly talks about you enough."

I let my mouth drop open at that. First, he talked about me, which could only be a really, really good sign. Second, I was like so embarrassed that his mom was telling me that. Oh my gosh.

I was totally blushing.

Mrs. Huisman said she would tell Mike that I'd called, and I thanked her.

After I hung up, I threw the broken part of the metal clasp into the trash and turned to put the envelope back on the stack of papers, but then hesitated, running the tip of my finger over Mindy's old name. Her real name.

Minh.

They'd never officially changed it to Mindy even though that's what everybody called her. Mom told me that I refused to call her Minh from the moment I met her. That I insisted that her name was Mindy from the very start. I totally didn't remember that.

I pulled up the remaining clasp of the envelope and looked inside.

It was mostly paperwork. Nothing interesting at all. When I went to slide everything back into place, I noticed something else in there. A picture of Mindy when she was little, holding a sign and totally not smiling for the camera.

The look in her eyes made me feel sad, so I shoved the photo into the envelope and dropped it back onto the bed.

It was blazing hot inside, so we set up a few card tables outside in the covered porch off the back of Grammy's house. It wasn't like they didn't have air-conditioning. Grumpy was just too much of a penny pincher to run it until it reached ninety degrees.

"It's only eighty-five," he said, pointing to the thermometer on the side of his garage.

"But it's hotter inside the house," I said.

"When I was a kid, we were so poor we didn't have a scrap of paper to make a fan out of," he said.

No matter how I tried talking him into it or batted my eyelashes, he wouldn't budge.

The air-conditioning stayed off, and we all ate in the covered porch.

Apparently I'd lost my cuteness at some point over the past few years.

It ended up being all right, though. Grammy made a cold pasta salad and Grumpy grilled burgers and hot dogs. Uncle Chris had brought over a cooler of ice and bottles of pop. After he was done eating, my little cousin challenged Mindy and me to a watermelon-seed-spitting contest.

Grumpy joined us and won by a ton.

"Teddy," Aunt Dana called to him. "Come clear your place."

"It's Ted," he said, slumping back to his spot and picking up his plate. "I'm not six anymore, Mom."

The teen years were going to be something else with that kid.

"Well, Sonny was just over eight pounds," Mom said, continuing whatever weird conversation they were having at the table. "She was a good chunk of a baby."

"Mom," I said. "I wasn't a chunky baby."

"How would you know?" She moved her hands along her belly. "And, yes, honey, you were."

"Teddy was, what, seven, seven and a half?" Uncle Chris asked.

"Ten," Aunt Dana said, grabbing a handful of chips from the bag on the table. "Ten, Chris. He was ten pounds."

"I don't know how she remembers that," Uncle Chris said.

The look Aunt Dana shot him should have knocked him out of his chair. Too bad he didn't notice.

"Dale came early," Grammy said.

No one moved after she said that. First, she never talked about things like having babies. It wasn't proper, especially not at the table. Second, in my whole life I'd only ever heard her mention Uncle Dale a few times. And especially not when Mindy was around. The few times Grammy had said his name was in whispers that I overheard.

It was like he was some well-guarded family secret.

"Yup," Grumpy said. "He was just a little guy."

That was it. All they said about him.

We stayed until it started getting dark, and when we went out to our car the fireflies were out and blinking. Grumpy lifted his hands, catching one and letting it crawl up his arm before it flew away.

Soon we were all hopping off the ground, catching fireflies and watching as they blinked their butts at us.

Grammy, though, stood on the bottom step of the porch, arms crossed and face scowling. I wondered if she'd ever been a little girl or if she was just born a crabby old woman.

It was so disrespectful, and I knew it. I just couldn't understand why someone would ever choose to be miserable all the time. And not only that, but to hold it against anyone who was having a good time.

If she wasn't going to join the fun on her own, I thought I should force her hand a little.

"Come on, Grammy," I said. "I'll catch one for you."

"I could catch one if I wanted to," she said.

Mindy skipped up to the porch, her hand out to Grammy. Grammy didn't budge. So Mindy grabbed her hand.

"Please, Grammy," she said.

Mindy's hand dropped when Grammy pulled away from her and went inside.

Dad and I dropped Mom and Mindy off at home before rushing to the grocery store before it closed. Apparently Mom was out of green olives and potato strings and the baby needed them right away.

"We'll be fast," Dad said before Mom got out of the car. "Can you think of anything else we need?"

"Circus peanuts, please," she said.

I thought I was going to upchuck right there in the back seat of Mom's station wagon. I hoped she didn't plan on eating all of those things at the same time.

"You got it."

"Thanks."

Mom gave him a peck on the cheek before struggling to get her belly up and out of the car, insisting that she didn't need help.

I switched from the back seat to the front while Dad waited to make sure Mom and Mindy made it inside okay.

"I would've thought you'd be going out tonight," he said, turning to check behind us as he pulled out of the driveway.

"Everybody went to see a movie," I said. "It's all right." I mean, it wasn't all right. But I wasn't going to tell my dad that.

"Was Mike going to be there?"

"Dad."

"I'm just asking, honey." He turned onto the road toward town. "I like him."

"Seriously, Dad."

"All right. All right. I'll stop talking about him."

A few minutes went by with neither of us saying anything. Dad turned up the radio and sang along to some old band. They sounded like the kind of guys that would have beards down to their belly buttons and greasy hair under their grungy cowboy hats.

The music was twangy, and I was not a fan.

Lucky for me, we only caught the last half of the song, and then it switched to Aretha Franklin. I hummed along, not wanting Dad to have the satisfaction of knowing that I liked music from when he was my age.

The parking lot at the store was only half full. Probably

mostly employees at that time of night, mopping the floors and restocking the shelves. Dad found a spot and put the car into park.

"Okay. Olives, potato strings, probably get some ice cream," Dad said, counting on his fingers. "What else will this baby want?"

"Circus peanuts," I said.

"That's right."

"Seriously, if the baby is this demanding when he comes, I will lose my mind," I said.

"You won't even be home."

"Lucky me." I smiled even if I felt a little pang about leaving home. "What did Mom crave when she was pregnant with me?"

"Gosh. Um." He closed his eyes tight, squishing up his face. "I seem to remember her asking for SpaghettiOs a lot."

"Ew," I said. "So gross."

"It drove Grammy crazy to see her eat so much junk food. Ready?"

We got out of the truck and walked across the parking lot. Dad let me step through the automatic door first and the air-conditioning made my arms all goose bumpy. The overhead speakers played a musical arrangement of some old Fleetwood Mac song, and Dad sang along with it.

If anybody I'd known was at the store I would have died on the spot of embarrassment. Lucky for me, there were just a handful of people there, all of them at least as old as my dad.

"Come on, Sonny," he said, grabbing a cart. "You know this one."

"No, I don't," I said.

"Well, you used to sing it whenever it was on the radio." He grinned at me and sang way too loud, "Rhia-aaa-nnon!"

"Dad, stop."

"Couldn't even if I wanted to."

"I'll get the olives," I said, headed toward the aisle where all the pickles and stuff were shelved.

As I went I couldn't help but hum along with the song. Quietly. So quietly that nobody would have been able to hear it. Fine. I *did* remember the song. And, to be honest, I still sort of liked it. I remembered this one day when Mom had it playing on the stereo at our old house, turned up all the way.

Even as loud as it was, I could still hear her voice over Stevie Nicks's.

I started crying and went to my room so Mom wouldn't see me.

Grabbing two jars of olives from the shelf, I rolled my eyes at myself for how dumb I was when I was five.

I cried because I worried that somebody would hear my mom sing and take her away to become a rock star, and I wanted to keep her all to myself.

When Mindy came into our room and saw me, she tried to give me a hug.

I'd pushed her down.

Ugh. I was such a jerk sometimes.

I found Dad in the freezer section. In addition to the potato strings, he'd also grabbed a few cans of Pringles and a bag of Doritos.

"Just in case," he said when he saw me inspecting his cart.

"Uh-huh," I said.

"Should I get mint chocolate chip or Neapolitan?"

My favorite flavors. I was tempted to say that we should get both, but then I thought about Mindy and the look she had on her face when I'd pushed her so long ago.

It had been the same hurt look as when Grammy pulled away from her. The same as in the picture I'd found in the envelope in Mom and Dad's room.

"Pecan praline," I said.

Every once in a while I could let Mindy have her favorite.

Twenty-Eight

Bruce, 2013

Dad and I sit across from each other at Fiona's, each of us with a mug of coffee on our paper placemats. His hand is curved around his cup, and I can't help but notice his crooked fingers and the liver spots and the raised, purple veins.

He hasn't been able to get his wedding ring off for years, the thickened knuckles now far bigger than when he and my mother got married.

I don't believe he'd want to take it off even if he could.

It's a rare thing, a man being as devoted as he is to my mom, even though it couldn't have been easy.

Mom is many things. Easy to live with isn't one of them.

But my dad always was one for a challenge, I suppose.

"Well," Dad says after the two of us sit quietly for several minutes, "your mother got her hair done yesterday."

"Oh yeah?" I say.

"Yup. The hairdresser came right up to our apartment." He takes a slurp of his coffee. "It's quite a setup. She's got this whole cart with a sink and everything."

"How about that."

"Hooks right up to our faucet."

"I bet Mom liked that."

"Nope." He closes his eyes and shakes his head. "She hated every minute of it."

Dad chuckles as he unrolls his silverware and spreads the napkin on his thigh.

"I've loved her my whole life," he says. "Ever since we were kids and I put a worm in her hair."

"Such a romantic," I say.

"She hauled off and socked me right in the eye." He laughs. "First shiner I ever had."

I don't mention that Mom would refute that story if she was here. She'd say she hit him by accident when she was flailing to get the worm out of her curls. I don't know who to believe, but it's a good story either way.

He turns and looks out the window, his eyes watery. Using the knuckle of his veiny hand, he knocks a tear out from the corner of his eye. Being a man of his generation, he's never been one to cry. Especially not in front of his son. Growing older, though, has softened up the waterworks, I guess.

"What's up, Dad?" I ask.

He doesn't look at me, just swallows hard and pulls the hanky out of his pants pocket to wipe his nose. It takes a good couple of minutes before he's able to speak, and in that time I've got to blink back more than a couple tears of my own.

It doesn't matter how old a man gets, it's always hard for him to see his father cry.

"She's not doing so good, son," he says. "Her body's had about enough."

The kid who's helping Fiona out today swings by and refills

our coffee cups. I tell him thanks, but Dad doesn't turn away from the window until the kid's left the table.

When Dad faces me I think how much I resemble him. It's strange to know exactly what I'll look like in twenty-some years.

"I always thought I'd go first," he says before reaching for the sugar packets and dumping too many of them in his cup. "I know she's hard to love. That's no secret, I guess."

I shake my head and pass him the little bowl of creamers.

"But a promise like the one I made to her at our wedding isn't supposed to be easy, is it?" He peels the top off a container of cream. "Loving her is the best thing I've ever had to work at. I guess that's why I'm scared of letting her go."

Fiona carries over an armload of plates, setting them in front of us. Of course, Dad's breaking all the dietary rules his doctor imposed. Who cares? That's what I want to know.

He's eighty-eight years old and still does the morning workouts he learned while he was in the Army—maybe a little slower these days, but still. He deserves a couple of strips of bacon every once in a while.

"I think that's all for you boys," she says. "Need anything else?"

"Nope, I think we're fine," I say. "Thanks."

"How's Hilda doing?" She puts her hands on her hips.

"All right," Dad says, doing his best to smile. "Beautiful as ever."

"That's what I like to hear," Fiona says. "You tell her I say hi, all right?"

"Will do."

"I've always liked Hilda. She's a real sweetie."

I have to admit, I've not heard that word used for my mother before.

Fiona leaves us to it, and Dad bows his head to pray before even touching his fork. His mouth moves along with the words he's praying silently in his head.

It takes me back to the time after Dale died and I came home to a house full of sadness. We had dinner together every night, whether we ate a bite or not. And Dad insisted on the four of us holding hands to offer grace before we passed around the dishes of food.

That was a time when my faith was shaky at best and I couldn't pray even when I tried. Just hearing the prayers of my father, as simple as they were, steadied me.

"We won't be afraid, we will trust in you," he'd say every single time, even as his voice shook.

I'm certain I see his lips form those very words as he prays over the breakfast Fiona made for him.

We won't be afraid.

We will trust in you.

Mindy's hand shakes when she lifts it to move the mouse, pointing the cursor on the screen to the post button.

"Why is this so scary?" she asks.

She's at the desk in the study, sitting in front of the big monitor of my computer. She's uploaded two pictures—the one of her that was taken at the orphanage in Vietnam and one of her Linda took earlier today. Attached to the photos is a paragraph explaining who she is and who she's looking for.

I've read it over four or five times to assure her that it's good enough.

"The name I was given at birth is Pham Quyen Minh. I now go by the name Mindy Quyen Matthews," it reads. "I believe I was born sometime in the early seventies but am unsure of the date—I know little of my earlier years living in Vietnam. It's unlikely, I know, but I would really like to reconnect with my birth mother or any living relatives. Honestly, I'd be interested in learning anything about who I am."

She presses a finger on the mouse, and it makes its clicking sound. The post is published. There's no looking back now.

Mindy takes a good breath, and we both stare at the screen. Her post is just one of many on that site, most of them with a very similar story to Mindy's.

"Now what?" I ask.

"We wait to see if anyone comments," she says.

"You know, I brought cinnamon rolls home from Fiona's." I cock my head in the direction of the kitchen. "You wanna split one while we wait?"

"You know you're my favorite person, right?"

"I've always known it."

By the time I decide to go to bed for the night, Mindy has gotten a handful of comments on her post. Nothing conclusive about her birth family, but everyone is encouraging.

My favorite came in pretty early on.

"I'm sorry that I don't know about your family," it says. "But I can tell you what your name means. Minh means bright. Quyen means bird. It's not much, but maybe it will make you smile."

It makes us all smile.

Our bright bird. Couldn't be more fitting.

I lie in bed, holding hands with Linda as we both drift off to sleep, thinking of this adventure Mindy's inching up to.

She might find some of her relatives over there, or she might never meet a single one of them. There's a chance she'll buy a ticket and fly back to the land of her birth, or she might hold off on that for a while.

We don't know what's coming. No matter what, I've got to be ready to let her fly.

I whisper a prayer just as I'm turning the corner into sleep.

We will not be afraid.

We will trust in you.

CHAPTER Twenty-Nine

Linda, 1975

Minh held my hand as we stood on the porch, watching Bruce back his big old truck out of the driveway. Sonny knelt on the front seat, half hanging out the window to wave back at us.

"Bye, Mindy," she yelled. "I'll be back after school, okay?"

"Sit on your bumper, Sonny," I hollered after her, hand cupped to the side of my mouth.

Minh blinked up at me.

"What are we going to do today?" I whispered once the truck was out of sight.

It was the first time it was just the two of us, and I had no idea of how to keep her occupied until we had to go pick up Sonny at noon.

We started with a little walk, wandering around the yard. Taking it slow, we headed to the backyard, where we had plenty of open space and freshly cut grass. I slipped off my shoes, feeling the cool ground on my bare feet.

"Green grass," I said, stooping and running my finger through the blades.

Minh sat on her rump, tugging on her sneakers until they popped off and pulling at her socks until her little tootsies were free in the fresh air. I sat facing her, taking her tiny feet in my hands.

"Minh's feet," I said. Then I pointed at mine. "Mommy's feet."

Repeating it, I dared to tickle her toes and was rewarded with a giggle. It was small, but such a wonderful sound.

"That's a tickle," I said.

She nodded, the smile still lifting her face as she stretched out her legs, wiggling her toes so I'd do it again.

I was more than happy to oblige.

Sunshine on a cloudy day, that's what her smile was.

We put our shoes on the back stoop and circled the yard while I pointed to the flowers along the edges of the house, naming them as we went.

Red geranium and yellow dandelion. Purple iris, green hosta, pink echinacea. When I stopped to sniff a flower, she did too. When I picked one and held it out to her, she took it from me, holding it as carefully as she could, a small bouquet collecting in her hands. Wherever I walked in the yard, she was close by my side.

We went inside around ten o'clock, and I turned and aimed the rabbit ears on the television until I was able to get PBS. We caught just the tail end of the opening song of *Sesame Street*, and it came in clear as crystal.

Miracle of miracles.

"You have fun watching this," I said, putting my hand on the top of the set. "I have to go make a telephone call. All right?"

She nodded and turned her eyes to the puppets on the TV screen.

One of the few things on my checklist for the day was calling to get Minh appointments with our pediatrician and dentist. Grabbing my address book from the junk drawer and Minh's immunization record from the envelope, I dialed the number for the doctor first.

The receptionist at the doctor's office told me I'd need to get everything square with our health insurance before I made an appointment. The insurance agent told me I'd need all my paperwork in order before I added Minh to our policy. The adoption agency told me that they still weren't sure how immigration status worked for these kids brought over from Vietnam.

"Does that mean she's here illegally?" I asked.

"Not necessarily," they answered. "We'll let you know how all that's going to work when we've got it sorted out."

That was not confidence inspiring.

I hung up the phone, feeling dizzy and not an inch closer to getting a doctor's appointment for Minh.

What was left over in the Mr. Coffee from first thing in the morning had gone tepid, so I poured the java into a pan to heat up on the stove. While I waited for the coffee to warm up, I hummed along with the familiar song playing on the TV.

Once it was warm enough, I poured the coffee into my cup, careful not to make it slosh over onto my hand, and stirred in my cream and sugar.

It wasn't fresh and it wasn't nearly as hot as I would have liked, but it would hopefully work to stimulate my brain into figuring it all out so we could get Minh in to see the doctor. And soon.

Oscar the Grouch's voice carried through the television, and

I stepped into the living room to see Minh still sitting in her spot in front of the screen.

"Everything okay in here?" I asked.

Minh glanced at me before turning her attention back to Oscar.

"I guess so," I said under my breath.

Sipping my coffee, I turned toward the piano, fingers itching to play. It had been a few days since I'd had the chance. If anything could clear my head, it was playing something languid and emotionally charged. Debussy might just do the trick for me that day.

It would have to wait, though. Minh was settled and I had lots of chores to get done before Sonny came home at lunchtime.

I started in the girls' room, not worrying too much about making their beds. They'd just be in them again for a nap that afternoon. I picked up stray socks and teddy bears from the floor and carried the dirty laundry to the hamper in the hallway.

It was when I was in the bathroom, wiping down the sink and countertop, that I heard a loud noise from outside. Figuring it was just a tractor backfiring in the field next door, I went on with my work. That was until I heard the high-pitched screams from the living room.

Panicked, I rushed to Minh, having no idea what could have happened. I'd only been in the bathroom, a handful of steps away.

Still on the floor, she had half turned toward the front door, her mouth turned into a gaping frown, her eyes enormous and unblinking. She screamed over and over.

"Minh?" I said, trying to keep calm but not doing such a good job at it. "Did you get hurt?"

I put my hands on her arms, moving her little body so I could see if she was bleeding or . . . or . . . I didn't know. When I couldn't find anything, I pulled her to me, trying to soothe her.

She clung to me, still screaming, as I carried her to the kitchen and wouldn't let me go when I tried to put her on the counter.

We stayed like that for a very long time. I imagined it was the banging sound that had terrified her so. I thought of Chris and how he stayed inside on the Fourth of July and flinched at sudden noises. All since coming home from Vietnam.

I wished I could know what Minh had seen of the war, what she remembered.

Was it even possible for a child to have shell shock?

Her screams had dissolved into whimpers, her breath deepening. Still, she trembled, clinging to me for dear life.

"Oh, sweetie," I said. "It's okay. You're safe."

After a while she let me go long enough for me to wet a washcloth with cool water to dab on her forehead.

"Doesn't that feel better?" I asked.

She looked directly into my eyes. Her irises were so deeply brown it almost seemed impossible. I cupped her cheek with my hand and gave her a gentle smile.

Her poor little face showed how exhausted all that fear had made her.

I took her to the couch and held her while she slept. Not long. Just twenty minutes or so. But all the while I tried not to imagine what horrors she held in her memory.

I wished I could erase them all.

Bruce came home at the end of the day with an apple pie from his boss's wife and a couple dozen cookies from the bakery in town.

"They wanted to congratulate us," he said, handing the box of cookies to me. "And they really mean it. They didn't just give us oatmeal raisin."

"Chocolate chip," I said, grabbing a cookie from the box.

"How did Minh do?" he asked, glancing out the kitchen window to watch the girls as they played in the yard. "Did you have a good day?"

"Well, we all survived," I answered before taking a bite of the cookie.

"That's something, I guess."

Outside, Sonny curled her body for a somersault, rolling across the yard. When she tried to stand up, she tumbled onto her behind. I could hear her laughter all the way inside the house.

"I found out that Minh's feet are ticklish," I said. "And that she likes applesauce."

"Well, that sounds like a pretty great day."

"And I learned that loud noises send her into hysterics." I regarded my half-eaten cookie before handing it to Bruce to finish. "The poor little lady."

He accepted my cookie, and we watched the girls for a few minutes longer. It appeared that Sonny was busy teaching Minh how to do a somersault. When Minh tried it, she ended up flat on her back, arms stretched out at her sides. Then she rolled over, her back toward us. At first I worried that she'd gotten hurt.

But then she got to her feet and I saw the wide smile on her face and the way her little body shook with laughter.

CHAPTER Thirty

Sonny, 1988

E very year on the weekend of Fourth of July, we rented a
cabin at this little resort in Fort Colson. I mean, it wasn't
a resort with a spa and massages or anything like that. It was a
lot more rustic with a row of cottages to rent and a campground
where people could park their RVs or set up their tents.

There was a little camp store, though, that sold penny candy
and served scoops of ice cream as big as my dad's fist. So, at least
there was that luxury.

We always stayed in Cabin 9, which had the best view of
Chippewa Lake.

All day we'd swim or take a rowboat out on the lake. In the
afternoons Mindy and I would take a rest on the beach, catching
as much sun as we could, checking our tan lines every once in a
while to see how dark we were getting. In the evenings we'd sit
in the screened-in porch, drinking root beers we'd bought from
the little store and playing Michigan rummy, Mom fretting over
our sunburned noses and shoulders.

Every night I'd lie in the top bunk in the room Mindy and I claimed and listen to the loons call back and forth to each other.

Their song was creepy and beautiful at the same time.

Without a question, our trips to Chippewa Lake were the best memories of my childhood.

That year, packing for vacation, I wasn't sure if there'd be a family trip to the lake the next year. I couldn't know if Mom would want to drag an almost one-year-old along—I'd have a new sibling by then!—or if I'd even be back home for the summer.

I shoved my swimsuit into my bag, thinking about how growing up meant I had to let go of things little by little. Maybe going to the lake with my family was one of those things just like I'd given up my Barbie dolls when I was twelve.

It made me sad to think about.

But then I thought of all that I could grab hold of once my hands were free.

The day was blisteringly hot, and the cabin wasn't air-conditioned, so the only relief was in the lake. Mindy and I got into our swimsuits and held hands when we jumped off the end of the dock, the shock of cold water making us almost numb until we bobbed back up to the surface and into the sun.

Mindy got out after a little while, wrapping herself in her towel to read on the beach in the shade of a tree. I, on the other hand, wasn't ready to leave the water. It just felt too good being cool and weightless.

Floating on my back, I closed my eyes against the too-bright sun. The water rushed in and out of my ears, making a sloshing sound that drowned out any other noise. If I'd tried, I could have imagined I was the only one around.

It was peaceful and lonely at the same time.

Well, it was until something smacked down near me, sending a splash of lake water into my face. I gasped and got a lungful, making me hack and flail until I got my feet on the sandy bottom.

"Hey, sorry," somebody yelled from over by the dock. "You all right?"

I waved my hand over my head and took in a wheezing breath. "Fine," I croaked.

"I didn't even see you over there."

It was a boy. Of course it was. The sun made his bright-red hair look like flames curling up from his head, and from the way his skin bore a certain shade of lobster, I predicted he'd be sore later on.

"It's all right," I said.

"Could you grab my football?" he asked. "It's right over there. Yup. You got it."

Had I been a cool girl, I would have thrown that ball in a perfect spiral, impressing the socks off that boy. Instead, I tossed it using both hands, as if it was a basketball. The problem was, I didn't let go of it in time and it dropped, nose first, into the water in front of me, going no more than a foot.

"Well, good try," he said.

I grabbed the ball and tucked it under my arm, side-paddling my way to the dock. When I handed it up to him, he sat down, dipping his feet into the water.

"Thanks," he said. "You wanna play catch?"

"Not really."

I made sure my swimsuit wasn't riding up where it shouldn't

have before climbing the ladder up and out of the water. The wood of the dock was rough and hot under my feet.

"You staying in one of the cabins?" he asked.

"Yup."

"I live just down the road," he said. "Maybe could I buy you an ice cream cone sometime?"

"No thanks," I said. "I have a boyfriend."

It wasn't totally the truth. Not yet at least. I mean, Mike hadn't asked me to be his girlfriend, but whatever. I knew he liked me.

I grabbed my towel and wrapped it around my chest so football boy might stop ogling. When I turned to walk back to the beach, I saw that Mindy wasn't alone with her book.

There was a boy sitting with her. His hair was just as dark as hers, and when he tilted his head upward, I saw that he was cute. Like, really cute.

And my sister was talking to him.

She even laughed. But not her quiet, shy laugh. It was full-on, head-thrown-back laughter.

"Who's that?" I asked.

"My brother," football boy answered.

"Really?"

"Yeah, he's adopted." He held the football under his arm. "We got him from Korea."

"You mean he was *born* in Korea?"

The kid shrugged his rounded, sunburned shoulders.

When I rolled my eyes and turned away from him, he yelled "See ya!" at me.

I wanted to yell back "I hope not," but I didn't want to interrupt whatever kind of love connection Mindy was making with the cute boy on the beach.

I walked back to our cabin, trying to act cool, like my heart wasn't beating a million miles a minute. Once I got inside, though, I let myself spaz out a little before calling for my mom.

"What?" she asked, jolting up from the nap she was taking on the couch. "Is everybody okay?"

"Yes." I waved her over to the screened-in porch. "You've got to see this."

Bleary eyed and having a very hard time getting up—I didn't know how that belly could possibly get any bigger—Mom made her way to my side.

"Is that a boy?" she asked, whispering.

"Uh-huh."

"And Mindy?"

"Yup."

"Is she flirting with him?"

"I think so," I said.

"I didn't know she even knew how to do that."

"Isn't it great?"

Mom and I huddled together behind the screen and watched Mindy and the boy for at least fifteen minutes before we got bored and walked down to the store for ice cream.

Mom and I helped Mindy pick an outfit—we didn't have much to work with from her suitcase, so I let her borrow one of my tank tops and cut-off jean shorts. Then we did her makeup and hair, and I was glad I'd thought to bring an extra can of hairspray.

"I need to sit down," Mom said, pulling out a chair at the table. "My ankles are killing me."

"Ew, Mom," I said, looking at her legs. "They're huge."

"Sorry for being so gross." She sat, fanning herself with her hand. "Can you pull that chair over so I can put my feet up?"

"Is that normal?" Mindy asked, helping her lift her legs to the seat of the second chair.

"No clue. It is pretty hot today," Mom answered. "But don't worry about me. You get ready for your date."

"It's not a date." Mindy's eyes got wide. "Is it?"

"Might be," I answered, using the point of a safety pin to separate her lashes. "Don't move or I'll accidentally poke your eye out."

She pulled away from me. "No thank you with the safety pin, please."

"That's the weirdest sentence I've ever heard." I dropped the safety pin back into my Caboodle. "You look pretty, Mins."

"What's his name again?" Mom asked.

"Eric," Mindy said. "I don't remember if he told me his last name."

"You might want to figure it out," I said, backcombing her bangs just a little more so they'd have more lift. "See if it sounds good with Mindy."

"Oh my goodness, Sonny." She slumped her shoulders. "It's not like I'm going to marry him."

"You might." I winked at her.

Dad came in, tackle box in one hand and a bag of quickly melting ie in the other.

"Whoa, what's going on in here?" he asked, setting the tackle box on the table next to Mom. "I didn't know you girls were bringing makeup."

"Dad, I bring makeup wherever I go," I said.

"Why?"

"You wouldn't understand."

"Mindy has a date," Mom said.

"A what?"

"We're just getting a pop or something, Dad," Mindy said. "Don't panic."

"With who?" He dumped the ice into his cooler. "Do we know this boy?"

"Dad, she'll be fine," I said. "It's a boy she met down by the beach."

"Today?"

"He's nice, Dad," Mindy said. "I promise, I won't be gone long. Okay?"

"All right." Dad smiled at her. "You look pretty."

She laughed and looked down, cheeks pinking even deeper than the blush I'd brushed on.

Mindy was pretty. So pretty. I wasn't sure she knew that.

We all went quiet when we heard the knock on the door of our cabin.

"I'll get that," Dad said.

Mom went to bed early, saying she didn't feel very well. It wasn't too hard to see that the heat was draining her. Poor Mom. So that left Dad and me to sit on the porch and play rummy while waiting for Mindy to come back. We placed bets with M&M's, and my pile grew with each game.

I liked to win.

Dad checked his watch while I shuffled the cards.

"Are you worried about her?" I asked.

"Nah," he said.

"It's okay if you are." I started dealing, moving my lips while counting.

"Well, I don't know." He picked up his cards, fanning them in his hands. "But I'm sure worried about this hand. Did you even shuffle?"

"Yes. Don't be a spoilsport."

"I'm not. I just don't want to lose all my candy."

I rolled my eyes. "Just play."

Dad checked his watch again.

"She won't be late," I said.

He nodded and popped an M&M into his mouth.

"I know you still see us as your little girls," I said, grabbing a tan candy and putting it in my mouth. "But we're growing up. You can trust us."

He huffed out a laugh.

"What?" I asked.

"It's not you girls I don't trust," he answered. "I was a boy once. I know how they are."

We finished that game, and I let him have half the M&M's.

When someone set off a firework on the other side of the lake, I worried that it would make Mindy jump. She hated loud noises like that.

Thirty-One

Bruce, 2013

All the ladies of the family got up extra early this morning, headed for a bridal shop in Grand Rapids to find the very most perfect wedding dress for Holly. Off the rack, of course. There's no time to wait for an order to come in.

Dana came to spend the day with Mom, giving Dad a pass for a few hours.

That means the men have the day to eat junk, smell bad, and burp without the expectation of us excusing ourselves.

My dad's the worst offender of that last one.

When we found out that Zach had never been fishing before, we decided to remedy that while the girls were away. Mike had all the live bait we could need, Chris brought an extra pole, Dad lent the kid one of his bucket hats, and I drove all of us and our gear—including Mike's motorboat—out to a lake not too far outside Bear Run.

There's nobody else out here today. It's too cold for most people to even think about fishing. But we're plenty bundled up and have a couple of thermoses of hot coffee. We'll be just fine.

Zach's not necessarily comfortable putting a worm on the hook yet, and his cast leaves a little something to be desired, but his willingness to try is impressing the socks off me. When he reels in his first bite and we snap a shot of him with it before tossing it back in—it was on the small side—the pride on his face makes me like him even more than I already did.

We eat a lunch of the fish we caught this morning, sitting at a picnic table in Mike's workshop so we don't stink up the house while the girls are away. Dad's in the middle of telling about a time he nearly got dragged downstream by what he thought was an enormous catfish when he was a kid.

"Hardly old enough to shave, even," he always said when he started the story.

The way the tale goes, he went out with his line and a bucket to catch a few sunfish for his mother to cook up for dinner. They were poor in those days, still recovering from the Depression, even though it seemed the rest of the country had moved on, all their attention on the war in Japan and Germany.

"We couldn't afford to buy meat at the market most of the time," Dad says. "My father always said it took an idiot to starve in a place like this, though. Deer and squirrel and raccoon all over the place."

"You never ate raccoon," Mike says.

"Sure did, smarty pants." Dad shakes his head. "It's stringy and has got a strong flavor, but it'll do in a pinch."

"Probably tastes like garbage," Chris says.

"Well, that's what it eats, isn't it?" Dad says. "Well, anyways . . ."

He moves on to the part of the story where he stands in the stream all day long without a fish so much as swimming past his line.

"It was starting to get dark," he goes on. "And I wanted to go home. But my mother said I better not without something for our supper, so I stayed put."

Soon it was so dark he couldn't see his hand in front of his face. Not even the moon offered any glow. He got nervous, knowing he'd never find his way home with no light.

"What did you do?" Zach asks, sitting on the edge of the bench.

"Well, I stayed where I was," Dad says. "I sure didn't want to make my mother mad by coming home without anything for her to cook."

"Were you there until morning?"

"Nope."

Dad tells us how that was when he felt the first tug on his line. It was slight but got his attention. Then another pull and another. Each stronger than the one before it.

"Back in those days there was a rumor around that a monster-sized catfish swam through the waterways of Bear Run. So terrified were folks around here, they wouldn't let their kids swim in the rivers because they were sure the freak of nature was a man-eater," Dad says. "We even had a name for it. We called him Hans."

Chris and Mike meet eyes and both shake their heads, knowing how this story goes.

"Hans?" Zach asks. "Why?"

"Some kid claimed to have seen it moving down a deep run of river," Dad says. "Here's the crazy part. The kid swore that the fish yelled 'Hans!' as it went."

Zach scratches his head, and by now I think he's wondering how much baloney he's being sold.

"Anyway, I was sure it was Hans that I'd caught on my line," Dad goes on. "I thought how this beast could feed my entire neighborhood for a week if I managed to bring it in, so I held on, determined not to let it go."

It dragged him for a mile down the river, and he was afraid it would take him clear into Lake Michigan if he didn't dig his heels in and hold it firm.

"There was no way I'd let it get away with my pole," Dad says. "I got myself wedged on the other side of a boulder and held on for dear life."

Hans struggled against the hold of the line but couldn't break free. Dad reeled it in, slow and steady, until his catch was in reach.

"I put my hand in the water, feeling of its tail. It was smooth, but not exactly fishlike," Dad says, letting his voice get quiet. "Boy, was it ever big. I ran my hand along it, thinking it felt more like metal than anything. When I got about halfway down . . ."

Zach doesn't blink, his eyes focused on my dad's face.

"POP!"

Zach flinches.

"Up comes a man from the top of the fish," Dad says. "He had his hands up in the air and he was yelling all this stuff I couldn't understand. That was when I realized I hadn't caught a fish after all."

Dad pauses, takes a long drink of his iced tea, luxuriates in the quiet. The man knows he's got Zach on the line and is toying with him right before he reels him in.

"What was it?" Zach asks, desperate.

Dad turns his eyes one way and then the other as if making

sure no stragglers are listening to his story, even though it's just the five of us sitting there.

"A German," he says. "I hadn't caught myself a catfish. I'd caught myself a U-boat."

"What?" Zach squints his eyes and crinkles his nose. "I don't get it. Is that real?"

"He's pulling your leg," Chris says, nudging Zach.

The boy's going to have to get used to the ways of old Grumpy. I'll tell him on the way home that Dad only ever tells that particular big-fish story to the people he's coming to love. It's a rite of passage into the family.

It's Dad's way of saying, "You belong with us."

Linda and I are both satisfyingly beat after the days we've had. We turn in at an hour we might have once thought obscenely early—it's not even all the way dark yet. Exhausted as we are, though, we stay up a little longer, talking in bed.

"Dad told his Hans story," I say.

"Oh. That's good," Linda says. "I'm glad he likes Zach."

"He's a good kid."

I roll to my side so I can see her profile in the fading light coming in through the window. When she catches me watching her, she smiles and I inch over and give her a kiss.

For as much attention that new love gets in the movies and such, it can't hold a candle to love that's had time to age, to mature. A slow burn is always better than a flash in the pan as far as I'm concerned.

"I think everyone has a dress for the wedding now," Linda says, yawning. "I can't tell you how many Holly tried on. There are so many choices these days."

"Can't even imagine."

"She found the perfect one." She lets her eyes close. "Just you wait until you see it."

The dress is currently hanging in the closet in the room that used to be Holly's. I've been made to promise that under no circumstances am I to look at that dress. I'm to wait until the wedding day.

I guess that's so the photographer can snap a picture of my first glimpse of Holly in her gown.

They always like to get a shot of the dad crying.

CHAPTER Thirty-Two

Linda, 1975

The article about our adoption of Minh ran in the *Bear Run Herald* on the Thursday after she came home to us. It was right there on the front page along with a picture of the four of us standing on our front porch. Sonny and Minh held hands and looked so sweet together.

The editor of the paper promised us a copy of the picture by way of thanking us for letting them publish our story. I'd already figured out where I'd hang it in the living room.

That morning I loaded Minh and Sonny up in the Dart, and we listened to Carole King on the radio. While we might not have been able to feel the earth move like Carole did, we certainly did shake along with the car, and I hoped nothing was about to tumble down. From the way the muffler sounded, it wouldn't have surprised me one bit if it did.

Minh pressed her face against the window when we pulled up in front of the school, watching all the kids running around the playground while they waited for the bell to ring.

We'd decided to hold off and not enroll her in kindergarten in the fall. Four months just wasn't enough time to get her ready

for school. Bruce and I hoped to teach her as much English as
we could before sending her off for kindergarten.

I couldn't begin to imagine how frightening it would be for
her to be in a class full of kids, not understanding more than a
word here or there that they said.

But from the way Minh watched those kids with such long-
ing, I wondered if I'd done the wrong thing.

I was convinced that half of my time was spent second-
guessing my decisions.

"Bye, Mom," Sonny said, grabbing her bag. "Bye, Mindy."

"Bye," Minh said.

Sonny and I both looked at her, big smiles spreading on our
faces.

I had no idea if she knew what the word meant, but it little
mattered. It counted as a victory.

I held Minh's hand, and she held her doll's as we made our
way across the parking lot, and when we reached a cart, I lifted
her into the seat. She was so light. It surprised me every time I
picked her up.

"Ready?" I asked, putting my forehead against hers.

"Bye," she said.

"Oh, you silly."

I rolled the cart into the store, a blast of cold air making
gooseflesh prickle on Minh's arms. I rubbed one hand on her
skin, hoping to warm her up a little bit.

"It's cold in here, isn't it?" I said, pretending to chatter my
teeth. "Brr."

But her attention wasn't on me. Her eyes darted all around
the store at everything there was to see.

"See the bright lights?" I said, pointing up. "And, oh, do you see the red apples?"

When we neared the bananas, her eyes lit with recognition, and I grabbed a bunch, letting her hold them in her lap. When I turned my back on her for one second, she tore one of the bananas free and peeled it before I could stop her.

"Oh, we're supposed to pay for those first," I said, taking the rest of the bunch and putting it in the cart where she couldn't reach it.

Apparently she'd had bananas before.

I sang along to the elevator music playing over the speakers as we moved from produce to meat to dairy to dry goods, and all the while I kept a running tally of how much I was spending so I'd stay within my budget. Things weren't as tight as they'd been, but we still needed to be careful. Thank goodness for the stack of coupons in my wallet.

When Minh finished her banana, I took the peel, making a mental note that I'd need to ask the cashier to add a dime to our total to pay for it.

We meandered into the cereal aisle for a box of Wheaties. As soon as we rounded the corner, two women looked up at us. One was reading the side of a canister of oatmeal. The other had just dropped a box of Froot Loops into her cart.

"Linda Matthews," the woman with the oatmeal said, pointing at me. "How in the world are you?"

"I'm well," I answered, searching her face for a trace of familiarity.

She was an older woman, right around the same age as Hilda give or take a few years. I tried to place her. Church? No. The school? I didn't think so.

"You don't remember me." She scrunched her nose.

"I'm sorry."

"It's all right." She nodded at Minh. "I understand you have other things on your mind these days."

"Well, yes."

"I do your mother-in-law's hair," she said, touching her chest. "Dixie Chapman."

"Oh, right." I still had no memory of ever meeting the woman.

"You should come by the beauty parlor." She looked at my hair with a hint of a scowl. "I could do something with that."

"Maybe," I said, glancing up at her football-helmet-shaped bouffant.

I determined never to get my hair done by that woman.

"Anyway," Dixie said, "I saw you were in the paper this morning."

The woman with the Froot Loops glanced at me before grabbing a box of Golden Grahams.

"Yes," I said, cringing. "We didn't realize we'd be on the front page."

"And is this her?" The woman took a step toward our cart. "What's her name again?"

"Minh."

My little girl looked up at the sound of her name.

"I could never do it," Dixie said, leaning toward me as if sharing a secret. "But good for you."

"I'm sorry, I don't know what you mean."

"I mean raise a child that wasn't mine."

"Well . . ." I started, but then didn't know what to say next.

I grabbed my box of Wheaties. There was no celebrity athlete on it that time. Just a normal person riding a bike. Minh gladly took it from me, letting it rest on her lap.

"My nephew was over there, you know," Dixie said. "I'm sure Hilda's told you about him."

She hadn't, but I nodded anyway.

"You know what he told me? He said that the countryside is real pretty. Lots of trees and flowers." She sucked her teeth. "But he said those people over there just don't know how to take care of it. Let it go all to trash."

"Well, I don't know how true that is," I said, moving my cart forward in hopes of putting some distance between Minh and that woman. "They've had a war, you know."

"I'm just saying what he told me," she said. "My nephew's no liar."

"Well, I think I should . . ." I started, trying to move along so I could begin the process of forgetting what horrible things that woman was saying.

"He said they were backward people. Real primitive," she interrupted. She tipped her head and raised her eyebrows. "Not quite with the times like people over here."

"That's just not true . . ."

"Well, I won't keep you. She's very cute," Dixie said. "I just think of all the orphans in our own country."

"If you're so worried about them, why don't you adopt one yourself?"

I looked up to see the other woman standing at her cart full of sugary cereal, arms crossed.

"Well, excuse me," Dixie said. "I don't think that's any of your business."

"But it's your business to bully this woman?" Froot Loops asked.

"I don't like your tone."

"That's fine."

"Can you believe this?" Dixie said, looking at me for solidarity, I supposed.

"Mrs. Chapman, what you said was unkind." My hands shook, so I gripped on to the cart. "Someday soon my daughter will be able to understand English, and I hope she never hears anyone say such horribly mean things about her place of birth like what you said today."

"Well, I . . ."

"There's no need to apologize," I said. "But please remember that she's a person just like you or me, and she can be hurt by what people say."

Dixie harrumphed and pushed her cart away from us.

Minh was completely oblivious to the entire affair. She just kicked her little feet and stared at the box of Wheaties.

As for me, I thought I was going to burst into tears I was so upset.

"You did good," Froot Loops said.

"Thanks." I swallowed.

"I think your mother-in-law's going to have to find a new hairdresser," she said.

"You're probably right," I said, letting go of the cart and stretching out my fingers. "She'll be furious when she hears how I talked to her friend."

"Well, I'm proud of you." She winked at me. "Don't let people like that get to you, okay?"

I nodded.

"If anybody's backwards it's people who think they're better than everybody else," she said.

"Thank you." I glanced down at Minh then up again.

When I rolled my cart away, Minh called out to the woman, "Bye."

The girls were meant to be napping in their room after lunch. But when I came in after weeding the side flower boxes, I heard them giggling. It was fine with me if they didn't sleep, just so long as they were on their beds not making a mess of anything.

An eruption of laughter came again and then shushing from Sonny, I had to imagine.

Sneaking to their bedroom door, making sure to avoid the creaky floorboard in the hall, I tried to hear what in the world was so funny in there.

"Say it again," Sonny said. "Sonny."

"Sonny," Minh said, sending them both into giggles. "Sonny."

"Now Mindy," Sonny said. "Go on."

"Minh-dee."

More laughs.

"Minh-dee, Minh-dee."

"Now say Daddy."

"Daddy," Minh said.

I stood perfectly still when Sonny told her to say Mommy. When Minh did, it stole the breath right out of me.

Thirty-Three

Sonny, 1988

I'd seen it happen a million times. A girl would get her first boyfriend, and all the rest of the world would melt away into unimportance. All she'd want to do is talk to him on the phone, write gushy love letters to him, and practice writing their names together in her diary.

When a girl got her first boyfriend, she'd annoy everyone else by only ever talking about him—how much she missed him when he wasn't around or worrying that he was upset with her or talking about how dreamy his eyes were.

I had to admit to having been that girl at least once. In my defense, though, I was in eighth grade at the time. I hadn't known any better.

So, when a week after meeting her at the lake in Fort Colson Eric asked Mindy to be his girlfriend, I totally expected her to become the most annoying person in all the world.

Much to my surprise, though, she turned him down.

"Don't you even like him?" I asked on the way home from work the day she told me.

"I guess," she said. "But he'll just dump me eventually. I'm saving myself from getting my heart broken."

"You're kidding, right?"

"Sonny, I'm not like you." She put her hands up and shrugged. "You're pretty and interesting and fun to be around."

"Oh, whatever, Mindy. You're so pretty."

"Thanks." She sighed. "I'd rather be fun to be around, though."

I paused at a four-way stop before rolling through, expecting Mindy to yell at me. She didn't disappoint.

"There were no other cars," I said. "Maybe you'd be more fun if you weren't always criticizing my driving."

"Whatever."

"So, like, are you just never going to talk to him again?" I asked. "I mean, he's so nice. And really cute."

"We're going to be pen pals," she said.

"Seriously?" I turned toward her. "Pen pals?"

"Keep your eyes on the road," she said. "Don't forget we have to pick up some gummy bears for Mom."

"I just don't get why you'd stay in touch with him if you're not interested in going out."

"Um, because he's a good friend. And because we have a lot in common."

"Like that you're both adopted?" I asked.

"For real, Sonny, if we forget the gummy bears, Mom is going to spaz out."

Apparently she was done with the Eric conversation even if I had so many questions I still wanted to ask.

I drove to the convenience store where the candy was cheapest, letting the car idle while Mindy ran inside.

When we got home, Mom was up in her bedroom with the door closed.

"I'm on the phone with Aunt Dana," she called through the door, almost shrilly. "You can put the gummy bears on the kitchen counter. Thanks."

"Do you want us to make you a sandwich?" Mindy asked.

"Nope. I'll get something to eat in a little while."

Mindy and I walked down the stairs, side by side, whispering.

"She sounds funny," Mindy said.

"I know. Like she's crying or freaking out or something."

"Should we call Dad?"

"She's on the phone." I shook my head. "It's probably just the baby making her feel crazy again. She'll be better soon."

"It must be so horrible to be pregnant." Mindy hopped off the bottom step and turned toward me. "You have to pee all the time."

"I don't know. I think it sounds like fun."

We rounded the corner into the kitchen.

"Fun?" Mindy grabbed a loaf of bread from the box on the counter. "All the mood swings?"

"People bring you candy whenever you want it," I said, opening the fridge for the Goober Grape peanut butter. "You get so much attention."

"Strangers touch your belly." Mindy grimaced.

"And tell you that you're glowing."

She untwisted the tie on the bread, spinning the bag open before handing me two slices. I got out a knife and dug into the peanut butter and jelly mixture in the jar. We ate in the family room, watching a rerun of *The Facts of Life* and trying to figure out which girl we were most like.

Mindy thought I was like Blair, and I said she was most like Tootie.

"Really?" Mindy asked. "I kind of thought I was more like Jo."

"No," I said. "You aren't a tomboy."

From the kitchen we heard a bag being opened. Mom had found her gummy bears. All must have been right with the world.

"What are you girls watching?" she asked, walking past us and slowly lowering herself into the loveseat.

I glanced over at her, watching as her jaw worked, chewing the candy. As soon as I turned back toward the TV, though, I realized something was different about her. Very different.

"Mom," I said, horrified. "Um, did you get a haircut?"

"Yes," she answered, a forced smile on her face. "I thought maybe it would be easy once the baby comes, you know, to have it a little shorter. Besides, with how hot it's been, I just wanted it off my neck. So, I called and made an appointment. I took in a magazine with Princess Diana in it, thinking that would look nice."

"Oh," Mindy said, dropping her half-eaten sandwich on her plate.

"But then the hairdresser said I wouldn't look good with that style." Mom sniffled and shoved a few gummy bears into her mouth. "So she did this to me."

She put her hand on her head, feeling the very, very short hair.

"It's like Mia Farrow from *Rosemary's Baby*," she sobbed. "Did she think I was having Satan's child or something?"

"I don't know," Mindy said. "I haven't seen that movie."

I shot my sister a look, and she picked her sandwich back up, taking a big bite.

"It's not that bad, Mom," I said.

"I look like a pinhead!" Mom yelled before shoving a handful of gummies in her mouth.

"No, you don't." I slid my plate onto the coffee table. "You're beautiful."

"But all my pretty hair is gone." She covered her face with both hands and wailed, her mouth totally full of candy. "Your dad is going to be so upset with me."

"It will grow back," I said. "And Dad won't be mad. I promise."

Eventually Mindy and I managed to get Mom to eat something that wasn't full of sugar and helped her back up to her bed, where she fell asleep just a few minutes after her head hit the pillow.

Once back downstairs, I called Dad and told him what happened.

"Dad, she needs you to be Prince Charming today," I said. "You know what I mean?"

"Yeah." He cleared his throat. "I'll see what I can do."

"I mean it. You can't, like, blow this off. She needs to feel like the most special woman in the world." I was being bossy, I knew it. But if ever there was a time for it, this was it. "And bring flowers. Not red roses, though. You know she hates those."

"Got it," he said. "I'll be home in an hour."

He came home exactly one hour later with a bouquet of flowers that looked very expensive. Daisies and irises and even a sunflower. Not a red rose in sight. When he saw Mom, he smiled and told her how beautiful she was. He said that she should get dressed up because they were going out for dinner. And at a place that took reservations.

She came downstairs in a sleeveless maternity dress that she'd cinched so it didn't hang like a tent. Somehow she'd done her makeup so that her eyes stood out even more than usual with a shimmery eyeshadow she'd borrowed from me.

With that look she could have been cue-ball bald and no one would have even noticed.

Well, they might have noticed. But they would have thought the bald woman was super gorgeous.

"Pretty as the day I met you," Dad said, taking her hand. "Let's go, babe."

She put arms around him, pulling him as close as she could to her so she could give him a giant, loud kiss on the lips.

I was a teenager, and so my obligation to the world was to be grossed out by the display of affection mere feet from me.

They walked outside, and Mindy and I watched Dad get Mom's door and help her into the truck. Before he shut her in, he put a hand on her cheek and said something that made her smile.

My word. My mom was gorgeous.

CHAPTER Thirty-Four

Bruce, 2013

When Holly was first born, I held her every moment I could. My mother warned me that I'd spoil the girl if I didn't put her down every once in a while, but I wouldn't hear of it. While I knew it was possible to ruin a child with too much sugar or too many toys or never saying no to anything, I knew there was no such thing as giving too much love.

I still believe that with all my heart.

I'm standing in the narthex of the church where I've been playing double roles as a father of the bride and greeter, welcoming the handful of guests who have come to celebrate with us. It's mostly family, ours and Zach's with a couple of college friends who were able to drop everything and make the trip.

It's not the grand wedding I'd always expected to throw for Holly, but that doesn't take any of the goodness out of the occasion.

It's not every day I get to give my baby girl away to a man I've grown to admire.

I saw Zach for a minute before he walked his mother down the aisle. The kid's a mess of nerves. It's all right. So am I.

It's my third time, and I might have thought it would get easier. It does not. But I wouldn't trade it for the world.

The only piano player we could get on such short notice is the old choir teacher from the school. Thank goodness she's got "Canon in D" memorized. When she starts playing, Mindy and Sonny link arms and start the slow walk to the altar.

That's when my Holly rounds the corner and I get my first glimpse of her in all her finery.

"Daddy," she whispers, holding the skirt of her dress to the sides just like she did a hundred times when she was little. She turns a twirl and all I see is my little bird all grown up. How did it happen so fast?

If my heart stops right now, I won't be surprised at all.

"You're beautiful, honey," I say.

"Daddy, don't cry," she says, smiling. "You'll make me cry and then my makeup will be ruined."

"We can't have that, can we?" I knuckle a tear out of the corner of my eye.

She hugs me, and even though I worry about messing up her hair or crinkling her dress, I hold my daughter in my arms. She lets me go before I'm ready. It's probably for the best. I'd never be ready.

Twining her arm in mine, she rests her head on my shoulder.

"I'm so excited," she says.

I'd planned what I might say to her when we got to this place, but I can't seem to remember a single word of it. It was this way when I walked Sonny to Mike and Mindy to Eric.

It's not often that I find myself completely at a loss like this.

The pianist starts up with the wedding march and Holly and I step to the threshold of the sanctuary.

Linda stands, locking eyes with me and making me want to cry. I guess it would be all right if I did. Nobody would think anything of it. Besides, Linda's already dabbing under her eyes with the hanky I let her borrow earlier.

I wink at her before turning to Holly. "You ready?"

"Yes," she whispers.

During the rehearsal last night, this felt like the longest walk in history. Today it's too short. In no time we're at the front of the sanctuary, where Linda joins us, kissing Holly on the cheek before taking her hand.

When the pastor asks who is giving this woman away, Lin and I say "We are" at the same time, and I'm sure everybody hears how my voice shakes.

Before I know it, I let her go.

In lieu of a reception, we've rented out Fiona's for the evening. It's not swanky by any means, but Fi did a fine job on the food and even let us decorate a little bit.

Good thing Holly's favorite meal is breakfast because that's all Fiona ever makes.

It's a small party but loud, and I find myself in need of a little breather out on the bench in front of the diner. The air's crisp and the stars bright. What a really good day it's been.

The door opens and Sonny steps out, still in her dress but with a denim jacket on to keep her warm.

"Scoot over," she says. "No hogging the bench."

I move to my left and she sits beside me.

"You okay?" she asks.

"Yup. Just needed a little air."

She puts an elbow on the back of the bench, resting her head in her hand.

"He'll be good to her, Dad," she says.

"I believe it." I rub my palms against the legs of my dress pants. "It always takes a little getting used to, though. She was, after all, only born five minutes ago."

"Is it harder this time?" she asks. "Since she's your last?"

"Between you and me?" I say. "It was hardest on me when you got married."

"Really? I wouldn't have expected that."

"Our first little bird out of the nest." I pat her knee. "Your mom and I raised all three of you girls so you could make it out in the world. Still, it's always come as a surprise when it's time to let one of you go."

"Good thing we haven't gone too far." She gets up. "Come on, Daddy-O. It's almost time for the love birds to cut the cake."

"I'll be right in," I say.

"Promise?"

"Yup."

When she opens the door, a rush of glad-making sound escapes from the party, and I'm eager to get back to the fun.

I take in a couple more fortifying gulps of autumn air before getting up from the bench.

The scene through the window is one I want to remember for the rest of my life. All the people I love most together in one place. Dad's eyeballing the cake, rubbing his hands together. Linda's sitting in a booth with Zach's folks, making friends with them. Our granddaughters have started an impromptu dance party in the middle of the diner.

Even Mom's smiling, Holly crouched down beside her wheelchair so Mindy can take their picture.

The poet Mary Oliver—a favorite of mine—once posed the question about what it is one plans to do with their "wild and precious life." I've pondered that a whole lot since first reading it.

But today, looking in on my family, I think I've come upon the answer.

If all I've done with this one life is be a son, husband, brother, dad, grandpa to these remarkable people, that's good enough for me.

I pull open the door and get back to the celebration.

CHAPTER Thirty-Five

Linda, 1975

The heat of a hundred bodies mingled to make the elementary school gym even smellier than it usually was. Add to that discomfort the indignity of adults trying to fit their behinds on the tiny chairs that were in rows placed too close together. I thought Hilda was going to blow an artery with how put out she felt.

It was the first we'd seen her since Minh came, and she didn't say anything to us when she took her tiny seat. Every minute or two she looked at Minh out of the corner of her eye as if sizing her up.

When the kindergarteners came in, marching in a single-file line, all wearing little white robes and construction paper graduation caps with yarn tassels, all of our attention turned to them.

Once up front, Sonny waved at us, smiling wide and showing off the space where her front teeth had been just the week before.

"See Sonny?" Bruce whispered to Minh, who stood between his knees.

"Sonny," she whispered.

Minh lifted up on tiptoe to see between the heads of the people in front of her. But when Ivan snapped a picture from the seat beside Bruce, the flash exploding light, Minh flinched. From all around the room came an echo of clicking cameras and bursts of flashbulbs. She scrambled up onto Bruce's lap, pressing her face into his chest. The meat of her hands covered her ears, her fingers wrapped around the back of her head, assuming the position we'd all been taught as kids during air-raid drills.

For us as kids, the air raids never came. They'd been some abstract fear of what-if.

Not when.

I reached for Minh, touching her shoulder. It only made her jerk away from me and let out a terrified little yelping sound.

Bruce put his hand on the back of her head and wrapped his other arm around her behind and eased himself up from the chair.

Sonny watched from the front as her daddy stepped out into the hall with Minh.

Her smile faded.

I tried to get her attention so I could smile and flash her a thumbs-up. But she kept her eyes on the door, waiting for Bruce to come back.

The teacher knelt on the floor in front of her class, leading them in a song that was undoubtedly meant as a heartstring tugger, about growing up so fast. Sonny went through the motions along with her classmates, but without her usual *joie de vivre*.

Halfway through the song, though, she got her smile back and that bright sparkle in her eye.

Turning, I saw Bruce standing at the back of the gym, Minh in his arms. He'd managed to get her calmed down, and she snuggled right up to him. When he noticed me watching them, he whispered something into Minh's ear and pointed in my direction.

She met my eyes across the room and smiled, lifting her hand in a wave.

"Looks like she's all right now," Ivan whispered.

I nodded.

Little by little, we were figuring it all out.

Hilda insisted that we have a party for Sonny's kindergarten graduation. On the phone a few days before she told us to be at her house for supper by six o'clock and that she would take care of the food and decorations. We just needed to show up. And on time.

She said nothing about Minh or how she'd snubbed us the past several weeks. She didn't apologize or so much as acknowledge that she might have caused some harm.

Everything was supposed to go back to normal just because she was ready for it to.

If only I was a stronger woman I would have put my foot down and demanded that she say sorry before we would step into her house or her into ours.

But I was lily-livered and wanted so desperately to make everyone happy. So to Grammy and Grumpy's we went. And on time.

Hilda kept the food in her warm oven, waiting for Chris and Dana to come with baby Teddy. But when Dana came, just her and the baby, my heart sank.

"Where's Uncle Chris?" Sonny asked, giving Teddy's foot a shake between her thumb and finger.

"I don't think he'll be here this time, honey," Dana said. "I'm sorry. He wanted me to tell you how proud he is of you, though."

"Is he okay?" I asked, putting out my hands to take the baby.

"Yeah," she answered, putting the diaper bag on the floor by the stairs. "He just has this car in the shop that's turning out to be a difficult nut to crack. You know. He has to work late to fix it."

From the way she didn't meet my eyes when she said it, I wondered if it was true.

Hilda wasn't the only one in the family who had tender feelings about us adopting Minh. For some reason, though, it hurt less that Chris had kept his distance. Somehow, I had more grace for him than I ever did for Hilda.

"Sweetie," I said to Sonny. "How about you go get washed up for supper. All right?"

I held Teddy against my shoulder and bounced, waiting for Sonny to make her way out of earshot.

"Dana?" I said. "I know having Minh here is probably hard for him."

"It'll be fine," she said. Then she met my eyes. "Being over there stole a lot from him. But he's still a good man."

"Without a doubt."

"It might take him a little time."

"We can be patient."

Teddy squirmed in my arms, and I adjusted my hold of him until he eased back into comfort.

Hilda had asked Ivan earlier in the week to put in an order for a sheet cake that was to say "Congrats, Sonny!" in pink frosting. When he'd gone to pick it up from the bakery that afternoon, she'd told him to check it before he left to make sure everything was correct.

So, when she brought out the cake box after supper and lifted the lid, she scowled.

"I thought you checked it," she said.

"Yup," Ivan answered.

"But they spelled her name wrong." Hilda pointed. "They wrote 'Sunny.'"

"Like I told them to."

"Dad, you know her name's spelled with an *o*, right?" Bruce asked, spelling it out loud.

Ivan tapped the end of his chin and looked from Hilda to Bruce as if trying to decide if they were pulling his leg.

"Are you sure?" he asked.

"I'm certain," Bruce answered.

"Her real name's Sondra," I said by way of explaining.

"It is?" Ivan pulled his mouth into a thoughtful frown. "How about that?"

"Oh, for pity's sake," Hilda said, cutting into the cake as if to teach it a lesson.

Dana and I met glances and I had to bite the inside of my cheek to keep from laughing.

Out the window behind Dana I saw Chris's Pinto parked in the driveway. He stood against it, examining his nails.

"Chris is here," I told her. "Do you mind if I go talk to him?"

She took Teddy from me—I was, admittedly, a baby hog that day—and told me to go ahead.

Chris looked up when I stepped out the front door.

"You know, doesn't matter how much I scrub my hands," he said. "They'll always be grease stained, I guess."

"Just shows you're a hard worker," I said.

"Maybe."

"Hilda saved a plate for you."

"That's nice of her." He focused his eyes on the cement between our feet. "I don't talk about Nam much."

He worked his mouth like he was trying to figure out what he needed to say next. I didn't want to step over his words, so I didn't say anything.

"Try not to think about it either." He shrugged. "Not that I can help it."

One of the neighbors drove by and tapped their horn in a friendly honk. I waved.

"The memories that bother me most are of the kids." He bit his top lip. "Too much happened to them that no kid should ever have to live through."

He lifted his eyes. Chris Francis had the most earnest eyes I'd ever seen. Truly. And that day they were full of hurt, so much that it made me want to cry.

"I never hated them," he said. "The folks over there."

"I know you didn't," I said.

"In fact, I wanted to help them." He closed his eyes. "Wish I could've done more for them."

He pushed his lips together and breathed in and out through his nose a few times before opening his eyes, again with that sincere expression.

"I'd like to meet my niece now. If that's okay," he said.

"Of course." I nodded toward the house. "Come on."

I had Chris wait on the steps off the entryway and went to find Minh who, blessedly, had finished eating her piece of cake.

"She gobbled it right down," Bruce said, wiping the frosting from the corners of her mouth.

"Chris is ready to see her," I whispered into his ear. "But maybe not with everybody watching."

"Oh," Bruce said, nodding to let me know he got it.

He scooped up Minh and the two of us did our best at sneaking out of the dining room without drawing too much attention.

When he saw us walk in, Chris stood and pulled on the bottom of his T-shirt.

"This is Minh," Bruce said, lowering her to the floor. Then to her, "That's your Uncle Chris."

Chris squatted down, putting out his right hand to her. "Chào," he said.

She took his hand with her left, not shaking it. Just holding it. "Hi," she said.

"Hey, that's pretty good."

"Bye." Her eyes sparkled.

"She's just showing off now," Bruce said.

"I can see that." Chris turned his eyes to their hands. Hers tiny and with a little smudge of frosting on her thumb, his big and with nails rimmed black from years of working on cars. "It's good to meet you."

"You better come and get some cake before Sonny and Dad eat it all," Bruce said.

"Sonny," Minh said.

Chris stood, Minh still holding his hand. He took two steps toward Bruce and pulled him into a hug.

There was something fierce, almost wild about that hug. As if all the past hurts between them stood no chance against the way they slapped each other's backs. As if they put it all behind them right that moment.

CHAPTER Thirty-Six

Sonny, 1988

By the end of July all anybody talked about was the drought we seemed to be in the middle of. The grass in everybody's yard turned yellow then brown because of the watering ban. At church on Sundays the prayer request list had a new section headed with "Pray for Our Farmers! Pray for Rain!" listing all the farming families by name.

It was hot. It was dry. It was completely miserable.

"It was 108 in Arizona yesterday," Mindy said when I complained.

"They're used to it," I said back. "I, on the other hand, am not used to it being ninety degrees at eight o'clock in the morning."

"I'm just saying that it's hotter in Arizona."

"Yeah. Because it's supposed to be."

Dad set the air-conditioning to blast our house with freezing air all day and all night for Mom's sake. He told her not to go outside for any reason, not to get the mail or to run to the store or anything.

"Stay inside no matter what," he told her.

"What if there's a fire?" Mindy asked.

"Well, it'd probably be cooler inside than out anyway," he said. Then, to Mom, "Linda, I'm serious. I don't want you risking it."

Mom, ever the free spirit who wasn't all that fond of being told what to do, nodded.

It wouldn't have surprised me at all if she pointed one toe out the door once we were all gone for the day just because she could.

The only person in the history of the world who looked good in a muumuu was Mrs. Olds. On her, the oversized dress didn't look shapeless or frumpy, it was flowing, and the bright print of green leaves and pink hibiscus wasn't cheesy, it was exotic.

"I bought this in Hawaii when I was there in the late sixties," she said, running her hands along the fabric. "I was there with my second husband for our anniversary and fell in love with this as soon as I saw it."

"It's pretty," Mindy said.

"Thank you." Mrs. Olds put a hand to her heart. "Now, I think we should do our work in the cellar again. What do you think?"

Neither Mindy nor I needed to give it a second thought. It was at least twenty degrees cooler in the cellar. We grabbed the boxes Mrs. Olds pointed to and hauled them downstairs to sort through them.

I didn't even care if I got cobwebs in my bangs.

On one side of the cellar we had a table for all the things to keep, and on the other side Mrs. Olds had set a garbage can for the things that were to go. For most things, it was pretty clear which side of the room they belonged on. Other things were a little more complicated, and Mindy and I debated each other over the fate of the particular artifact.

Our most heated argument was when we found a set of clown figurines. I said that they were chic and Parisian. She said that all clowns—French or not—were creepy and that she didn't want to be responsible for giving every kid in Bear Run nightmares.

I thought she read too much Stephen King for her own good.

In the end, Mrs. Olds had the final say—as she did with all things—and she decided to put them in the yard sale to raise money for the museum.

It was a good thing that most of the stuff was either obviously a keep—a strand of pearls that had belonged to Mrs. Huebert or a first-edition copy of *To Kill a Mockingbird*—or toss—an old, crumpled-up hamburger wrapper from McDonald's or a decapitated Cabbage Patch Kid. Otherwise we would never finish the job of sorting.

The box I'd picked that morning was, so far, all toss, and I was getting bored.

"Why do people donate trash?" I asked, picking a doily up between my thumb and finger, holding it far away from myself. The lacy trim was pulled all out of shape and the whole thing was stained and nasty. I could just tell that it would stink if I got it too close to my nose. "Gross."

"Well, I'll tell you something," Mrs. Olds said, putting her hand out so I'd drop the doily into it. "When something holds a memory for someone, it can be very difficult to let go of."

"Even if it's ruined?"

"Imagine this belonged to a dear auntie of yours," she said. "It was pinned on the back of a velvety chair she had in her sitting room where you used to sit with her and read stories when you were little."

"Okay?" I said.

"You've grown up. Your auntie has passed away. Even the velvety chair is gone, sold to some yahoo that came to a garage sale and paid twenty dollars for it." She held up the doily, letting it spin. "All that's left is this, and when you see it, you feel all those happy memories like they're brand new."

She pulled at the trim, trying to reshape it, and scratched at a bit of filth with her thumbnail.

"Eventually," she went on, "you realize that you can't keep everything that was someone else's. If you did, you'd have no room for what is yours. But it's too difficult to throw it out. It would feel like tossing that memory of sitting in the chair, sharing stories with your aunt."

"So, I donate it to the museum instead?" I asked.

"Exactly. Because that feels more honoring of her memory."

She considered the ratty thing before shrugging and flinging it in the direction of the garbage can. When she noticed Mindy and my shocked faces, she put her hands on her hips.

"Well, she wasn't *my* auntie," she said.

Coldhearted.

She was so awesome.

Mom was in the baby's room when we got home, standing at one end of the crib and looking down at the duckling print of the sheets and the fuzzy duck stuffed animal in the corner. It still smelled like fresh paint in there, the walls a happy yellow color that Mom begged Dad to paint them. A stack of tiny disposable diapers was lined up on the middle shelf of the changing table. Itty-bitty green-and-yellow footed pjs hung in the closet.

I stood in the hallway, watching her before she knew I was there. Mom rubbed her hands around the front of her stomach and hummed a gentle tune, just loud enough for me to hear over the noisy air conditioner.

When she'd been pregnant with me, Mom had Dad read books next to her belly so that I'd get used to his voice. I knew because there was a picture of it that Aunt Dana took. Even though she hated spinach, she forced it down so that I'd grow healthy. She quit her band to settle down and be a mom.

That last one made me feel a pinch of guilt when I thought about it even though she'd never said she regretted it.

"Oh, honey," Mom said, catching a glimpse of me out of the corner of her eye. "I didn't know you were home."

"We are." I took a step into the room. "It's coming together, huh?"

"Yup." She shook her head. "Baby will be here before we know it."

"Are you nervous?" I tapped one of the ducks hanging from the mobile over the crib.

"Not really," she said. "This isn't my first rodeo."

"I don't think they let pregnant women participate in rodeos."

"That's probably true." She reached out and put her hand on my cheek. "But I might have considered it when I went into labor with you."

"What?" I said. "Why?"

"Oh, Sonny. You were a stubborn one," she said. "I was in labor for thirty hours with you."

"Is that a long time?"

She closed her eyes and nodded slowly. "A very long time."

"Did it hurt?"

"Yes," she answered. "They always say you forget the pain. It's sort of a lie."

I grimaced. "Sorry."

"You were worth every single moment of it." She smiled. "How's that for a self-esteem boost?"

"Actually, pretty good."

"I was so scared when we brought you home from the hospital." She reached into the crib to smooth a crease in the sheet. "I worried that I'd mess everything up."

"But you didn't."

"Oh, honey. I made mistakes," she said. "Plenty of them. And as soon as you started talking, you had no problem letting me know about them."

"That sounds about right." I laughed.

"I used to sing to you at night."

"I remember."

"If I sang a song that was high, you'd stop me and tell me to 'sing it right.'" She smiled. "I think you wanted me to use my lower voice."

"I'm sorry."

"Don't be, sweetheart," she said, grabbing my hand. "I love the person you are. Bossy pants and all."

"Stop it," I said. "You're just trying to make me cry."

But instead of my eyes welling up, hers did.

"I can't believe you're moving in a month," she said. "I'm going to miss seeing you every day."

"You'll get used to me being gone," I said.

"No. I don't think I ever will."

In my mother's room, tucked away in a keepsake box, was a

little green dress and a pair of white lace-up shoes. She used to pull those out for me to look at when I was little, telling me it was what she brought me home in.

I hadn't seen them in years. To be honest, I hadn't thought about them much either.

Still, I knew they were there.

I wondered if, while I was away at college, Mom would pull them out, letting them remind her of the good feelings of the first moment she saw me, held me, called me hers.

CHAPTER Thirty-Seven

Bruce, 2013

There was a sunrise today like every morning, I just couldn't see it for the cloud cover that obscured my view. It's all right. I still enjoyed a cup of coffee while I looked out my living room window to greet the day.

A murmuration of starlings has descended on my yard recently. I suspect there are a good number of them that fledged in the early summer. Since then they've grown so as to be indistinguishable among the others.

They grow up so fast.

"Goodness, they're noisy this morning," Mindy says from the bottom of the steps. "I could hear them all the way upstairs."

She crosses the room and turns the old rocking chair so she can sit and watch out the window.

"You ever heard of Eugene Schieffelin?" she asks.

"Can't say that I have." I take the wingback chair and angle my body so I'm looking straight at her.

"I read about him in a book, gosh, forever ago. He was alive in the nineteenth century, I think," she says. "Lived in New York. He loved Shakespeare and got this crazy idea to bring all the birds from the plays to live in Central Park."

"In captivity?"

"No. Just in the wild, I guess." She pushes a strand of hair behind her ear. "He imported a couple different species. House sparrows, bull finches, nightingales, starlings. A few others. I just can't remember all of them right now."

"Huh. How about that?" I say.

"Most of them couldn't make it here. But the sparrows and starlings were fruitful and multiplied aplenty."

"Boy, I'd say."

"I think they're doing okay for themselves." She leans back in her chair and crosses one leg over the other. "There's your little bird nerd lesson for the day."

"I look forward to another one soon." I wink at her before looking once more out the window.

"I'm going to look at a few apartments today," she says. "If you aren't too busy, I'd love to have you come with me."

I want to tell her there's no hurry for her to move out, that we love having her here. But I know she needs her space, a little more independence than she's afforded by living under her folks' roof.

"I can do that," I say.

We sit there watching the starlings just a little bit longer until they all at once take off, filling the sky with their dipping and divings, a single unit of flight with hundreds of independent wings.

I whisper a line from a Mary Oliver poem about thinking of dangerous and noble things. Mindy recognizes it. Of course she does. And she recites back to me the end of the verse, declaring a desire to be afraid of nothing.

Afraid of nothing like those winged wonders taking flight on a chilly November morning.

One window of the apartment overlooks Fiona's; out another I can see the public library. The last one offers a stunning view of the brick building next door.

The landlord left us alone to walk across hardwood floors that could use a little care and walls that need a coat of paint. It's nothing fancy, but the price is right and it's within walking distance of Mindy's office.

Besides, Mindy's smitten with the place.

"I can put my desk here," she says, pointing at one wall. "And my bookshelf next to it."

"Your mom might have an area rug in the attic that would look nice in here," I say.

"The braided one?" She nods. "That would be pretty."

I take a few pictures on my phone to send to Linda, and Mindy tests the appliances to make sure they work okay. They seem to, even if they're anything but new.

"You know," she says, shutting the door of the fridge that's not too much taller than she is, "this will be the first time I've ever lived on my own."

"Yup." I tap a loose floor tile in the bathroom with the toe of my shoe. "You think you'll like it?"

"Without a doubt."

I offer to treat her to a good cup of coffee, and she's happy to accept. We leave the truck parked along the street and walk, even if it is a bit chilly.

"You know, this is where I first met your mother," I say, holding the door of the coffee shop for her. "Did I ever tell you that?"

"Only a hundred times." She smiles. "But tell me again."

And I do.

Some stories bear much repeating.

CHAPTER Thirty-Eight

Linda, 1975

June days had a way of joining all together into one. Settling into an easy summer routine was natural for Sonny, Minh, and me. Get up for a bowl of cereal. Play in the morning sun, weed, worry over the tomatoes that showed no promise of bearing fruit. Inside for sandwiches and a quiet time. Up to play some more or walk to the park or drive to the library to pick out a few books. Home to make dinner and welcome Bruce.

Dinner.

Baths.

Bedtime.

Then again the next day.

Not such a terrible way to spend a life.

Not terrible, no. But a little less than exciting.

Still, that wonderful, monotonous, predictable life was precisely the one I'd signed on to when I married Bruce, and I didn't regret a single moment of it.

June became July, and even those days passed me by in a blur of routine.

Saturdays were different because Bruce got up to make French toast or pancakes, and we'd spend the day doing odd jobs around the house or packing into the car to have a picnic lunch beside the creek, letting the girls splash in the water until they were completely worn out.

Sundays were for church and sometimes lunch at Hilda's, then for naps in the afternoon and cereal for dinner.

Sure, time flew when we were having fun. But it went even faster when we were about the business of the every day, every hour, every minute. No matter how I tried to slow it down, to rein it in, it kept taking off on me, always hovering just out of reach.

The last night of July, I put the girls in the bath together. Sitting on the closed lid of the toilet, I watched them splash in the water and scoop up cupfuls of it to dump on their own heads. I was exhausted and eager to get them into bed so I could have time alone with Bruce while we sat in front of the television, watching reruns before dropping into bed.

"All right, girls," I said. "Scrub-a-dub-dub, please. Let's not make this last all night."

"Aw, but we're having fun," Sonny said, letting her shoulders slump. "Can't we play a little bit longer?"

"Play," Minh said, holding up her red plastic cup. "Please, Mommy."

She tipped that cup over, water spilling down her hair and face as she and Sonny both got a hearty case of the giggles.

I thought about what a little old lady had said to me at church the Sunday before. She'd taken my hand in hers and told me that I was in the "golden time" of parenting and that it would never get better than it was right then.

"Enjoy them now, sweetie," she'd said. "Don't take a single moment for granted."

Simply remembering what that old church lady had said made my chest tighten and my head spin.

Someday I'll miss this, I thought. *I'll kick myself for not enjoying it more.*

I ached for those little girls even though they were right there, within my reach.

Sooner than I wanted, they'd be big.

I gave them five more minutes.

I decided to enjoy them sufficiently the next day. And the next.

But in that moment, my backside on the hard toilet lid, I was tired.

Exhausted to the bone.

"Uh, Lin," Bruce said, cracking the door open and peeking in. "Maybe get the girls out of the tub."

"What's going on?" I asked.

"I just opened the mail. We got something from the adoption agency." He reached his arm in, handing me a piece of paper. "Don't freak out, okay?"

"Don't bathe your adopted child with other children," the letter read. "They may have been infected with parasites. Take them to the doctor immediately for medicine."

We got the girls out of the water and wrapped them in towels, not knowing what in the world we were supposed to do.

"You can never tell your mother about this," I told Bruce. "Never."

I tossed and turned all night, unable to sleep even as exhausted as I was. All I could do was worry about getting Minh to the doctor the next day, finding money for the anti-parasitic, and keeping Sonny healthy.

I didn't want to take a moment of these golden years for granted.

Of course I didn't.

Still, it would have been a lie to say that some of those golden moments weren't so very hard.

Minh liked to sit beside me on the piano bench while I played. She'd put her fingers on the very edges of the keys, never daring to press down on them to make the notes sound, even when I told her she could, that it would be all right.

That afternoon had grown so hot that being outside in the sun was more miserable than being inside with very little breeze. I set the fan to oscillate and sat at the piano, flipping through my sheet music until I found the song I wanted.

"Nocturne in C-sharp minor" by Chopin.

I'd played it a hundred years before in my high school recital when I'd still had dreams bigger than I could hold in my two arms. Those days I couldn't understand that I'd let all that go for life in a cramped house with a man who sometimes snored and two little girls who weren't always very good at putting away their toys.

Sometimes the dreams of the young were replaced by those they never could have dared to imagine.

It didn't mean that one dream was better than another. They were just different.

I was overwhelmingly, wholeheartedly, blissfully thankful for the life I had with Bruce and the girls.

My fingers found their way as I played, missing their place a few times. Nothing too horrible, though. I played the song the way I felt it instead of how it was written—a habit of mine that had vexed my piano teacher enough that she threatened weekly to expel me from my lessons.

If I looked closely enough, I could still see the scar from when she split my knuckle with her ruler.

During a trill in the song, Minh climbed up beside me. She watched as I passed my fingers over each other, an intricate dance, while I performed a run up the keys.

"Mommy," she said, her little voice holding so much awe that I had to stop the song.

"Want me to do it again?" I asked.

"Yes," she said.

So I did the run again. And again. Four times.

Then Minh extended her pointer fingers and pushed down one key, then the next. C, F, C, F.

"Very nice," I said.

"Again?" she asked.

"Yes."

And she did. The same two notes. Then she played them together, louder, making her eyebrows push together.

"Mom," Sonny said. "Mom."

"Just a minute," I said, still watching Minh play her two-note song.

"Can I have a popsicle?" Sonny asked, making her voice louder.

"Not now. It's almost time for dinner."

"But it's hot," Sonny said, taking a step closer to me. "Please."

"I said not now." My voice had a sharpness to it that I wasn't accustomed to using with her. I softened it as much as I was able. "I'm listening to Minh play a song."

"That's not a song," Sonny said. "It's just pounding."

"Don't be rude." I turned back to Minh.

"Why does she get all of your attention?" Sonny screamed, stomping her foot and slamming her fists into the sides of her thighs.

"Sondra Lynn Matthews, you go to your room." I stood up and pointed the way. "I won't have you throwing a tantrum."

Sonny tensed every muscle in her little body and screamed, her face reddening so deeply I might have worried had I not witnessed this brand of temper from her before.

It was a good thing we didn't have any neighbors, otherwise they might have called the police after hearing such a savage war cry from my sweet daughter.

Minh stopped her song and slid from the bench. I felt her press against my leg.

"Look at your sister, Sonny," I said, putting a hand on the back of Minh's head. "You've upset her."

Sonny, nostrils flared and lips pursed, glanced at Minh. Then she threw her head back and heaved out a sob. Big, round "wah" sounds came from her, and her shoulders jolted up and down with every intake of air.

"Oh, honey," I said, reaching for her. "Shoot. I didn't mean to make you cry."

Then I heard a sniffling from Minh that broke into a quiet weeping.

"Girls." I knelt on the floor. "I'm sorry for yelling. I don't want to be the kind of mom who yells."

Before I knew it, I was joining in on the crying.

As hot as it was, the three of us huddled together until we were all wailed out. By the time Bruce got home, we were on the couch, one girl on either side of me, *Free to Be You and Me* on the record player and dinner entirely unmade.

Good man that he was, he rolled up his sleeves and put together a handful of peanut butter and jellies.

"You're a good mom," he said when he handed me mine, cut into quarters. "These girls are lucky to have you."

He'd used strawberry jam. That was as good as him telling me that he loved me.

CHAPTER Thirty-Nine

Sonny, 1988

When I woke up that morning, I had a smile on my face. Not only was it exactly two weeks before I'd move away to college, it was also the day that Mike was taking me out on what he called a "date of surprises." The only thing he'd tell me was that I needed to wear my prom dress.

Mom and Dad had even agreed to abolish my curfew. Not that we'd be out too late. The whole town of Bear Run turned into a pumpkin when the clock struck midnight, leaving a whole lot of nothing for anyone to do but twiddle their thumbs.

Still, it was shaping up to be the very best day of my whole life.

I sat up in bed and stretched my arms over my head, feeling nothing but excitement for the day.

That excitement passed quickly once we got to work and Mrs. Olds asked Mindy and me to look through the collection of donated taxidermy for an "Animals of Michigan" room. I stared down a particular frozen-in-a-snarl possum for a full five minutes to make sure it didn't move before putting on two layers of work gloves and lifting him out of his box.

Mrs. Olds was conveniently busy elsewhere in the museum. That sneaky stinker.

"This is bogus," I said before squealing when the possum tail touched my skin. "I'm going to die now."

Mindy stood, looking down into a box, her hands up in surrender. "This one's full of birds."

"I hate this room so much."

Out of the corner of my eye I saw a rat scuttle into the room and I screamed, running to the wall and climbing on top of the radiator.

"Rat! Rat!" I yelled, keeping my eyes open and fixed on the thing. "Mindy, get help!"

But Mindy didn't move, and at first I thought it was because she was utterly horrified. Then I realized it was because she was laughing.

I looked back at the rat and noticed that it was stuck—glued?—onto a chunk of wood.

"Seriously?" I shouted, jumping down from the radiator and kicking the rat with the toe of my Keds.

Mrs. Olds came in, hands to her chest and laughing so hard I thought she was going to give herself a heart attack.

"Oh, Sonny," she said. "I'm sorry. I had to."

I opened my mouth to let her know that, no, she didn't when I heard a deep voice calling up the stairs.

"Hello?"

"Is that Grumpy?" Mindy asked.

I nodded and Mrs. Olds stepped to one side to let us out of the room.

"Girls?" Grumpy said when he saw us look over the banister to the landing. "We've got to go."

"What's wrong?" I asked, my heart sinking into my stomach.

"Grumpy?" Mindy said. "What are you doing here?"

"We have to go to the hospital," he said, waving us toward him.

"Is it the baby?" Mindy's face lit up.

"Yeah. Let's go."

"Mrs. Olds," I said, turning to look at the small woman.

"Go," she said. "Go. Don't worry about this. I'll take care of it."

Mindy and I ran side by side down the steps, so fast it was a wonder we made it to the bottom without falling.

Grumpy drove five miles per hour over the speed limit the whole way to the hospital, which, for him, was a pretty serious criminal offense. I wouldn't have doubted if he went down to the police station the next day to turn himself in.

For that day, though, the only important thing was to get us to the hospital.

We all knew even if we didn't say it that the baby wasn't supposed to come for another three weeks at the least. Something had gone wrong. All Grumpy said was that it was something to do with blood pressure.

Honestly, I thought he was saying that the stress of it all was raising *his* blood pressure.

It wasn't until we were in the waiting room that Aunt Dana explained it.

Mom was the one with high blood pressure—it might have even been why her ankles were swollen like balloons. It was best for both of them, Mom and the baby, if the doctor delivered the baby right away.

"Will they be okay?" Mindy asked.

"I think so," Aunt Dana said, taking our hands.

We waited for a long time. Uncle Chris gave me a dime so

I could call Mike. It was a bummer to call off our date, but I wouldn't have left the hospital that evening for anything. Not even to wear my prom dress one more time.

"I'm just disappointed I have to go see *Big Top Pee-wee* by myself," Mike said on the other end of the line.

"We were not going to see that," I said.

"Well, *we* aren't now. But *I* am."

"You're so weird," I said.

"Yeah," he answered. "Hey, do you want me to come to the hospital? I could steal a wheelchair and see how fast I can push you down the hall."

"No." I put my forehead against the top of the pay phone, the metal cool against my skin. "That's all right."

"Okay. Call me tomorrow, though?"

"Sure. Bye."

"Wait, Sonny?"

"Yeah?" I said.

"I just wanted to ask you something." He hesitated. "I, uh . . ."

"Yes?" I felt queasy and lightheaded and wasn't sure I was ready for whatever he was about to say next.

If I'd learned anything from watching Molly Ringwald movies, it was that a boy always picked the weirdest times to ask a girl to go steady with him.

"This is kind of weird to ask on the phone."

"Okay."

Even through the receiver I could hear him pull in a quick breath.

"Well, I was wondering if . . ." he started.

"Wait," I interrupted him. "Don't do it like this."

"Do what?"

"Ask me to be your girlfriend."

"Why not?" he asked.

"Because what if we end up getting married and having kids?" I said. "Do you really want to tell our children that you asked me to be your girlfriend over the phone?"

"We're getting married?"

"Well, we might. Who knows?"

"Okay, I guess."

"So, save it. Ask me later."

"Roger that."

"Goodbye, Mike."

"Bye, Sonny," he said. "I like you."

"I like you too."

It was almost midnight when Dad came into the waiting room. Grammy and Grumpy had already gone home, leaving us to wait with Aunt Dana. The doctor had come out half an hour before to tell us that everybody was all right, but that was all she'd say.

She wanted our dad to be the one to tell us everything.

When Dad came out, he had his hand on his heart like he worried it would burst right out of his chest, and he had to swallow and take a breath before saying anything.

"She's perfect" was all he could get out.

"It's a girl?" I jumped out of my seat and clapped my hands.

"Can we see her?" Mindy asked, moving to the edge of her chair.

Dad answered by putting out both arms and nodding. The two of us fit up against him and he wrapped his arms around our shoulders.

"Aunt Dana?" I said, looking behind me.

"I'll come back tomorrow," she said, getting up and slinging her purse over her shoulder. "Tell your mom I love her, okay?"

I nodded, swallowing past the rock in my throat.

The hallway from the waiting room to where Mom was took forever to walk, and I wanted to break away from under Dad's arm to run and skid around the corner to see them. To see my baby sister.

My legs felt like jelly, though, and I thought I'd probably biff if I tried going fast anyway.

Mom was propped up in her bed, a little bundle in her arms. She glanced at us as we walked in, but only for a second before setting her eyes on the baby again.

"Is she okay?" I asked, stopping a few feet from the bed, suddenly nervous for the baby. "She's so early."

Mom nodded. "She came out screaming her head off, so her lungs are just fine."

"Check this out." Dad sat next to Mom and pulled the knit hat off the baby's tiny head, where a bunch of crinkly red hair stood on end. The baby had her fingers curled, hands held against her cheeks.

"Does she have a name yet?" I asked.

"Holly Anne," Mom said.

It was the most perfect name in the world.

I rushed to the side of the bed opposite Dad and looked into Holly's face. I'd never seen a newborn that was so beautiful, so dainty.

"Mindy?" Dad said, patting a space on the bed. "Come meet your sister."

She hesitated just a second before rushing to the rest of us.

We hovered, feeling the baby's soft skin, peach-fuzzed cheeks, counting fingers and toes even though Mom promised they were all there.

CHAPTER Forty

Bruce, 2013

The old orange cat from down the street usually makes his way to our yard about eleven o'clock every morning. He slinks up to the property line, crouching as he goes and stopping under the cover of a shrub I planted a couple of years ago next to the patio. His focus is sharp and trained on the bird feeder where the goldfinches congregate.

They seem completely unaware of his presence. They go about feasting on the little black nyjer seeds. If I happen to be watching from inside the house, like I am today, the cat sits in wait for a bird to fly close to the ground. When one does, he pounces.

Good thing those finches are savvier than he.

I rap my knuckles against the glass of the patio door, and Buttons—that's what Linda and I call him, at least—freezes, ears swiveling. When I knock again, he turns his head.

"Scat," I say, feeling foolish because there's no way he can hear me.

When he sees that it's just me, he eases up the tension in his body and plops right down on the ground, rolling a little bit in the grass as if in deference to the master of the house.

I can't help but think he's being a little sarcastic.

Cats are weird critters.

"Go on," I say.

"Who are you talking to?" Linda asks from the kitchen. She's got a wooden spoon in her hand, using it to reach something on the top shelf of the cupboard.

"Buttons," I answer. "What are you trying to get?"

"The foil." A box of sandwich bags falls to the floor. "Darn it. Who put these up there?"

"I did." I tilt my head. "That's where they go, right?"

She turns toward me with a look of exasperation that makes me cringe.

"They go in the drawer by the sink," she says. "Where I can reach them."

"Need help?"

"No, I can do it."

Any bit of determination my girls have they got from their mama. I've always been equally impressed and annoyed by how resolved she is.

"Just let me . . ." I start.

But that's when the long box of foil slides to the edge of the cupboard and she grabs it.

"Told ya," she says.

"Yup. And you only knocked down one thing in the process."

"Oh, shush." She pulls out a near-perfect square of foil, tearing it off and forming it around the top of the pumpkin pie she made late last night. "You almost ready to go? We should leave in the next ten minutes or so."

"Okey-doke," I say.

Her sigh is about as deep as they come, and she stills her hands, palms down, on the counter. When she closes her eyes, a tear slides down her cheek.

"Are you crying?" I ask.

It's a stupid question, I know it as soon as it comes out of my mouth. Of course she's crying. I take a step toward her and put two fingers under her chin, lifting as gently as I can.

When she lets her eyes focus right into mine, my heart skips a beat.

I don't think I'll ever get used to how beautiful she is.

"It's a different kind of Thanksgiving, isn't it?" I ask.

She pinches her eyes closed again and sniffles. "Yes."

As far back as I can remember, Mom hosted dinner at her house, insisting on the whole crew being in attendance regardless of any other plans they might want to make. Even with all the leaves in her dining room table, we still had to set up a couple of card tables to make sure we had a seat for everybody.

She'd put the ladies to work, directing all the jobs from basting the turkey to opening the cans of olives for the relish tray. With all those women buzzing around the kitchen, slicing the canned cranberry sauce and standing on the step stool to find the gravy boat, my mother was in her element.

All the men would do their part to stay out of the way by watching the Macy's Thanksgiving Day parade and performing feats of strength like cracking a macadamia nut.

We, of course, would switch over to the Lions game, hoping that Mom would let us get in the first half before calling us to the table.

Matthews Thanksgiving was the most chaotic, stressful, exhausting day of the year. For the ladies, at least. Especially Linda. Boy, my mother never let her off easy on those days. She worked her hard, wore her out. And, no matter what, nothing Linda did was ever quite good enough.

I sort of thought it would be a relief for the day to not be the same old thing.

"I'm going to miss it," she whispers. "Isn't that crazy?"

"Nah." I lean forward and kiss her forehead.

I get it.

This year Sonny and Mike surprised the girls with a trip to Florida to see their other set of grandparents. Zach and Holly decided to drive across state to spend the day with his brother in LaFontaine.

Linda offered to host the rest of us here, but Dad said it would be too hard to get Mom in the car. She's staying put within the walls of the retirement home these days for better or for worse. So the plan was for us—including Chris and Dana—to go to them and be their guests in the dining room there.

We were able to reserve a table for the seven of us.

This morning, though, Mindy called to beg off, claiming that she's just not up to it.

It's our first Thanksgiving in over forty years without our kids.

It's the first of my whole life to not be celebrated in my child-hood home.

I'm a man given to occasional fits of nostalgia. Today it's hitting pretty hard.

I've had better meals in my life, but the kitchen staff at the retirement home did the best they could with the compressed turkey breast and powdered mashed potatoes. Well, and I was glad Dad snuck a contraband saltshaker in his jacket pocket.

It's the simple gifts we sometimes find ourselves most thankful for.

We're back in Mom and Dad's apartment, where Linda and Dana pass out little plates of pie with Cool Whip dolloped on top. Boy, does it taste good. There's nothing like pumpkin pie.

Mom's pulled up to the small drop-leaf table, trying to work the fork with her left hand, her right sitting limp in her lap.

We know of at least two separate strokes that have hit her over the past month. Her doctor wonders if maybe she's had a few more that we don't know about.

There are some hard decisions coming our way.

I always knew there would be a time when I'd have to face losing my folks. Still, it aches to think about not having them. How fortunate I am that I've still got them even at my age.

Dad's got the Lions game on, and we're hoping against hope that they can pull it off against the Packers. So far, so good.

When they score a touchdown, Dad claps his hands and hollers and I expect Mom to scold him for being too loud. She doesn't, though, and I turn to see what she's up to.

"It's all right, Mom," Linda says. "These things happen."

I've never heard her use that name for my mother before, and it surprises me.

She kneels and I see the piece of pie, whipped cream side down, on the floor.

"I'll get you another piece," Dana says. "It's no trouble."

Mom just shakes her head, her lips held in a tight line.

One of the only places open on Thanksgiving Day is the little movie theater in downtown Bear Run. It's the sort of place that only has room to show one film at a time, and this week it's *Frozen*.

It's usually the kind of movie I save to watch with my grand-daughters, but today's been hard for both Linda and me. So, I buy us a couple of tickets and even spring for popcorn and pop. We've got the entire theater all to ourselves and sit in the smack-dab middle.

And since it's just the two of us, I don't get embarrassed when I tear up.

Boy, when that Olaf tells Anna that she's worth melting for, I lose it.

Good thing I've got that old hanky in my pocket. It always comes in handy.

"I think that's the best princess movie I've ever seen," Linda says when I open the passenger side door for her.

"You think so, huh?" I ask.

"I'm going to have that song stuck in my head for the rest of the year, and I'm not upset about it at all." Her eyebrows furrow. "Is that your phone?"

"Yeah," I say. "It was going off through the whole movie."

"Well, what if it was an emergency?"

"I figured they'd call you too." I reach into my pocket for my phone, and the screen is lit up with a message from Mindy.

It's just two sentences.

Call me. I've found something.

CHAPTER Forty-One

Linda, 1975

All summer long, the radio deejays seemed to have favored Captain and Tennille, playing "Love Will Keep Us To-gether" every opportunity they could. I, for one, had had more than enough of that song and cringed every time I heard the bouncy bass line at the beginning.

Sonny, however, didn't get sick of it, proclaiming that it was her favorite song in the world and singing every single word at the top of her lungs. Minh bobbed her head and watched Sonny's dramatic dancing.

So, when the song came on in the car on the way home from Kmart, I didn't switch stations, as much as I wanted to. And I told Sonny to be careful not to move too wildly in the back seat. We'd just spent far too much on school supplies and I was feel-ing a little on edge. The last thing I needed was to be distracted by her arms flailing in the rearview mirror.

All I kept thinking about was how I'd need to stretch the groceries a little tighter that week and drive a little less to save on gas. So preoccupied was I that I didn't notice the black car in the driveway until I pulled in behind it.

I turned down the radio and shushed Sonny when she complained about missing the end of the song.

"It'll be on again in half an hour," I said.

"Who's that?" Sonny asked, leaning forward against the front seat and pointing toward our porch.

"I don't know, but don't point, please," I said, putting the car into park. "He's probably just selling something. Stay here, all right?"

A man stood on the porch in a very official black suit and tie, a clipboard in hand.

Getting out of the car, I bemoaned that I was wearing a well-loved John Lennon T-shirt and scrubby bellbottoms and that my hair was all a tangle from driving with the windows down. I ran my hands over it, hoping to tame the wildness out of it but not sure I did much good.

"Can I help you?" I asked.

"Mrs. Matthews?" he said from where he stood, consulting the clipboard.

"Yes."

"I'm from Immigration Services. You might remember getting a letter from us." He looked up, cocking an eyebrow in quite a severe and unwelcoming way.

"I'm afraid I don't know which letter that is," I said. "It was from Immigration?"

"You should have received it last month," he said. "Informing you that I'd be coming to talk about the immigration status of one Pham Quyen Minh."

I glanced over my shoulder to see the girls watching me from the car. When I lifted my hand to wave at them, I noticed that

I was shaking. I shoved my hands into my back pockets so the man in the suit wouldn't see me trembling.

"I'm sorry, I don't recall a letter like that," I said, trying to sound more confident than I felt.

He jotted something down on the paper clipped to his board and made a humming sound that told me he didn't believe me.

"At any rate," he said, still writing, "the legality of Operation Babylift is in question and we're attempting to reunite the children with their parents."

"Excuse me?"

"We learned in May that some of the children were not surrendered to the orphanages willingly by their parents and therefore were displaced unlawfully," he said, glancing up at the last word. "And so they need to be returned."

I tried to swallow but my throat had gone completely dry.

"I think I need to call my husband." I pressed the palm of my hand into the middle of my chest, feeling my heartbeat speed up.

"I'm not here to take the child. Not today." His eyebrow lowered and his face softened, even if just a little. "Ma'am, you need to understand. If any of these kids were taken from parents who wanted them, we've got a real problem on our hands. Nobody wants to support state-sanctioned kidnapping. Wouldn't you agree?"

"Right." It felt as if my heart dropped all the way to my toes. "What do you need me to do?"

"It's more of what *I* need to do today." He lowered the clipboard and slipped the pen into his shirt pocket. "I'll need to get her fingerprints and take a few photos of her. That's all for now."

"Then what?"

"We'll review her paperwork . . ."

"Good luck," I interrupted. "We were given hardly anything for her."

"And if there's a question about her status, we'll do some digging," he said. "If there's any hint of doubt, we'll ask you to pause any and all filings for adoption."

"If there isn't?"

"Then you may proceed."

"And we have no say in the matter?"

"None whatsoever," he said. Then he lowered his voice. "I know this is scary, Mrs. Matthews, but we must do what's right."

I nodded.

"Now, if we can go inside, I'll get my things from the car. I can be out of your hair real fast. Okay?"

"All right."

I got the girls out of the car and sent Sonny to the backyard. Miraculously, she didn't argue or ask any questions.

The man sat beside Minh at the table, and she didn't take her eyes off his face while he rolled her fingertips on the ink pad and then pressed them onto a sheet of paper. He took half a dozen pictures of her at different angles and she didn't smile, even when he tried to make her laugh.

He was out of our hair fast, as promised.

I, however, held my teeth clenched for the rest of the day.

It stormed that night. Buckets of rain fell, gathering into a pond at the low spot in our backyard, and I was for once glad we didn't have a basement that would surely get flooded by such a downpour. Lightning sliced the sky, followed by cracks of thunder that boomed so that I felt each one all the way through my body.

Sonny sat as close to the living room window as we'd allow, cheering with each lightning bolt that lit up the sky as if it was a Fourth of July fireworks show.

My fearless girl. I wondered what plans God had for her. Whatever it was, there was no doubt in my mind that Sonny would charge in, taking on the world.

On the other hand, there was Minh, curled up on Bruce's lap, eyes shut tight and hands—fingers still stained from the ink earlier in the day—covering her ears.

My timid girl. The plans God had for her were no less spectacular. Whatever they were, I was confident that she would rise to them.

Another big boomer thundered and the electricity cut out, leaving us in pitch dark.

"I'll get the candles," I said, feeling my way to the kitchen.

Pulling open the junk drawer, I ran my hands over odds and ends—cookie cutter, twist ties, a couple of ketchup packets—until I felt the rough-sided box of matches.

"Daddy?" Minh said. "No light?"

"No light," Bruce echoed her. "But it's still okay."

I fumbled to get the box open and pick out just one match without spilling them all over the floor. Dragging the match head across the striker, sparks flashing from the friction, I breathed in the sulfur smell.

The little flame lit up the whole kitchen, and I touched the fire to the wick of a candle I kept on the counter.

From the living room I heard Sonny start to sing, doing her very best Toni Tennille impression. Bruce joined in and I heard the tiniest giggle that could only have belonged to Minh.

Oh, this little family of mine.

I carried the candle to the coffee table just in time for another chorus. When Sonny told me to sing along, I did if only to make Minh happy.

There wasn't a way of knowing what would happen the next day or the next month. I couldn't guess what would happen with Immigration.

All I could do was hold on to that moment, the sound of Sonny's voice and the way Minh's eyes crinkled in the corners when she smiled.

I held on for dear life.

CHAPTER Forty-Two

Sonny, 1988

I'd never, ever really enjoyed holding babies. They were squirmy and fussy and totally boring. Besides, they were kind of stinky and gross. So, whenever somebody offered to let me hold their baby at church, I usually pretended that I had to go to the bathroom or said I had a sore throat so I could get out of it.

I wasn't a baby person.

Well, that was until I met Holly.

When I picked her up it didn't matter if she was screaming her head off, she'd calm right down, fitting perfectly into the crook of my arm. She had all these adorable little faces she'd make, and I couldn't help but laugh at her.

Sometimes when I'd talk to her, she'd open her eyes and look right at my face.

Mom said that it was just gas, but I swore she was smiling at me half the time.

After work, I totally drove way over the speed limit so I could get home faster and see Holly. Mindy yelled at me to slow down, but I ignored her. I didn't want to miss any time I had with my baby sister.

That day, I paced the family room, holding on to Holly after Mom finished feeding her. She was wrapped up in a blanket just like a little burrito, and when Mom looked away, I loosened it so her arms could be free.

"Mom," I said, "why are her hands black?"

"Oh." Mom looked up from her lunch, bleary eyed. "Huh?"

"Is this ink?"

"I tried cleaning it off." She shrugged.

"What, did she, like, break the law and have to get finger-printed or something?"

"Who had to get fingerprinted?" Mindy asked, rounding the corner into the room.

"The baby," I answered.

"It's not a big deal," Mom said. "They took her handprint at the doctor's office today. That's all."

"Didn't they do that at the hospital?" I asked, grabbing a baby wipe and rubbing it against Holly's hand.

"It got smudged."

"I remember when someone came to get my fingerprints," Mindy said. "Remember that, Mom?"

"How do you remember that?" Mom asked. "You were so little."

"I remember a lot more than you know."

"Was that the guy in the black suit?" I asked. "I thought he was there to arrest you, Mom."

"Oh, you did?" she asks, her mouth full of ham sandwich.

"Why did they need those anyway?"

"You know what," she said. "I haven't thought about that in a really long time. It had something to do with a few kids from Vietnam who weren't supposed to have been brought here. They were trying to get it all sorted out and return those kids to their families."

"Are you serious?" I asked. "And they thought Mindy had a family over there still?"

"I don't really know." Mom pulled the tomato slice off her sandwich and dropped it onto her plate. "We never heard from them again, so we just assumed everything was fine."

"Like, they just dropped it?" I asked. "And you never followed up?"

"I guess so."

"So, wait." I turned toward Mindy. "Do you still have family over there?"

Mindy got her deer-in-the-headlights look she had whenever someone put her on the spot, and she pushed her mouth all to one side.

But before I could press Mindy for more information, Holly tensed her whole body and made the cutest little grunting sound.

Well, it was cute until I realized what she was doing.

Who knew a baby would poop that much? Gag me!

Holly went down for a nap and so did Mom, leaving Mindy and me to fold the baskets of clean laundry that had piled up. I didn't mind, really. It was actually kind of fun to look at all the tiny clothes.

"I had a mother in Vietnam," Mindy said.

"What?" I asked, looking up from a little onesie with ducks on it.

"I remember my Vietnamese mom." Mindy bit her lower lip. "I mean, not what her face looked like or anything. For some reason I can't remember that. But I know she was alive when I went to live at the orphanage."

She grabbed a cloth diaper and folded it into quarters.

"Was she nice?" I asked.

Mindy nodded.

"She had this hat that I used to like to wear. It was kind of shaped like a pyramid." She used her hands to draw a triangle over her head. "I have this memory of her running with me, like she was carrying me."

"You mean, she was running from something?"

Mindy nodded.

"What was it?"

"No idea," she said. "It's a little foggy. You know? But when she was running, I dropped her hat, and someone stepped on it. Then she took me to the orphanage. I thought she was sending me away because I broke her hat."

"But that wasn't why, right?" I asked.

"No." She shrugged. "I'm sure it was because she wanted me to be safe."

Through the baby monitor we heard Holly stir, and both Mindy and I held our breath, waiting to see if she'd start screaming. She didn't and we both relaxed our shoulders.

"Do you miss her?" I asked after a few minutes.

"My Vietnamese mom?" Mindy wrinkled up her forehead. "Sometimes."

She got up and grabbed a stack of baby undershirts to put away upstairs in Holly's room. When she didn't come back down, I went to see what was up.

The door to our bedroom was only closed partway, and I looked through the gap to see Mindy sitting on the edge of her bed, her back toward me. My sister who hardly ever cried was sniffling and her shoulders bobbed up and down. Her fists clenched and unclenched on the bedspread.

Holly squawked and Mindy turned at the sound, seeing me looking in.

"Are you okay?" I whispered, letting myself in and making my way to sit with her.

She closed her eyes and nodded.

"Someday we'll find her," I said. "I'll help you."

"It might be impossible," she said, resting her head against my shoulder.

I reached my arm around her and leaned my head against hers.

"Maybe," I said. "But at least we can try. Right?"

"I guess so."

"And once we find her, we'll go meet her," I said. "Together."

"We will?"

"Like I'd let you go there without me."

We sat like that for a few minutes while I tried to think of something really smart and really compassionate to say. I even ran through all the memory verses I'd learned in Sunday school, trying to find just the right one for that moment.

But all I could think about was the cross-stitch that Mom had hanging in the family room. Aunt Dana gave it to her one Christmas, and it was pretty much the cheesiest thing I'd ever seen. It had these cutesy little baby birds in a nest and a mama bird with her wings stretched out over them like an umbrella, shielding them from the abnormally large, sky-blue raindrops.

He shall cover thee with his feathers, was stitched above the birds. Then below them, *And under his wings shalt thou rest.*

When I heard the verse in my head, it was in an English accent. That always happened when I read the King James Version.

I tightened my hold on Mindy.

"Hey, Sonny," she said.

"Yeah?" I said.

"You're hurting me a little."

"That's all right."

I didn't ease up.

After spending so much of my life trying to protect her, trying to fix everything for her, I realized that it wasn't my job. It never had been.

I wasn't the mama bird in the cross-stitch.

I was one of her chicks.

CHAPTER Forty-Three

Bruce, 2013

W hen Dale died, I didn't necessarily lose my faith in God. It was more like I gave up believing that he cared. If he had, then he wouldn't have allowed my brother to die. He could have protected Dale, but he didn't.

The image that I'd kept of God holding us in the palm of his hand didn't seem to be true to me anymore.

It wasn't until I became a father that I weighed the burden of protecting my own kids and realized I couldn't shoulder it alone. I'd need a whole lot of help.

I made the choice to suspend my disbelief.

I've seen shimmers of God's interest every once in a while ever since.

Sitting in front of the computer screen, I can't help but think what a holy moment I'm in, Mindy standing behind me and Linda in a chair next to me.

"See?" Mindy asks. "Right there."

On the screen are two photographs, side by side. The one is of little Minh at the orphanage in Vietnam, holding the sign with her name. The second is of a group of kids, arms around each other. A few smile or flash a peace sign. But those kids don't hold my attention. There's only one child in that picture that has my heart skipping all over the place.

"It's me," Mindy whispers, pointing at the one off to the side.

Even in black and white, the impetigo marks on her face stand out. It is, without a shadow of doubt, her.

"How did you find this?" Linda asks.

"This boy," Mindy says, pointing to one of the kids holding his fingers in a *V*, "saw my post and emailed me this picture. We were there together, I guess."

"Oh, honey."

"He said these were taken at an orphanage in Thu Duc right outside Saigon," she says. "Well, it's Ho Chi Minh City now. Anyway, he gave me a few phone numbers to try for the orphanage and an email address."

"The orphanage is still open?" I ask.

"Well, it's changed hands a few times, but they've kept some of their records." She leans back in her chair. "It can't hurt to see if they've got anything that can help me."

"Was he able to find his birth family?" Linda points at the boy.

"Yes." Mindy nods. "He visited them last year. He has all these pictures from his trip. It's incredible."

She clicks on a few links so we can see. Pictures taken through the airplane window as it landed on a runway lined with palm trees. One of the man approaching a cluster of people and another of a woman pulling him into a deep embrace. And on and on.

He even posted a video of him touring his childhood home.

"I remember this," he says several times, pointing to this or that.

His experience has me feeling a whole lot more hopeful than Paula's documentary that we watched on Halloween.

"You'll need to learn some Vietnamese," Linda says.

"There's a woman who gives lessons over Skype," she says. "I've had a few sessions already."

"Good for you, honey."

"Are you going to call that number?" I ask.

Mindy nods. "I did right before I came over here."

I hold my breath, waiting for her to say more.

"And?" Linda asks.

"They said they'd let me know if they find anything." She shrugs. "So, now I wait."

Linda's the kind of woman to start watching Christmas movies as soon as the Thanksgiving leftovers are packed away in the fridge. I guess that's better than getting up in the wee hours of the next morning to stand elbow-to-elbow with other shoppers at the mall.

We pop *A Christmas Story* into the DVD player and the three of us settle in.

I'm glad Mindy agreed to stick around for a little bit. It feels more like a holiday with her here.

Right about the time when Santa tells Ralphie that he'll shoot his eye out, Mindy's phone rings. I hit pause on the movie, and we all look at the screen of the phone.

"This is it," Mindy whispers, covering her mouth. "I'm kind of scared."

"Answer it, honey," Linda says. "We'll be right here, won't we, Bruce?"

"As always," I answer.

Mindy swipes on the screen to answer and gets up from the couch, headed toward the kitchen. On our end we just hear a couple of "uh-huhs" and "I understands." She jots a few notes on a tablet of paper on the counter.

"Yes, thank you," she says before hanging up.

I hold my breath, waiting for her to tell us what's up. But I let it out when she turns, leaning back against the edge of the counter and tapping the phone on her forehead.

"Mindy?" Linda says. "Okay?" She tilts her head toward Mindy, her way of saying we should get up off our rears and go to our daughter. We do, and Linda uses her hand to smooth Mindy's hair.

"What did they say?" she asks.

"According to their records, her name is Hoa," Mindy says, not turning toward us. "She told whoever filled out the paperwork that she was a house cleaner in Saigon."

Linda smiles. "It's something. More than you knew ten minutes ago. Right?"

That's my babe. Always seeing those sunny sides.

"Maybe." Mindy turns and drops her phone next to the pad of paper. "I don't know. I'm not really sure how I'm feeling right now. Maybe I should go home and sleep on this. I can think about it in the morning."

"Makes good sense," I say.

"Are you okay to drive?" Linda asks. "You could just stay here."

"I'll be fine. I need to be alone with this, I think." She sighs. "Is that all right?"

"Of course it is, sweetheart," Linda says. "Don't worry about us, okay?"

"Thanks, Mom."

She puts on her coat and grabs her purse. Linda makes sure she takes a piece of pumpkin pie with her, handing it to her before pulling her into a tight hug.

"I love you, Mindy," she says. "We'll find her, okay?"

Mindy nods and kisses her mama on the cheek.

"I'll walk you out," I say, shoving my arms into a jacket.

The night's gone icy cold, and I know everything will be frosted over come morning. Soon enough we'll have piles and piles of snow to contend with. Well, that is if we have the kind of winter I prefer.

"Fiona's is open tomorrow," I say. "We can pick you up for breakfast if you want."

"Can I call you when I wake up and let you know?"

"That's fine."

She opens her car door but doesn't get in right away.

"I shouldn't get my hopes up," she says. "It's probably best if I manage my expectations better. I might not find anything. I need to prepare my heart for that."

"But you did find something, didn't you? You've got her name. That's a start." I put my hands into the front pockets of my jeans. "We've made progress."

"There could be a hundred thousand women named Hoa in Vietnam."

"Well, that may be true, but don't stop hoping yet. All right?"

"I'll try not to."

"This is just a little dip," I say. "Not a crash landing."

I watch her back out of the driveway, and I follow her tail-lights until she turns right on the road that'll take her to her apartment.

Emily Dickinson said that hope is a little bird, singing her heart out during a terrible storm. Even on cold nights like this one, that feathered friend trills on.

One thing Emily didn't say—had she even known?—was how all that singing got the attention of the one who formed that bird by hand.

It's the nature of small birds to sing their little hearts out.

And it's the nature of God to hear them.

CHAPTER Forty-Four

Linda, 1975

I hadn't kept much from my rockstar days. But deep in the closet I shared with Bruce was a getup I used to wear when my band was playing a set with a bunch of Janis Joplin songs. It was a flouncy blouse that I put together with a knit vest and a micro-mini skirt that drew all the wrong kind of attention.

It was what I was wearing the day I met Bruce.

He, of course, paid me the right kind of attention. I didn't catch him peeking at my legs at all that first time we talked. Instead, he looked me right in the eye.

What a guy.

It pleased me to no end when he stuck around at the coffee shop until our show that night, and when I sang "Piece of My Heart"—my version a more vampy, smooth one than Janis's—I tried not to look in his direction because I knew I'd crack, I was so nervous.

I'd long ago sold all the other ridiculous clothing to a friend who was heading out to LA to seek her big break. Every feather boa and wide-brimmed hat went. My leather pants that I'd saved every penny to buy and my go-go boots too.

But that outfit I couldn't so easily part with.

The girls were outside and Bruce wasn't due home for another hour, so I pulled the whole ensemble out of the closet, curious to see if it might still fit.

Thankfully, that kind of top was more than a little forgiving and didn't cling to anything I'd rather it not. The skirt, on the other hand, I couldn't get up and over the hips that I'd acquired while pregnant with Sonny.

It was just as well.

Taking off that skirt—which required a lot of pulling and praying—and hanging it all back up, I felt such relief that I'd let all of that go when Bruce and I started our little family.

It was a fair bargain for all I got in exchange.

Besides, I'd always have music.

I slipped on my soft jeans and an old T-shirt of Bruce's, making my way to the kitchen.

I had a tuna noodle casserole to get in the oven.

Sonny insisted on checking and double-checking her paper bag full of school supplies. She simply would not get ready for bed without making sure that every last thing was at the ready for the first day of school.

"First grade is a big deal," she told Minh. "This is the year we learn to read."

Minh nodded and smiled as if her sister was saying the most wonderful things.

"Okay. It's all there," Sonny said, getting up from the floor and crossing the room. "Good night."

"I'll be right there to tuck you in," Bruce said.

"You don't have to do that anymore, Dad." She put her hands on her hips. "I'm in first grade now."

"Is that so?"

"Unless you *really* want to," she said. "Then it's all right."

"I really want to, honey."

"That's fine." She turned toward the bathroom. "Come on, Mindy. Time to brush our teeth."

The two of them went together, Sonny giving instructions the whole time.

Bruce lifted his eyebrows at me, and the only thing I could think of to say was, "First grade is a big deal."

It really was.

CHAPTER Forty-Five

Sonny, 1988

Mrs. Olds baked a batch of brownies for my last day at the museum, and she refused to let us lift a finger other than to eat, claiming that this was our official office party. She'd even brought kazoos.

"Don't worry," she said. "You're still getting paid."

She tossed a handful of confetti in the air when she said it, and I knew Mindy would have to sweep that up the next week.

"When I was your age, I longed to leave home again," she said. "If you'll remember, I was already a divorcée by the time I turned eighteen."

Mindy and I nodded, our mouths full of brownie.

"I was certain that I'd become an old maid." She scratched her head. "Although, technically, I don't know that a divorced woman would be considered a spinster. Hm. Anyway, I got a job watching the Huebert children. Of course, they were the very great-grandchildren of the original Mr. Huebert. Would you believe that they still lived in this very house?"

"Did you have quarters here?" Mindy asked.

"Oh no. Nothing like that," Mrs. Olds answered. "I just came to sit with them during the days. Their nursery was upstairs in the critter room."

I shuddered just thinking about the stuffed beasts on display up there.

"They had a map on the wall of the entire world," Mrs. Olds said. "I'd stand looking at it, trying to pronounce the names of all the different countries and dreaming of traveling from one corner of the earth to the next."

She pressed her fingertip into a crumb of brownie on her plate, lifting it to her mouth. She closed her eyes and sighed. They really were that yummy.

"Well, I didn't last long in that job," she went on. "I got fired when the stock market crashed."

"Bummer," I said.

"It was just as well. Those children were monstrous." She pushed her hands together. "Anyway, to keep the story short, I eventually met and married Mr. Olds, who just happened to be a pilot. He made good on his promise to show me the world."

"Where did you go?" Mindy asked before polishing off the rest of her brownie.

"All over," Mrs. Olds answered. "I'll tell you what. I always considered myself to be a brave woman until the first time I got on an airplane. I just kept thinking about poor Amelia Earhart and how she went missing in her plane. I was certain that would happen to me too."

"But it didn't," I said. "You were all right."

"Obviously." Mrs. Olds winked at me. "Life requires so much courage out of us, doesn't it? Even putting our feet on the floor in the morning is an act of bravery, don't you think so?"

"Well, I'm not very brave," Mindy said.

"My dear," Mrs. Olds said. "Give yourself some credit."

Then she plopped another brownie on each of our plates.

Bear Run had only one cemetery, and it was way out in the boonies. Not too far from where we lived when Mindy and I were kids. On one side were the oldest graves with cracked, sun-baked tombstones that were nearly impossible to read. On the other end were the more recently departed of the town. The rows on that side were straighter, and some of the planters had flowers in them, even if they were dried up after a full summer of no rain.

Dad had told me that Grammy and Grumpy already had their plots picked out and paid for, even if they wouldn't need them for a really long time. At least I hoped they wouldn't.

I wondered if, someday, Mom and Dad would buy a spot there too. It gave me the creeps to think about them dying.

It wasn't like I was the kind of teen to moon around, reading Poe and contemplating death all the time. It was just, like, when I drove past the cemetery I was reminded that everybody would die someday.

It made me think of a John Donne poem I memorized for my English class. Like, it was kind of depressing but sort of beautiful at the same time. All about how nobody is an island but instead part of a continent made up of everyone. Each time a person dies, it matters to everyone else.

I turned the El down the road that would take Mins and me to the cemetery, even if it was really far out of the way, and thought of the last lines of that poem.

> *Therefore, send not to know*
> *For whom the bell tolls,*
> *It tolls for thee.*

Metallica so totally ripped off John Donne.

"Why are we going this way?" Mindy asked.

"I just wanted to go for a ride through the cemetery," I answered.

"Um, why?"

"You're going to drive," I answered, slowing down where the dirt road got rough with craters.

"No, I'm not."

"Yeah, you are."

"I don't even have a permit," she said, shaking her head. "What if I hit something?"

"Well, fortunately for you, you can't hurt any of the people who live here," I said. "And you can't break this car. Trust me. I've tried."

"I don't know about this, Sonny."

"Are you scared?"

"Yes. Duh."

"All the more reason to."

I pulled into the narrow lane of the cemetery, glad nobody else was there. It was pretty iffy, giving my sister a driving lesson there, and I knew some people would think it was disrespectful.

I parked beside the gigantic Huebert family monument.

"Ready?" I asked.

"I don't want to do this," Mindy said.

"Mins, life is too short to avoid everything that scares you."

"It's a completely rational fear, Sonny." She crossed her arms.

"You saw those videos in driver's ed. People die in car crashes every day."

"Yeah, but more people *don't*." I got out of my side and around to hers, pushing her across the seat and behind the steering wheel. "Now drive."

The driving path in the cemetery wasn't paved, but was straight and flat, and Mindy took it at maybe ten miles per hour. Whenever there was a bend or a turn, she slammed on the brake before spinning the steering wheel. After the first five minutes of white-knuckling it, she relaxed.

By the end of the first time around, she was smiling.

She never even came close to grazing a gravestone.

When we got home there was a letter from Eric on the counter, and Mindy ran up to our room to read it, locking the door behind her. The only reason I didn't pound on the door for her to let me in was that Holly was sleeping and Mom threatened to banish me if I woke her up.

After ten minutes of me begging in whispers to be let in, Mindy finally opened the door, a goofy smile on her face. She handed me the one-page letter.

"You can read it if you want," she said, her voice dreamy and both hands resting on her chest, right over her heart.

I skimmed the note. It was mostly about how beautiful she was—which was true—and how he couldn't stop thinking about her—which was corny—and how he only ever wanted to be with her—which was gag-worthy.

Blah, blah, blah.

But then, at the very bottom of the page were the three words that every girl wanted to hear from a boy.

I love you.

"He loves you?" I whispered, wanting to yell but afraid of banishment. "What in the world?"

"I know," Mindy said, practically swooning onto her bed.

"Do you love him?" I plopped down beside her.

"I don't think so. At least not yet." She took the letter from me, folding it and putting it on her bedside table. "I guess I like him, though."

"Okay." I pulled my legs up under me. "Why?"

"Well, he's nice and he likes *Star Trek*," she said.

I resisted calling him a nerd because I was a good sister.

"We have a lot in common." She swallowed and looked down at her comforter. "He's the only person I've ever met who really knows what it's like to be me."

The mood in the room changed with that last sentence she said.

It wasn't about me and I knew it. So I tried to ignore my hurt feelings for a couple of minutes at least.

"I just mean that he understands what it's like to be adopted," she said. "I didn't mean . . ."

"It's okay," I said.

"He was a baby when he was adopted, so he doesn't remember Korea or anything. Still."

"I get it," I said, even if I didn't really understand. Not totally. "So, do you want to go out with him?"

"I guess." She shrugged. "I kind of wish we could just be friends for a little while longer, though. It's scary."

"Why?"

"Because he might break my heart."

"Not if you break his first." I smiled at her.

It was nice when she smiled back.

She grabbed a piece of paper and her favorite pen from her desk to write him back. Just to tell him she was ready to be his girlfriend. When she'd finished, she asked me to read it, like to make sure it all made sense and that it wasn't too cheesy. It was fine, even if she did quote Spock once toward the end.

What tripped me up, though, was how she signed the letter.

"Your girlfriend, Minh?" I read out loud. "Does he call you that?"

She lowered her eyes and nodded like she felt guilty about it.

"It's not bad," I said. "I mean, it's your name."

"I know," she said. "Do you think it's weird?"

"No." I paused for a second. "It's just that I thought you liked being called Mindy."

"I guess it's fine," she said. "It's not like I have a choice, though."

"What do you mean?"

"You decided that everybody would call me Mindy, not Minh." She shrugged. "I just went along with it to make you happy."

"Well, that's dumb."

She scowled and shook her head, rolling her lips between her teeth like she was trying to keep her yapper from saying the wrong thing.

"I'm sorry, okay?" I said. "I was, what, five? I didn't realize at the time that I was wrecking your life."

"You don't have to be so dramatic about it," she said. "It's fine. I'm not mad about it."

I thought about storming out of the room and stomping down the stairs. That, however, would have been dramatic, just proving Mindy's point.

"Me being Mindy is easier for everyone, I guess," she said.

"But it's nice to have one person in the world call me by my real name."

From the other room Holly cooed and Mom started singing a little song to her.

I looked back at Mindy's letter and the way she signed it at the bottom. Even if I lived until I was a hundred years old, I would never be able to understand what it was like to be adopted. I'd never know how it felt to look different from the rest of my family. There was no way I'd ever get it.

But Eric did.

And I'd just have to be okay with her giving him a part of her life that she'd never be able to share with me.

It wasn't about me. Not even a little.

"Your letter's fine," I said.

"Should I have said that I love him back?" she asked.

I told her to hold off on that for now.

A girl could only do just so many brave things in one day.

CHAPTER Forty-Six

Bruce, 2013

Mom fell again this morning. When Dad called, he said this might be *it*. I sat with him in the hospital waiting room until the doctors and nurses finished all manner of testing and got Mom set up in a room.

Their best guess is that it was another stroke, probably her biggest yet. She's unresponsive, and this time around we can't say she's just being stubborn.

Still, Dad talks to her, whispering pleas for her to open her eyes, to see who's here to see her.

"It's Brucie," he says, using the name they called me when I was little. "You wanna say hi to him?"

When she doesn't move, not even a fluttering eyelash, he reaches up and tries his best to fix her hair.

"I'll have to ask her nurse for a comb," he mutters. Then he looks toward me. "You think they've got some here?"

"I'm sure they have a whole drawerful," I say.

He nods as if satisfied, and gives her bangs one last swipe to the left. I don't tell him that she's always worn them to the right.

He's trying.

We each find a chair and settle in, watching her and letting the time slide by.

Just about suppertime Dad tells everybody to go get some grub. Everybody but Dana and me. With most of our family vacated, the room feels empty, colder. The sounds of the machines hooked up to Mom are more pronounced. There's a click over here, a whooshing over there. Every couple of seconds something beeps.

It's uncomfortable, that discordant song. When Dad starts to talk, I'm relieved.

"I know we've talked about this before," he says. "But I just wanted to remind you of your mother's wishes."

He glances at Mom and clears his throat.

"Her advance directive?" Dana asks.

Dad nods.

"We remember," I say.

Mom's made it clear that, at the end, she doesn't want doctors keeping her alive longer than she has to be. Dana puts her arm around my shoulder, and the kindness is enough to undo me a little.

"Hey, hey, son," Dad says. "I didn't mean to make you cry."

"I know it." I rub the meat of my hand under my eyes. "It's just hard."

Dana pulls me closer to her, wrapping her free arm around me in a sideways hug.

"If she has to go, it'll be okay," Dad says. "We'll be okay. Won't we?"

"Yeah, Dad," Dana says. "We will."

He takes Mom's hand and leans down, pressing it against his lips.

Then he returns it to the bed so carefully.

Over the next few days, we all take shifts at the hospital with Mom. Nobody can stand the thought of her being in that room by herself, so somebody's there at any time of day and night.

Thank goodness the nurses keep the coffeepot going at all times in a hospitality room at the end of the ward.

Last night all three of my girls kept watch, and when I step into the room first thing in the morning, it looks like they've had a bit of a party. The trash can is full of candy wrappers, pop cans, and an empty box of pizza sits on the counter in the corner.

"You didn't save me a slice?" I ask.

"Sorry," Holly answers. "Staying up all night makes a girl hungry."

"I bet." I turn toward Mom. "Any change?"

Sonny shakes her head. "The nurse said her vitals are steady."

"That's good, I guess." I feel my coat pocket, pulling out a cell phone. "Oh, Mindy. You left this on the charger at home."

"I know," she says, taking it. "Thanks for bringing it."

She yawns and clicks on the screen, typing with her thumbs.

"Why don't the three of you go home and get a little rest," I say, sloughing off my coat and hanging it on a hook by the door. "Grumpy'll be here soon."

"I'm in no hurry," Sonny says, checking the clock on the wall. "Evie's probably on her third living room performance of 'Let It Go' by now. I'd bet she'll have at least a dozen more to do by lunch."

"It's a great song," Holly says.

"You want to go be her audience for a couple of hours?"

"I'd love to."

"Guys," Mindy says, staring at her phone. "I just got an email from Vietnam."

When she looks up, her red-rimmed eyes are wide and there's just a hint of a smile in the corners of her mouth.

"What does it say?" Holly asks. "Is it from your birth mom?"

"I haven't opened it yet." She shakes her head and then swallows hard. "I'm nervous and excited and terrified."

Holly leans over and gives her a peck on the cheek. "We're here."

"I know." Mindy makes the screen dark. "And I love you for it. But I kind of need to read this by myself."

"We get it," Sonny says. "Right, Hol?"

"Sure." But from the way she dips her head I can tell she doesn't really get it.

Sonny and Holly left an hour ago, headed for home and Evie's never-ending concert. Holly was a little put out when Mindy sent a text to let us all know that she was getting some fresh air, that she'd catch up with us later.

If it were up to Holly, we'd all give her daily updates on all the goings-on of our lives. Not so much because she's snoopy, but more because she cares that much. She just has a different way of showing it.

The cup of coffee I brought for Dad after he showed up has already gone cold, forgotten on the rolling tray next to Mom's bed. His head is resting against the back of the recliner and he's snoring with abandon.

I'll let him sleep as long as he needs to.

The poor guy.

I brought my copy of Robert Service's poems to read to Dad if he wanted me to. It's the book he gave my brother for his sixteenth birthday. After Dale died, I pilfered it, knowing that nobody would notice.

There were a few pages that had the corners folded down. Mostly the ones about adventures in Alaska. Dale had always dreamed of the Yukon. My heart is still tender when I think about how he never made it there. Not on this side of life, at least.

I liked to have hope that heaven would hold adventures we couldn't have here and that Dale got his chance to face down a grizzly without any fear of being eaten.

Anyway, there's one dog-eared page that always catches me off guard when I look through this book. It's for a poem about the reason that birds sing.

It's a bouncy verse, so very happy-go-lucky, and I wonder what made Dale pick that one as a favorite. I guess I can't know.

So absorbed am I in the poem that I jump at the touch on my shoulder.

"Sorry," Linda says. "I didn't mean to scare you."

"That's all right," I say. "Everything okay?"

There's a smudge of mascara under her right eye and her nose is red the way it often is after she's been crying.

I glance at Mom and see that her chest is still rising and falling and the heart rate monitor showing activity. Dad's still snoozing away.

"Yeah." She puts her lips on mine in a gentle kiss. "Mindy got some news."

"Oh?"

"It's not what we were hoping for," she says. "But it's not all bad."

I meet Mindy at our trail, the two of us bundled up in coats and scarves, hats and mittens. I've got a thermos of hot tea and a couple of chocolate bars in my pack. I remember that it was Dale who told me years ago that I should always take chocolate on cold weather excursions.

I never hit a snowy trail without it.

It's quiet out here today, and the only sound we made is the crunching of our boots on the hard-packed snow. Every minute or so Mindy sniffles. Other than that, it's darn near silent for the first quarter mile or so.

That's when she stops, breath steaming out of her mouth. I turn to face her, wondering if now is the time to pull out the chocolate.

"The email was from a man named Thi," she says, pronouncing it as *Tie*. "I guess he's my half-brother."

"Mindy, this is excellent," I say.

"Hold on." She puts her hands in her coat pockets. "Don't get too excited yet."

"All right."

"He said that they've been looking for me the past couple of years but weren't sure where I'd ended up." She closes her eyes. "He said that for a while they were afraid I was on the plane that crashed."

There's this clenching in my core at the thought of it.

"But then someone told him about my posts on the Babylift page." She licks her lips. "He knew as soon as he saw the pictures that it was me. That I'm his half-sister."

"And you're sure he's legitimate?"

"I think so," she says. "He knew about the impetigo I had on my face. His—our mother told him about it. And he had a picture of me."

She yanks off one mitten with her teeth before pulling the phone from her pocket and searching for a photograph.

It's black and white and grainy, a little faded as pictures from that long ago are. Still, it's clearly our little Minh sitting on the lap of a woman who looks startlingly like our grown-up daughter.

"That's your birth mother?" I ask.

"Yeah."

"You look just like her."

"Do you think so?"

"For sure."

From the way she smiles, I can tell she thinks so too. I can tell she's proud of it.

She takes one last look at the picture and then puts the phone away, fitting her hand back into the mitten.

"Anyway, Thi lives in Thu Duc, right outside Ho Chi Minh City," she says, starting to walk again. "He said there's a lot to see there, some nice hotels for Sonny and me to stay in."

"Then you're really going?"

She nods. "Sonny's calling the travel agent tomorrow."

"And passports?"

"All set," she says. "I think we're just worried about leaving while Grammy's sick."

"None of us want you worrying about that, sweetie," I say. "We'll manage while you girls are gone."

We move along on the trail, not talking for a good amount of time. Something niggles at me, though. Something she hasn't said more than a few words about. It isn't until we reach the halfway mark on our walk that I get the tea and chocolate out of my pack. I hand Mindy one of the tin cups of chamomile before pouring one for myself.

"And what about your birth mother?" I ask, peeling the wrapper off my candy bar. "You think you'll get a chance to meet her?"

I've caught her mid-sip and she swallows before looking into my eyes and shaking her head.

"She passed away a couple of years ago." When she sighs, her breath makes a cloud of steam in the cold air. "Thi said it was cancer."

I feel sick, suddenly no longer hungry for the chocolate.

"I'm sorry," I say. "You must be heartbroken."

She nods, looking into her cup.

"It's sort of anticlimactic, isn't it?" she says.

She kicks a clod of dirty snow, and it falls apart.

"Well, I'm not sure that real life is all that much like a movie."

"Yeah. I know." She sniffles and rubs her nose with the back of her mittened hand. "I had my hopes up."

"I know, honey."

"I really wanted to know what kind of person she was," she says. "I wanted to get to know her."

I do my best not to spill tea on her as I pull her close, remembering one of the first times I held her. Then I wanted so desperately for her to feel safe. These days I'm aware of how incapable I am of sheltering her. It's more likely that I can offer a small measure of comfort.

Something tells me that's enough for her.

We finish our tea and get back to walking. Out of the corner of my eye, I see the red streak of a cardinal zip by and keep my ears open.

Of all the birds in these woods, the cardinal is the only one who sings all winter long. The fellow lights on a branch and gives a tender serenade before taking back to the sky.

CHAPTER Forty-Seven

Linda, 1975

I turned on the radio, hoping for a happy tune on the way to drop Sonny off at school. My heart felt so raw at the idea that summer was over and that I wouldn't have her with me all day long. So, when "Landslide" came on, I got all kinds of sappy and weepy.

Time just went along too quickly. Life changed constantly. The last thing I needed was another reminder that, before I knew it, my girls would be all grown up. First days of first grade would turn into high school graduations and moving away to college. Then came weddings and babies of their own.

If I was this emotional sending Sonny off to school for seven hours, how much of a wreck would I be when she moved to another town or state?

I told myself to get it together, blinked against the tears, and took a good, deep breath.

Motherhood wasn't for wimps.

"Now, Mindy," Sonny said, hanging over the front seat to

talk to her sister in the back, "I'll be at school all day and there won't be any naps, so when I get home I'll be a little grumpy, so don't do anything to make me mad. Okay?"

"Okay," Minh said. "Sonny bye?"

"Yes. Remember? I'm going to school." Sonny held up her hand and waved at her sister. "Bye."

"Bye," Minh repeated.

When I looked in the rearview mirror, I saw Minh's little mouth turned down into a frown.

Pulling up to the curb in front of the school, I opened my mouth to tell Sonny to have a good day, that I loved her, to be kind to new kids. The whole rigamarole.

But before I could get a word out, she swung open the door and took off toward the playground, hollering a "bye" over her shoulder as she went.

It was a stab straight to my heart.

I had to shimmy myself across the seat to shut her door, and someone in a car behind me honked to let me know that I was in their way.

"Yeah, yeah," I said, straightening back up in my seat.

I took one last look at the playground before pulling away.

Sonny sat at the very top of the tallest slide, her arms lifted over her head and her face tilted toward the sky.

Ivan stopped over shortly before lunchtime, and I offered him a cup of tomato soup. It was from a can, not the homemade kind he was used to from Hilda, but he was still gracious enough to say it was the best thing he'd ever tasted.

For about the hundredth time I entertained the thought that Hilda did not deserve such a kind man.

"Say," he said after slurping up his last spoonful, "I happened to be at the toy store the other day."

"Oh you were?" I asked, taking his bowl to the sink.

"Can't an old man frequent a toy store?" He wiped his mouth with a napkin. "Thanks again for lunch."

"You're welcome any time."

"That's good of you." He leaned into the back of his chair. "Anyway, I was looking at the dolls and darned if I didn't find one with dark hair and eyes."

"You did?" I asked, putting a hand on my hip.

I'd bemoaned more than a couple of times the lack of non-blond-headed dolls in all the stores in Bear Run.

"I sure did. And she was a pretty doll too." He smiled at Minh. "If you think that might be something she'd like, I can get it."

"You don't have to buy her a doll."

"Well, I already did," he said. "It's in the car."

"Ivan . . ."

"Now, it's nothing special, so don't get too excited."

He went back outside, and Minh left her seat at the table to watch him out the living room window. Holding his hands behind him, he came back into the house.

"Grumpy?" she said.

"Hey, she said my name." His face lit up. "How about that?" He knelt on the floor before handing her the doll.

"Mindy?" she asked.

"Yup. That's for you, Minh."

The smile on her face was pure radiance.

She reached up and bopped him on the nose.

As she'd predicted, Sonny was tired and grouchy when she got home from school that afternoon. Somehow her shirt got stained with ketchup—even though I hadn't packed any in her lunch—and her piggytails were tangled and frizzy.

It looked more like she'd wrangled a mountain lion than spent a day in first grade.

"We didn't even learn how to read," she grumbled in the car on the way home. "They promised we would!"

"Well, honey," I said. "You can't learn to read in just one day."

"Why not?"

"Because it's a big thing." I pulled to a stop at an intersection, turning on my left turn signal. "You need to be patient."

"I don't like being patient." She made a harrumph sound and crossed her arms. "I want to read. Now!"

"Sonny, I love you," I said, "but you're going to have to learn to go with the flow a little bit."

She didn't like that, not even a little, and pouted for the last half of the drive home so I'd know of her great displeasure.

We were just about to turn down the road to our house when I heard Minh's tiny voice from the back seat.

It wasn't unusual for her to jabber away to herself, trying on words she'd heard one of us say, practicing them so she could use them.

"Did you hear what she said?" Sonny asked before scrambling up onto her knees to look back at her sister. "Say it again, Mindy."

"Sonny, I love you," Minh said, then giggled.

"That's good," Sonny said. "Did you hear her, Mommy?"

"I did," I answered.

"Mommy, I love you," Minh added.

"Oh, sweetie pie, I love you too," I said.

"Daddy, I love you."

I pulled into the driveway, only just, and put the car into reverse.

"How about we go surprise Daddy at work?" I said. "We could take him some ice cream."

"Can we have ice cream too?" Sonny asked.

"Daddy?" Minh asked.

"Let's go."

I pulled out of the drive, headed to Bruce's office, and reminded myself to take it slow, even if I was eager for him to hear the new thing Minh had learned to say.

We'd have time—our whole lives—to hear her tell us that she loved us.

Still, I couldn't bear the idea of him waiting until he got home from work.

I peeked at Minh in the rearview mirror. She had both of her dollies—the old yellow-headed one and the new one with hair as dark and silky as her own—tucked under each of her arms.

She'd insisted on bringing them both.

CHAPTER Forty-Eight

Sonny, 1988

I sat in the front seat of Mike's car. He kept the engine running and the radio was playing "Glory of Love," and I thought that if there was any time for him to ask me to be his girlfriend, it was right then.

In less than one hour, I'd be leaving for college and I wouldn't see him until Thanksgiving. That was a long stretch for a girl not to be around a guy she liked. Every inch of me ached just thinking about how much I'd miss him. Not to mention how my stomach twisted when I considered how many girls he could meet in that time.

I wasn't sure that I was in love with him—I wasn't even sure what that really meant—but whatever was going on in my heart was causing me a stupid amount of agony.

Was I totally overreacting? Sure. But I was saying goodbye to him for three months. I was allowed a certain amount of melodrama.

At least I was keeping it all bottled up inside so Mike didn't end up thinking I was a total spaz.

"So," he said, "you'll make sure to send me your phone number?"

"Yeah," I said. "I'm going to miss you."

He nodded and reached over for my hand, grazing my thigh with his knuckles.

"I think I should get inside," I said. "Don't you have anything you want to ask me first?"

"Yup." His Adam's apple bobbed up and down in his throat. "Do you really think college food is as bad as everybody says it is?"

"Michael."

"Give me a second," he said. "It's kind of scary."

"Are you saying that I'm scary?"

"Yeah. I am." He turned toward me. "Because I still don't believe I'm good enough to be your boyfriend. You're way out of my league."

"True."

"It's a big deal, asking a girl to be official and stuff. You know?"

"So, are you asking?"

"Of course I am," he answered. "Sonny, will you please be my girlfriend?"

"Okay, I guess so."

We kissed, and I was only a little bit annoyed when I noticed Mom spying on us out the front window. She pulled the curtain in front of her face once she knew she was busted.

Mike walked me to the front door and kissed me again. I wouldn't have said that we were really good at it yet, but we were getting there.

I checked and double-checked my packing list, making sure I'd grabbed everything that was going with me to college. Mom had promised to send anything I left behind; still I went through every drawer and peeked under my bed one last time.

I was stalling.

Not that I wasn't excited to get to college and move into my dorm or anything. I was just really, really nervous about leaving home.

The stack of books on my bedside table caught my eye, and I read their spines, trying to decide if I needed to take any of them. Pulling *The Glass Menagerie* out from the middle, I thought about the character Tom and how he abandoned his family, leaving them to fend for themselves.

If there was one thing I'd hated about that play, it was how he'd wrenched himself away from his mom and sister. What a jerk.

"Hey," Mindy said from the doorway. "You about ready to go?"

"Yeah," I said. "Just a sec."

"You don't want to be late." She crossed her arms and leaned into the doorjamb.

"I know."

"You know that we'll all miss you, right?" she said.

"I'm going to miss you too."

I tensed, like, every muscle in my face trying to stop myself from crying. Still, the inside corners of my eyes stung and my nose got runny.

"Oh, don't cry, Sonny." Mindy crossed the room and gave me a hug. "It's going to be great. You're going to love college. I know it."

"I mean, I know that," I said. "It's just, I feel bad leaving you behind."

She narrowed her eyes at me and shook her head.

"You aren't leaving me behind," she said. "Besides, it's not like you're going away forever."

"Yeah. I guess you're right."

"Girls," Mom called up the stairs. "We've got to get on the road."

"Yes, Mom," Mindy answered. Then to me, "Coming?"

"Yup. Be right down."

She let me have another minute alone in the room that would never really be mine again. It would just be a place I'd crash over breaks and during the summer months.

I put *The Glass Menagerie* at the foot of the bed that had been mine as long as I could remember.

Dad met me at the bottom of the steps, his eyes all crinkly when he smiled.

"You ready?"

I wasn't, but I walked out to the car with him anyway.

CHAPTER Forty-Nine

Bruce, 2014

It was a long, deeply cold winter. The kind that makes a man wonder if turning into a snowbird and making his way to Florida for a couple of months isn't a good idea. The snow drifted high against the house, and more than a couple families in Bear Run had the pipes burst in their basements.

But we're on the other side of it now. Gloriously, spring is making its slow entrance back into our lives. Just the other day I noticed that we've got what I call Robert Frost blooms on the trees. The little golden flowers will soon spread into leaves and we'll be in a world of green before we know it.

Spring is the time when I'm glad I didn't head south so easily.

Stuck inside as much as we were made for lots of movie nights and euchre tournaments with Dad and Mindy and more than a little baking. A couple of times we had the granddaughters over to make ice cream out of the piles of untouched snow that accumulated in the yard.

Mom made it through the winter. She's a fighter, that one. But we've moved her to the nursing home wing, something neither she or Dad is all too pleased with.

So much of life is out of our control.

Zach and Holly are settled in their house outside of Cleveland. It's a cute little place that needs a lot of fixing up. But they're happy, so I am too.

I'm up early this morning, playing taxi driver for Mindy and Sonny. They take off today for two weeks in Vietnam and, boy, am I excited for them.

So excited, it seems, I forgot my travel mug on the kitchen counter. That's all right. Sonny'll have plenty of coffee brewed for all of us.

There's a light on in Sonny's living room when I pull into her driveway. Otherwise, the house is dark and I try not to make too much noise when I get out of the truck and go to the front door. Mindy's Prius is already here and her luggage is on the porch. I go ahead and grab it, hauling it to the truck.

"Hey, Dad," Sonny whispers out the front door. "You want some coffee for the road?"

"Yes please," I say after lifting suitcases into the pickup's bed. "Where's your stuff?"

"Just inside the door." She waves me in. "Oh, and we might have a little stowaway."

Evie peeks at me out the living room window, giving me her toothiest smile.

"Hi, sweetie," I say when I step inside.

"Sorry," Sonny says.

"It's all right. I'll be glad for company on the way home."

"Thanks."

We make quick time of getting the truck loaded up, and I'm

354 The Nature of Small Birds

glad for the cup of coffee that Mindy hands me. I glance at her in the passenger seat before pulling the gearshift into reverse.

"You ready for this?" I ask.

"I can't believe it's actually happening," she answers.

There's this spark of excitement in her eyes that warms my heart.

This day has been a long time coming.

><

Evie holds my hand as we walk into the airport behind Sonny and Mindy. I'm sad that I can't take her in past security to watch the planes on the runway or the scrolling flight schedule on the wall. But we look at the artwork in the lobby while her mom and aunt get their luggage checked in.

She thinks it's pretty special anyway.

Before I know it—before I'm ready—Sonny and Mindy are saying their goodbyes.

Sonny crouches down and kisses Evie on the cheek, telling her to be a good girl for me. Evie promises that she will and I believe her. Sonny lifts her hand, cupping Evie's cheek, and looks her right in the eyes.

"I love you," she says. "And I'll miss you every minute."

"I'll miss you every second," Evie answers. "Will you call me?"

"Yes." Sonny gives her another kiss. "Will you make sure to help Daddy?"

Evie nods. "Love you, Mommy."

One last kiss and Sonny's up and giving me a hug.

"It's hard to go," she whispers.

I know exactly what she means.

"She'll be all right," I say. "And so will you."

Mindy hugs me next. It's a quick one, which is all right. Short and sweet.

"We'll call as soon as we land," she says. "Keep your phone on, okay?"

"Will do," I say.

"See you in a couple of weeks." She bends down and gives Evie a kiss on the forehead. "I'll bring back something special for you."

And then, just like that, they're on their way.

Evie and I watch them go through security and they turn and wave once before heading for the terminal and out of our sight.

I take Evie's hand, really glad to have her here with me.

"How about some breakfast?" I ask.

"All right," she answers.

Together, we turn and walk to where I parked the truck, her hand in mine.

Evie and I grab a couple egg sandwiches from a drive-thru place near the airport and bring them to a park that overlooks the runway. Just a couple of planes have taken off so far, but not the one I'm waiting for. Not yet, at least.

"Grandpa," Evie says, her mouth full of breakfast, "how do airplanes fly?"

"Oh, boy," I say. "I don't know exactly."

"That's okay." She chews and swallows before going on. "Mom says that it's okay not to know everything. All it means is that you get to learn something new."

"She's pretty smart, isn't she?"

"Yup."

My phone vibrates in my pocket, and when I pull it out, I see a selfie of Sonny and Mindy along with a text.

"About to take off!" it says.

"Ready?" I ask Evie, tapping her on the shoulder. "Watch."

It's a big airplane that taxis onto the runway, gaining speed as it goes.

When it lifts up off the ground, it takes my breath away.

I know there are at least a hundred planes that fly in and out of here every day. But only one of them carries two parts of my heart.

It sure is something to see them fly.

Author's Note
and Acknowledgments

I first heard about Operation Babylift as I was reading up about the Vietnam War, researching for *All Manner of Things*. I knew I couldn't mention the event in Annie's story—the timeframe didn't line up. But I decided to save the idea for later, having absolutely no clue if I'd ever get the chance to write about it.

A few years later I needed to come up with another novel to write. Rummaging through my files, I found a note I'd jotted down about the Babylift and listed it as a potential book idea. Honestly, I didn't think my editor would be interested. I sort of hoped she'd pass.

It's no exaggeration to say that it scared the socks off of me when she said yes.

Fortunately for me, I found fantastic resources that helped me tell the story. *The Life We Were Given* by Dana Sachs and *The War Cradle* by Shirley Peck-Barns were enlightening, helping me understand the social, economic, and diplomatic implications of the Babylift. *Last Airlift* by Marsha Forchuk Skrypuch,

Escape from Saigon by Andrew Warren, and *Beyond the Babylift* by Pamela Chatterton Purdy informed about the lives of the children and families who lived it.

I was also thankful for the documentaries I found that offered unique and visual insight. *Operation Babylift: The Lost Children of Vietnam*, *Daughter from Danang*, and *Hearts and Minds* each broke my heart, but also offered hope.

When I was a little girl, I often worried about what happened to the children of Vietnam. I was haunted by the picture I'd found in a magazine of the child who has become known as "The Napalm Girl" and had more than my share of nightmares about her.

When I started writing *The Nature of Small Birds* I had that question in the forefront of my mind. What about the kids? While it would be thick of me to imagine I could tell the story of an entire nation of children, I could at least try to tell the story of one of them.

I, gladly, wasn't left to my own devices to tell the story of the Matthews family. What a relief.

Writing a novel is an ambitious undertaking in a normal year. More so during a global pandemic. I am doubly thankful for those who came alongside me this time around.

Many thanks to Kelsey Bowen and Kristin Kornoelje for helping me polish up this novel. Editors are bright and kind and I'm so grateful that I have the pair of you working to make me look smarter than I am.

To the Revell marketing team I extend high fives and a round of lattes for their efforts in getting this book on shelves. Michele, Karen, Brianne, you ladies are remarkable. Thank you!

Thanks to my agent Tim Beals for being excited for this book and cheering me on to keep doing the best work I can.

Special thanks to my friends who check in, offer encouragement, and let me be my nutty self: Jocelyn Green, Alexis De Weese, Anne Ferris, Sonny Huisman, Bruce Matthews, Joanne Sher, Betsy Carter, Ginger Main . . . I could go on and on. I feel so blessed by all of you.

My kids deserve props for surviving, not only a pandemic, but also having to be shut up in the house with a novelist. You three are tough little birds and I'm so glad to share this nest with you. Love you!

Now for the sappy stuff. To my sweet husband, who loves me as I am, encourages me to be as God intended me, and always makes sure I have a fresh rose to make me smile. Jeff, you're my very favorite reader. You always will be. I love you.

But most of all, praise and gratitude to the Father who sees us when we fly and cares when we fall, all the while keeping his hand open to offer us shelter.

Susie Finkbeiner is the CBA bestselling author of *All Manner of Things*, which was selected as a 2020 Michigan Notable Book, and *Stories That Bind Us*, as well as *A Cup of Dust*, *A Trail of Crumbs*, and *A Song of Home*. She serves on the Fiction Readers Summit planning committee, volunteers her time at Ada Bible Church in Grand Rapids, Michigan, and speaks at retreats and women's events across the country. Susie and her husband have three children and live in West Michigan.

Meet Susie

"*All Manner of Things* should be at the top of everyone's reading stacks. Beautiful. Honest. Artfully written. A winning novel."

—Elizabeth Byler Younts, author of *The Solace of Water*

After Annie Jacobson's older brother is deployed to Vietnam during the war, tragedy at home brings their estranged father home without welcome. As tensions heighten, Annie and her family must find a way to move forward as they try to hold both hope and grief in the same hand.

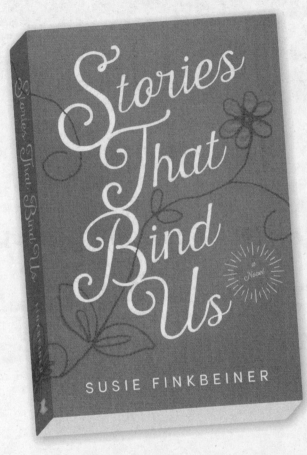

LET'S TALK ABOUT BOOKS

- Share or mention the book on your social media platforms. Use the hashtag **#NatureofSmallBirds**.

- Write a book review on your blog or on a retailer site.

- Pick up a copy for friends, family, or anyone who you think would enjoy and be challenged by its message!

- Share this message on Twitter, Facebook, or Instagram: **I loved #NatureofSmallBirds by @SusieFinkbeiner // @RevellBooks**

- Recommend this book for your church, workplace, book club, or small group.

- Follow Revell on social media and tell us what you like.

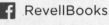 RevellBooks

 RevellBooks

 RevellBooks

 pinterest.com/RevellBooks